Mounting Danger

By the Author

Harmony

Worth the Risk

Sea Glass Inn

Improvisation

Mounting Danger

Mounting Danger

by

Karis Walsh

2013

MOUNTING DANGER

ISBN 10: 1-60282-951-9
ISBN 13: 978-1-60282-951-0

This Trade Paperback Original Is Published By
Bold Strokes Books, Inc.
P.O. Box 249
Valley Falls, NY 12185

First Edition: October 2013

Credits
Editor: Ruth Sternglantz
Production Design: Susan Ramundo
Cover Design By Sheri (graphicartist2020@hotmail.com)

Acknowledgments

Writing a book set in Tacoma was, for me, a literary return to my hometown. I'd like to take this opportunity to acknowledge the people who were instrumental in making me a lifelong reader and bibliophile. What a gift they gave me.

Thank you to my parents, for filling our house with books, and to my sister, Staci, because I cherish the memory of her reading to me by candlelight during a thunderstorm. And to the wonderful teachers who went beyond their curricula to give me extra encouragement and challenges: Mr. Thurston, Mr. Delorme, Mr. Nino, and Mr. Martin. And to Richard Sears—you are missed.

Many thanks to the people who are currently helping me transform my love of writing and words into novels. Radclyffe, Cindy, Stacia, Connie. Sheri, for her awesome covers, and the proofreaders for their important and exacting work. And, of course, thank you to Ruth Sternglantz. She is not only my editor, but also a teacher and a friend.

Dedication

For Cindy

Before you, I only wrote about love and romance.

Now, with you, I live them every day.

Thank you.

Chapter One

Blue lights flashed in eerie silence. No sirens, no sound. Sergeant Rachel Bryce got in her patrol car and slammed the door behind her, needing some noise, some proof she wasn't as invisible and incorporeal as a ghost. Rows of police vehicles—identical except for their small identifying numbers—lined the parking lot of Tacoma's Cheney Stadium. Small groups of officers—identical except for their faces, their body types, their name badges—formed clusters in between the rows of cars. They were a community, a family. Bound as strongly by unseen ties as by their similar uniforms. But not Rachel. She was alone.

She kept her features composed and calm, but her hands gripped the bottom of the steering wheel as she fought off her insistent and growing headache. She had already been to far too many funerals in her seven years with the Tacoma Police Department. Only a few years earlier, after she had signed up to take the sergeant's test, she and her colleagues in the TPD had joined with the other departments in Washington as they mourned the loss of seven officers over the course of a few months. Unlucky number seven. Shot and killed, like Alex Mayer. But then, she had been part of the solemn community. Comforting. Comforted. Standing together against the dangers they faced every day.

Anger and loneliness battled for her attention. She flipped off her radio, silencing its incessant updates on the funeral procession and route. She was somewhere in the middle of over one hundred cars, all wedged in the lot and about to drive slowly to the same destination. She was unlikely to make a wrong turn along the way. Too bad the same surety didn't apply to her career. Just one call, one choice had changed everything. She had made the right decision on that fateful call, even though no one else agreed with her. But being right didn't make up for being ostracized. Her decision had resulted in the arrest of a fellow officer. The law had been on her side, but the entire department had supported the more popular and senior officer. And an invisible, impenetrable wall had gone up between her and everyone she had considered family before that day.

The other officers started dispersing, heading to their cars, so Rachel turned her radio on again. At least it was another voice. Everyone else might turn away when she walked by, but the impersonal voice of the dispatcher still spoke to her. And would, as long as she put on this uniform.

A uniform she had been so proud to wear. She had spent plenty of time on the wrong side of a police car's safety glass. In trouble, in juvie, in yet another foster home, until a stroke of luck landed her in the home of a couple who cared enough to fight against her and with her until they pulled her out of a downward spiral and set her on the right course. A course that led her directly to the driver's seat of a patrol car. So much better than being trussed up in the back. She had gotten through college, through the police academy, through her rookie year by following the rules. Staying on the straight and narrow. But somehow, in some crazy way, doing what was right hadn't worked this time. Instead of giving her the security of a work family—any family—it had separated her once again.

Rachel inched forward as her row finally started to move through the maze of cones that brought order to the parking lot and under the arch formed by two fire trucks with an American flag fluttering under their extended ladders. Following the hearse and Alex's body. Volunteers from neighboring departments sat in each intersection, blocking traffic for the procession. Crowds of citizens lined the city streets, waving and holding signs in support. Rachel pried one hand loose from her steering wheel and waved back. To them, she must look like any other officer, but she knew better. She stopped waving and ran her fingers over her TPD badge, feeling the ridge of heavy black tape where it crossed the cold metal. She cracked her window for some fresh air, but instead of a sweet May breeze, she only let the smell of exhaust into her car. Still, she couldn't bear to shut the window again. The excruciatingly slow progress of the line of cars, the uncontrolled crowds pressing close as she crawled by, and the utter lack of escape routes aggravated the claustrophobia she had struggled with since childhood. She hadn't felt it this strongly for years, and she barely resisted the urge to pull out of the solid line of cars. Drive over the curb, over the sidewalk, over some pedestrians. Whatever it took to break free and be able to breathe again.

Safety wasn't in closed spaces. People hanging over the sides of bridges holding banners could easily drop something on her car. The ones lining the side of the road could shoot at her, grab her. Most cops learned to know where the exits were to keep from getting cornered and avoid walking into traps. Rachel hadn't needed those lessons from the academy or from her training officers. She had picked them up before she turned five. Don't go into a room if there isn't another way out. Don't turn your back on anyone. Ever. Don't trust the people who look so friendly as they wave and smile.

Inhale. Hold the breath. Exhale. Hold the emptiness. Rachel tried every breathing exercise she could remember. She was overreacting, being paranoid, but the panic she had felt in every funeral procession made the fifteen-minute drive to the Tacoma Dome seem like it lasted for hours. Before, she had been in the car with friends, with people she trusted to watch her back, to protect and support her. This time, the loneliness and isolation made her feel too vulnerable.

Finally, a motorcycle cop waved her toward the parking places reserved for Tacoma's officers. Rachel dragged a shaky hand over her forehead, wiping away a light sheen of sweat. No more crowds, and the congestion of cars eased as they separated and drove down different rows. Rachel backed into a spot and turned off her ignition. She had barely managed the drive here and she didn't know how she'd be able to handle the hot and crowded memorial service. She looked over at the Dome, its dirty blue-and-white patterned top a testament to the industrial area surrounding it. The smudged and grimy surface, defying the city's attempts to keep it clean, was courtesy of the Tideflats area, with its refineries and paper mills. Tacoma might not be the prettiest city Rachel had ever seen, but it had become her home—working-class and unpretentious, with the community spirit of a small town. She belonged here. So why was she being shut out?

Rachel finally got out of her car and walked past a group of officers. One had been in her academy class. One had been on her squad before she was promoted to sergeant in February. All of them she knew by name. She kept her head high, her face expressionless, as she passed them without a word. Not that they noticed. She wanted to stop and yell, wave her arms until they had to acknowledge her. Ask why they had sided against her without bothering to hear her side of the story. Ask why it was fair for the other officer—just because he was well-liked and had been around longer than she had—to turn everyone against her when her only sin was to uphold the law. But she didn't. Instead, she edged around the growing crowds and looked for a reasonably empty place to stand while she waited for the casket to be carried into the Dome.

She heard the horses before she saw them. The clatter of steel shoes on concrete, a shrill neigh that was immediately echoed by two other equine voices. Tacoma's new mounted unit. Led by Alex Mayer until a week ago. Rachel slipped behind the large white trailer, with the department's logo emblazoned on its side, and got her first glimpse of the recently formed unit.

She had forgotten they'd be here. Usually Seattle sent a few horses to escort a fallen officer to the memorial service, but of course Tacoma's unit would perform the duty today. Rachel looked over the four horses with her foster dad's voice in her head, pointing out their flaws and evaluating their conformation the way he had taught her to do. A handsome chestnut gelding, empty boots attached to the stirrups of his saddle, was obviously Alex's mount. He danced around as Clark Jensen tried to hold him with one hand and a bay quarter horse type with the other. Billie Mitchell, another officer from Rachel's academy class, was tightening the girth on her saddle while her flighty mare jigged in a tight circle. Lindstrom—Don… or Dan?—stood too far away from a pinto mare that was tied to the side of the trailer as he cleaned one of her hooves with a metal pick. He looked nervous around her, and with good reason apparently. Rachel didn't notice any glaring defects in the horses' conformation, but none of them seemed to be mentally ready for their public debut.

Rachel kept to the shadows behind the trailer. She wanted to help Clark untangle himself from the reins as the two horses twisted around him. And ask Billie why her mare didn't have Borium on her shoes to keep her from slipping on the pavement. And to tell Don, or Dan, that he seemed right to distrust the mare. The way her eye rolled back so Rachel could see its white rim, her switching tail, her pinned ears. Rachel had seen those signs in horses too many times before. And they were usually followed by a kick or a bite or a stomped-on foot.

But it wasn't her place to interfere. And the officers probably wouldn't want her help even if offered. She leaned against the aluminum trailer and felt the small jolts as the pinto mare pulled back against her tie rope. Of course the riders would be nervous on their first official outing. And sad and shocked because they were acting as escort for their dead sergeant. But, even shielded from the worst of the crowds and traffic noise by the huge trailer, the unit looked totally unprepared to be in public.

The aroma of hay and manure and sweating horses calmed Rachel and drove away the lingering scent of exhaust and claustrophobia. She took a deep breath and let the sounds and smells of the horses carry her away from the memorial and her lonely exile within the department, away from the disturbing prospect of a few hot hours in the Dome with hundreds of sweaty cops in wool dress uniforms. Back home to eastern Washington. Back to her foster family's ranch in the town of Cheney, where she could ride for miles without—

Rachel pushed off the trailer and moved toward Clark before she realized what she was doing. The bay gelding had pulled out of his grasp and wheeled away when Rachel reached out and grabbed his reins. He dragged her a few feet, but she held her ground and jerked him to a stop. Rachel stroked his neck, murmuring quietly until she felt the muscles beneath her hand relax a bit, and then she led him back to Clark.

"Thanks…Bryce," he said. He hesitated slightly before her name, as if merely saying it would give him cooties.

Rachel ignored the slight. She should be getting used to the way people said her name, but it hurt every time. She slipped the reins over the bay's head and handed them to Clark. "No problem," she said. She turned to walk away.

"Wait," Clark said.

Rachel stopped and faced him. His face was pale, and she could see red marks on his hand where the sweaty leather reins had burned him when the gelding pulled away.

"Really, thank you. If you hadn't caught him…"

Rachel didn't need him to finish the sentence. She knew too well what might have happened if the frightened horse had gotten loose among the crowds, on the city streets and so close to the freeway. "Just be careful out there," she said.

He nodded and followed the rest of the unit toward the street where the hearse and Alex's family were waiting. Rachel stayed near the trailer, where she could watch but not be noticed. Close enough to help if another of the horses got out of control. Usually, the police would be mounted while another officer led the riderless horse, but Rachel was relieved to see the whole unit stay on the ground. They could barely control their horses as it was, and Rachel gasped out loud when Alex's widow had to snatch her two young children out of the way of Lindstrom's mare. The four horses jigged and swerved around the coffin as if they were more likely to knock it over than to protect it, and Abby Hargrove, the unit's lieutenant, finally waved them off. Rachel was tempted to skip the service and stick around the trailer in case they needed help loading the horses, but Hargrove glared daggers at Rachel when she passed her.

No need to stick around where she wasn't wanted. Although she suspected she wouldn't be any more welcome inside the Dome than she was outside of it, Rachel joined the throngs of people filing through the entrance doors. For a brief moment, between the parking lot and the seating area, she belonged. Surrounded by officers from other departments, she was an anonymous TPD sergeant, receiving commiserating smiles and even the occasional shoulder squeeze or brush on the arm from strangers who accepted her more than her own people did. But it didn't last long.

Rachel paused at the edge of the bleachers. Tiers of seats were filled with people who had traveled to the memorial service. The distinctive red of Canadian Mounties, the navy and black of local uniforms. Rachel wanted to find a seat among them, but she'd be out of place yet again. Noticed because she wasn't sitting in the chairs reserved for Tacoma's officers, Alex's family, and visiting dignitaries. She hesitated, as unsure as she had been on every first day in every new school she had attended while growing up. Always hoping to be part of a group, but always expecting rejection. And rarely being disappointed in her expectations.

The feel of someone's hand on the small of her back, sliding over her duty belt, made Rachel flinch. She automatically reached toward her gun, but warm breath against her neck made her stop.

"Hey, Rach."

Warmth. The smell of her breath, the sound of her voice, the hand sliding over Rachel's ass and hip would have been very welcome if Christy hadn't been hiding behind her in the shadows of the bleachers. But the gestures were furtive, stolen. Not meant to be seen. Around the rest of the department, Christy was as cold as everyone else.

"What's up, Christy?" Rachel asked. She shifted her hips out of reach. She might be mad, furious because Christy had bailed on her when she needed her most, but her damned body still reacted to her ex-lover's touch.

"I miss you."

I miss you, too.

"Can you come over tonight? I don't want to be alone," Christy said. She pressed against Rachel's back, and Rachel could imagine the feel of her hard nipples, the smell of her sex, the wet touch of her tongue. "I need you."

And I needed you. Rachel had needed Christy to stand by her when everyone else turned their backs. Needed her support and her touch. But she had been surprised to discover that she hadn't meant enough to Christy to make her stick around. And Rachel had been even more surprised to find that the loss of her community, her police family, had meant more to her than the loss of her girlfriend.

"I have other plans," Rachel said. She walked away from the bleachers and into the crowd. Christy wouldn't follow her there. Rachel didn't look back into Christy's blue eyes, didn't want to see her dark strawberry-blond hair—so silky and long when Rachel unpinned it from Christy's usual tight bun. Definitely didn't want to see the way Christy's full breasts filled out her uniform top. Rachel walked resolutely toward the TPD seats and sat in a back corner. She tried not to watch when Christy walked by and joined her usual group of friends. Rachel's former friends.

Rachel had been so wrapped up in the emotions roiling through her, she thought she'd be distracted enough to make it through the service without any real tears. But the speeches by Alex's friends and the words of the chaplain broke through her personal issues and forced her to remain present. Her feelings for her fellow officers hadn't changed. They might be ignoring her, but she still cared. And she hated that she did. When Alex's young son, a boy who looked about eight, delivered a eulogy in his high, sweet voice, Rachel bit her lip and stared at the ceiling, the floor, the huge spray of flowers next to the casket. Anything to keep from seeing the fatherless little boy, anything to keep from crying. She had been holding so much inside, acting day after day as if nothing mattered to her. If she started crying now, she might not be able to stop.

Even the addresses by the government officials moved her. Ellen Laird, the state's governor. Eugene Varano, Tacoma's city manager. Rachel's cynical self knew they were only after televised publicity as they sympathized with the police so they'd secure union endorsements in the next election. Photo ops, as they shook hands with Alex's son and kissed his crying widow and patted his tiny daughter's head. But Rachel's cynicism couldn't keep her from the tug of connection as Alex was honored and remembered. One of her own had been killed, shot in the head when he accidentally stumbled on a drug deal in the park. Even the black sheep felt the loss of a family member.

Just make it through the service without crying. Just make it through the crowd without making eye contact with Christy and losing her grip. Rachel had her pride, although not much else. And tempting as the offer of a night of sex and cuddling was, it wasn't nearly enough to break Rachel's resolve. Private support meant nothing without any public support to back it up.

Rachel stood up when the seemingly interminable service finally ended. She took a deep breath and prepared to merge into the crowds again, push her way to the door and to the freedom of open air. She only made it a few feet before an authoritative voice stopped her.

"Bryce."

Damn. Rachel had been secretly hoping someone might talk to her, recognize her. Not in the shadows as Christy had done, but out here in the open. She got her wish, but why the hell did it have to be Abby Hargrove?

"Lieutenant," Rachel said, her voice formal and her posture tall as she turned around. Abby Hargrove had it all. Looks, success, respect. When Rachel had first been hired, she had hoped to find an ally, a mentor in the then-Sergeant Hargrove. She had quickly given up on that notion.

"Tomorrow, zero eight hundred. My office. You're being reassigned."

Fuck. Rachel hoped her expression wasn't giving away any of her internal swearing. She nodded as her lieutenant walked away without another word. Rachel didn't even bother going after her to try to find out more about this reassignment. She didn't need details to recognize bad news when she heard it.

CHAPTER TWO

Callan Lanford shifted her hips and wedged her right foot between her duffel bag and the metal frame of the seat in front of her. She was too tall to fly coach. A week of hard riding as she tried out for one of the East Coast's top polo teams hadn't even caused a twinge in her muscles, but two hours on an airplane and she was stiff and sore from inactivity. And restless. She tapped her fingers on the plastic tray table as she tried to muster some interest in the romantic comedy playing on the plane's small screen, but she gave up with a sigh and tugged out her earbuds.

Getting access to her laptop proved to be more challenging than any of the complex goal-scoring drills she'd performed during the previous week. She balanced her half-eaten fruit plate on her lap and tucked the plastic cup of ginger ale between her thighs before she closed the tray table. She groped for her duffel bag, careful not to spill her drink or hit her head on the seat in front of her. Once she had the laptop in hand, she maneuvered back to an upright position and opened the table again. She arranged her cup and plate and computer on the too-small plastic surface, hoping she had at least an hour of battery life and turbulence-free flying ahead of her.

Cal slid the window shade closed to keep the glare from the bright sun off her screen. She had spent the past months living in two worlds, practicing for and studying footage of the Virginia team while training her horses and coaching her own polo teams on her family's Washington farm. The scenery between the two coasts and the idle time spent traveling from one to the other were inconsequential to her. Too much time and space to think. She preferred action.

She opened a document full of notes she had made over the winter as her Pacific Northwest Polo Club teams had practiced in the indoor arena and played casual matches against other local clubs. Cal typed in the details of several new plays she had thought of over the past week of nonstop polo. She had suggested the Virginia team try them, but they had been politely uninterested. Cal had quickly learned that they were a smoothly functioning unit. Successful and established, they wanted nothing more than a qualified fourth player to step in and fill an empty space. They might be interested in her new ideas once Cal was settled on the team, but innovation wasn't a requirement for the job. Cal had adapted quickly, learning the team's plays and executing them flawlessly and without variation, but she hadn't been able to stop her mind from making changes and improving on their existing playbook. Her Northwest team wasn't at the same level yet, but they'd benefit from her week of exposure to new players and new methods.

Cal added some new drills she had learned in Virginia to her lengthy training file. Several of them could be adapted for the group of amateurs she coached in her limited spare time. She closed the document and checked her e-mail while she still had some power left, since, as she had suspected, she hadn't given her laptop enough time to charge before leaving the hotel. Silently praising the gods for in-flight WiFi, she scanned her e-mails quickly, deleting a few ads for riding paraphernalia as she skimmed through her in-box. A note from her friend Linda who played on a polo team in Portland, asking if Cal would be in Oregon for an upcoming meet. Cal smiled, remembering the last time she and Linda had gotten together on the field, and then later in Cal's hotel room. She'd make it a point to get to the meet. She had been too busy to give much attention to her social life over the spring, but she would have to change that—and soon.

Cal's smile faded as she read her dad's e-mail. He had sent an addendum to the long list of East Coast networking contacts her mother had sent a few days prior. Cal hadn't even made the Virginia team yet—technically, since she was certain she'd be picked to fill the empty position—and her parents already were planning her route to a different and better club. Cal read through the list of names, noting which ones she had met during her week of tryouts. She had felt it herself, that Virginia wasn't a place to get comfortable, a place to settle in and make her mark. She would gain some valuable experience, and then she would move forward. Always a new level to reach. Cal finished memorizing the list and read the more personal message her dad had written at the bottom of his e-mail. He had been contacted by a friend's daughter, asking Cal to train a mounted police unit. Cal could hear her father's laughter in his writing, and she laughed as well. As if she had the time or desire to devote to a new job. She lived and breathed polo, only resurfacing now and again for sex. Nothing else mattered.

Forty-five minutes later, as the plane taxied to the gate, Cal turned on her cell, pulled up her dad's e-mail, and dialed his friend's daughter's number. He could have answered for her since they both knew she wasn't about to take on a new project when the height of polo season was approaching and her time was scheduled to the minute, but he had respected her autonomy enough to let her make the call. She didn't have any trouble saying no to anything or anyone that might interfere with her priorities.

"Lieutenant Hargrove?" Cal asked when she heard an unintelligible voice answer the phone. "This is Callan Lanford, returning your call."

"Ms. Lanford?" a woman's voice repeated, breaking through the static. "I can barely hear you."

Cal turned toward the window, shielding her neighbor as much as possible as she increased the volume of her voice. "I'm sorry about that. I'm on a plane. My dad passed along your message about training the mounted police unit, but I have to decline the offer."

End of story. Cal had learned not to give excuses when she said no to someone who wanted to take time away from her career. If she said she was planning to leave the state soon, then the lieutenant would tell her they'd be glad to have her help on a temporary basis.

If she said she didn't have time available, she'd be given the unlikely story that the job wouldn't require much time at all. People usually had trouble arguing with a *no* that didn't have reasons attached.

Lieutenant Hargrove apparently wasn't one of those people. "We really need your help, so I hope you'll reconsider. The job offers decent compensation, and you can set your own hours. It's part-time work, so it shouldn't interfere with your own training. I'm going to have the officer-in-charge contact you, and she can explain in more detail what we—"

Cal heard her phone beep before the line went dead. Damn. Didn't she have anything with a fully charged battery? She wasn't accustomed to filling long hours of nothingness with technology. Cal would have liked to have ended this issue right now, but she'd have to wait until she got home. Maybe she could give the unknown officer-in-charge the names of other potential trainers, but Cal wouldn't accept the job.

She reset her watch to local time. After too many hours of stasis, she'd finally be able to *move*.

Rachel started her shift at six the next morning, still slightly hungover from too much beer the night before and exhausted from the struggle to keep from going to Christy's apartment. She spent the two hours before her meeting with Hargrove backed into a parking place at the station and sipping on a triple-shot latte. As a new sergeant, she still didn't have a set shift, so now she was doing a stint as fill-in for a vacationing day-shifter. The squad of old-timers, the patrol officers with enough seniority to qualify for a cushy day shift, suited her fine. They hated her because they were all long-time friends of Officer Sheehan—the man she had been unfortunate enough to arrest—but at least they didn't need or want her input on their calls. She spent her days hiding and staying out of everyone's way. Frustrated. Wanting to work, but relieved to have a place to lie low for a while, hoping the fuss over her decision would blow over and everything would return to normal.

Of course, her imminent reassignment blew that hope to bits. Rachel was tired of sitting on her lazy ass and not doing any actual police work, but she had a feeling that whatever post Hargrove stuck her in wouldn't make her life any easier. Still, how much worse could it get? A desk job? Rachel leaned against her headrest and stared at the modern glass-and-steel station. Working inside, constantly meeting up with other officers and their disapproving stares. The steel beams were as confining as prison bars, but at least people on the phone wouldn't know who she was. She'd spend her days listening to citizens complain about their neighbors' dogs and handing out theft report numbers for insurance claims. Better than the days when she could go her entire shift without talking to anyone who wasn't selling food out of a drive-through window.

Rachel finished her coffee and got out of her car. She swiped her card at the door and tossed the paper cup in the recycling bin before heading to the women's restroom to check her appearance. Lieutenant Hargrove never looked anything but perfectly polished. Rachel couldn't clean up her reputation, but at least she could give the impression of a model officer on the outside. She stood in front of the bathroom mirror and straightened her collar. Tucked her shirt a little tighter. Rubbed her sleeve over her already shining badge. Fuss and fuss, but she looked the same as she had when she'd started. She turned on the water and wet her hand, running it through her short dark hair to smooth down a few loose curls. If Hargrove had given her more notice, she would have gotten a fresh haircut. She sighed and dried her hand on a paper towel. She couldn't put it off any longer.

Rachel checked her watch as she walked up the metal stairs, her black boots echoing in the large open space. Nothing in the building was designed to muffle sounds or soften hard surfaces. Bright and utilitarian and austere. Judging and confining. The moment her watch's second hand hit the twelve, Rachel knocked on Hargrove's door.

"Come in, Bryce."

Rachel entered the small office. Abby didn't look up from the paperwork she was doing, but she motioned Rachel toward an uncomfortable-looking plastic-and-metal chair. Rachel sat on the edge of the hard plastic seat and watched her work.

Lieutenant Abby Hargrove was beautiful. Rachel had noticed her immediately when she had started with the department. Auburn hair wrapped neatly in an elegant chignon. Makeup perfectly applied. The body of an athlete and the curves of a sexy woman. All she needed was the sash and tiara, and she'd be able to win any title she wanted. But Rachel had no clue who was behind the stunning good looks. What kind of heart beat behind the bulletproof vest. What thoughts simmered behind those long eyelashes. The Hargrove name was well-known in the department, but not in a good way. Hints of violence, corruption. Nothing proven, but definitely something there. Abby Hargrove kept herself poised and aloof, separate not only from her family name but from everyone else on the department. Most of the other women on the force stuck together even across the barriers of rank, but not Abby.

She finally looked up and caught Rachel staring. Rachel didn't shift her gaze away. She was becoming quite adept at hiding anything she felt. Embarrassment, hurt, loneliness. They all were there, but under the surface. She couldn't change the way other officers treated her. She couldn't beg or cajole or demand their friendship. Her only recourse was to appear unfazed and untouched by everything. No sign of weakness allowed.

Abby stared back for a few seconds before she broke the silence. "Officer Jensen said you helped him with the horses at the memorial service," she said. "Do you ride?"

"Um, yes," Rachel said. She focused on the question and not her shock that Clark had bothered to mention her assistance. "My parents have a ranch in eastern Washington. I've ridden Western, and I played polo in college."

"Polo." Abby shuffled through some files on her desk and pulled out a slip of paper torn from a spiral notebook. "Have you heard of Callan Lanford?"

Rachel felt her confused response flicker over her face. She relaxed her forehead and blinked a couple of times before she answered. Of course she knew Callan Lanford. Golden girl of the polo world. Cal had been two years ahead of her in school, and the star of USC's national champion polo team. Far out of Washington State University's league. And Cal had been far out of Rachel's league. Cal still played—apparently both on the field and off. Every month, Rachel saw pictures of Cal in her polo magazines, either wearing the burgundy and royal of the Pacific Northwest Polo Team or wearing street clothes, with some gorgeous woman draped on her arm.

"I've heard of her," she said.

"Good." Abby slid the piece of paper over to Rachel. It had Cal's name on it, and a phone number. "She was recommended as one of the top trainers in the area."

"She is," Rachel said. Why were they talking about Cal? "But I don't need a—"

"Yes, you do," Abby picked up a small plastic container full of paper clips and leaned back in her leather chair. She flipped the box upside down so some of the clips stuck on the magnetic opening at the top. "You're Alex's replacement as sergeant for the mounted unit. Against my recommendation."

"I'm…what?" Special units like the mounted division were prestige and coveted positions, with their abundant grant money and the autonomy they offered. Rachel would have applied to be a rider in the unit if she had still been in patrol when it formed. She didn't have the seniority or the connections—even before her disgrace—needed to be in charge of it. "But…how?"

Abby shrugged. She pushed the paper clips back into the container with her long fingers and flipped it again. "Apparently you have a friend somewhere high up the food chain. You don't have any lower down." She leaned forward. "I'll be honest with you, Bryce. I don't want you in my unit, and I certainly don't want you in charge of it. The mounted division is dealing with enough crap. They're mourning their leader and they're pushing to be ready for the Fourth of July celebration, so they don't need to be handicapped with someone like you. You aren't a team player, you won't have their respect. You don't have a prayer of pulling them together in time."

Rachel struggled to pull her attention off the flipping paper-clip box and catch up with Abby's speech. She appreciated the honesty, at least. Abby was only saying out loud the things Rachel was thinking. Still, it hurt to hear them. "I never applied for the job," she said. "There must be some mistake."

"It's a mistake, all right, but not one I can fix. I'm stuck with you."

Anger finally pushed past Rachel's confusion. She held herself still with a tight grip on the cold metal arms of her chair. "Hey, I said I didn't ask for this. It's not my fault that the entire department is pissed at me. According to the domestic violence laws—"

Abby waved her hand. "Don't quote state laws to me, Bryce. Yes, you followed procedure to the letter. And yes, Sheehan's an ass and he belongs in jail. But sometimes playing the game has nothing to do with the rules. You lost the respect of the department and you're going to have a hell of a time getting it back. I don't want you dragging my unit down."

Rachel crossed her arms over her chest, feeling the comforting pressure of her Kevlar vest. Hargrove was crazy. Rules were the only thing holding society together. Without them, everything would fall apart. "So I'll refuse the job."

"Don't you think I tried to get someone else—anyone else—appointed? But you're the only sergeant with any riding experience."

So Abby had already known the answer when she asked Rachel if she was a rider. A few months ago, this posting would have been a dream come true. Now it was only a very public, very spectacular way to fail. "You saw how those horses were acting yesterday. There's no way anyone could have them ready in a little over a month."

"Alex assured me they'd be more than ready by the Fourth. Stick with his training plans and try not to make them worse than they are."

"But you said yourself, they won't listen to me."

"Exactly," Abby said. She tapped the paper with Cal's name on it. "So you get Callan Lanford to do the actual training. Your position as sergeant is merely a formality. You put on the uniform and sit on a horse. You're qualified to do that much, at least."

Abby handed Rachel a manila folder. “The security code for the stables and keys to the tack room and your new office. Remember, Alex was an experienced mounted officer and he kept detailed lesson plans. The riders will respect Callan. All you have to do is keep a low profile. Keep out of the way.”

Rachel left the office and walked down the stairs, keeping one hand firmly on the metal railing for support. Get outside. Get into the privacy of her patrol car before she gave in to her confusion and despair and frustration. Why had everything gone so wrong? She had just been appointed to a plum position on the force. Despite her short time as a sergeant, her bad reputation, her new superior’s wishes. If there was any smidgen of good feeling toward her left on the department, it’d be gone by the time news of her promotion spread. Rachel stepped outside and looked up at the flag flying at half-mast. She would have been delighted with this job if her squad liked her and her lieutenant had faith in her. Even more, if she didn’t have to call Cal Lanford and ask for her help.

❖

The soft crunch as Rachel’s sneakers hit the fir-needle-strewn path was a rhythmic accompaniment to her breath. Two footfalls for each inhale, two for each exhale. The park was quiet except for the ordered sound as Rachel jogged through the darkness. Her eyes had adjusted to the dim light of the quarter moon, but she could have run this trail blindfolded. She broke free of the trees and crossed the pavement, following the road for a few yards until another dirt path led her toward the bluff.

Point Defiance Park’s Five Mile Drive was a meandering road through a cool, dense forest. Rachel followed a series of hiking trails on her usual jogging route, crisscrossing the Drive at intervals. During the day, during the summer, the road was often filled with cars. Families driving at a leisurely pace among the fir trees and rhododendrons. Stopping to take photos of the raccoons and deer, pausing at viewpoints so they could watch eagles soaring over Commencement Bay. But at three in the morning, there weren’t any people except for Rachel. No sounds except for the slap of her shoes, the even rasp of her breath, the occasional scuffle as a small animal scurried through the brush. No city smells, only the wet odor of moss and fir and the fishy scent of Puget Sound. The park was officially closed at sundown, but this was the single rule Rachel ever broke. She needed the space, needed the solitude if she wanted to keep breathing through the rest of the day.

She hadn't heard the single shot, muffled by a silencer, which had killed Alex a week ago. She hadn't started her run until a few hours later. And by the time his body was found, she was already at work. She hadn't noticed anything unusual on her run, so why admit to anyone that she used the park after hours?

Rachel skirted the zoo's parking lot, keeping to the shadows out of habit, and ran downhill toward the ferry landing. She could barely make out the bulky shapes of the caribou where they clustered on a small knoll in their enclosure, their habits as predictable as hers. Normally she would head uphill here, back to her small apartment, but today she crossed the road leading to the ferry and paused to catch her breath.

Crouched over, with her hands supported on her knees, Rachel stretched her lower back as her respiration rate slowed. The long run had eased some of her tension, unkinking the muscles she relied on to keep her in control and calm every day at work. She was still in the park, but at its very edge where residential streets abutted the huge green space. An empty lot, once used as a storage dump for branches and dirt and rocks left behind after storms or landscaping projects, had been converted into a stable yard for the mounted unit. When Tacoma last had mounted police, they had been housed near the southwest corner of the park, where Rachel started her nightly run.

She had liked knowing there were horses in the park once again. Police and trail horses had once traveled the hiking trails now used only by people and deer. Occasionally during her runs over the past two months, since the horses had arrived, Rachel had heard them moving about in their stalls, snorting or whickering in the night. Sometimes she saw hoofprints on her trails, or she'd notice the lights on in the yard and know Alex or one of the officers was there. When the wind was just right, blowing off the Sound, familiar smells of barn and horse hit her as she turned for home. But she had never been inside the chain link fence surrounding the barn.

Rachel had her identification card on a cord around her neck. She fished it out from between her breasts and wiped off a light film of sweat before swiping it at the gate. She keyed in the security code she had memorized that afternoon and stepped into the mounted-police headquarters. *Her* mounted unit's headquarters. She belonged here. She might feel like a thief, sneaking around in the night, but this would be her new office starting tomorrow.

She walked around the small yard, familiarizing herself with its dimensions while she still felt in control, protected by the dark sky. Before she had to face the scowling faces of her new unit. She didn't have to guess how they must have reacted to the news. She'd be surprised if they didn't all resign from the division before she even spent one day in charge of them.

There was a small tanbark arena for schooling, cordoned off with bright orange pylons and crime-scene tape. Fancy. It would be tight quarters for four riders, but mounted horses didn't have the luxury of space. They'd spend their working hours in close quarters with citizens, perps, and cars. The barn was simple as well, an L-shaped structure with stalls for six horses, four of them occupied. No inside aisle, but a wide overhang offered a sheltered space for grooming and tacking the horses. She walked slowly past the stalls, peering over the top of the dutch doors. Three of the horses were asleep standing up, knees locked and a hind hoof cocked. The fourth, Clark's bay, was curled on a bed of clean shavings. Rachel kept her movements calm and quiet, humming softly under her breath as she moved past each stall. Ears flicked in her direction, the only sign that her presence was noted.

When she came to the short side of the L, she fished the key Hargrove had given her out of her pocket and opened the first door. A tack room. The meager light of the moon didn't reach into the darkened room, so Rachel ran her palm along the wall until she located the light switch. The sudden brightness startled her. She didn't like being backlit, visible to anyone who might be lurking in the deserted park, so she quickly turned the light off and plunged the room once more into blackness. She stood pressed against the wall until her eyes adjusted to the night again. A flashlight. She should have brought a flashlight with her.

She locked the tack room door and moved to the next one. Alex's office. No, her office. This time, she closed and bolted the door behind her before she fumbled for the light switch. The office was as tidy and well-ordered as the tack room had seemed to be in her brief glimpse of it. The desk was bare except for a plain Page-A-Day calendar and a metal in-box. A bunch of pens sat in a wooden cup next to a plastic paper-clip box like the one Hargrove had played with during Rachel's meeting with her.

Rachel sat in the cheap swivel chair, its lack of back support and loose casters sure signs of its advanced age. She opened the desk drawers one by one. More pens. Alex must have swiped a handful every time he walked by a supply closet. Miscellaneous office supplies. A stray hoof pick. The bottom drawer was wedged tight with file folders, and Rachel pulled them out one at a time. Hargrove hadn't been kidding. Alex had kept meticulous records on the health histories for each horse, plus expense accounts for tack and feed.

And training notes. Rachel flipped through the pages in the file. Alex had kept daily records of every ride, every lesson. And a notebook for each officer with their riding abilities and issues, how they performed in each lesson, their goals for the next ride. Rachel frowned as she tapped the stack of papers against the desk, tidying the pile before she stuck it back in the folder and wedged the whole thing back into the drawer. From the outside, the whole barn looked perfect. Perfectly managed, perfectly organized. And if Alex had been a riding instructor, preparing his students for a show or teaching them the fundamentals of riding, Rachel would have been as impressed with him as Hargrove seemed to be. But these officers and horses were preparing to be on the city streets in five weeks, chasing criminals, patrolling through rowdy holiday crowds, while being touched and bumped and spooked. They had barely made it through their short time at the memorial service without disaster. How would they handle Tacoma's jammed waterfront on the Fourth?

Rachel turned out the light before she unbolted the door and stepped out, locking the office behind her. She glanced at each horse once more before leaving the stable yard and walking slowly home. The first signs of dawn were glimmering in the east, and she heard the whistles and chirps as the park's residents greeted the new day. She wished she shared the birds' enthusiasm, but all she felt was puzzlement. After her meeting with Hargrove, Rachel had searched on-line for any information she could find about mounted police horses and their training. Her brief, slightly panicked search had given her plenty of information about desensitizing the horses and getting them accustomed to gunshots, cars, and contact with people. Alex had experience. He had spent a few years as a mounted officer in Portland before transferring to Tacoma. Why had he spent the past two months teaching these riders nothing more than how to sit in a saddle? Rachel jogged across a street and climbed the stairs to her apartment. Maybe Alex had more notes at home or in the tack room. She'd search for them later. In the meantime, she needed a shower before she had to go talk to Callan Lanford and admit she needed a babysitter to help her do her job.

CHAPTER THREE

After a shower and a quick breakfast of toast and coffee, Rachel drove out to the Lanford farm, home of the Pacific Northwest Polo Team. About a half mile beyond the city limits, she turned off the main road and crunched over a gravel driveway until she reached the large barn. She could have called Callan instead of driving so far, but she hated the words she had to say. *I need your help. I have no idea how to train a mounted unit, and even if I did, my squad won't respect me enough to listen.*

Rachel didn't want to ask for help. Didn't want to *need* Cal's help. It sucked. She wasn't qualified for her new job, but she didn't have a choice. She somehow had to become a success in this new post and earn back a little respect, or she'd have to resign. She couldn't keep going to work day after day and face the angry stares. Or worse, the vacant looks that passed right through her as if she weren't even there.

On the phone, Cal would only have heard Rachel's voice. At least in person she could wear her uniform. Give the impression she was strong and capable. Rachel got out of her patrol car and looked around. Exactly the kind of place where she'd expect to find Cal. Acres of mesh-fenced green pastures dotted with shiny, grazing horses. A huge indoor arena and an even huger outdoor polo field with pristine grass that would rival any PGA putting green. Three barns, a clubhouse, the main house that looked like a mansion. Every building was surrounded by neat, multihued gardens filled with fresh red beauty bark and colorful spring flowers. The Lanfords must have a battalion of workers to maintain the yard. And another one to clean the stalls and take care of so many horses.

A frenzied salvo of barks made Rachel stop admiring the view of Mount Rainier and turn toward the barn. A flurry of white came at her like a tornado. She might have been more concerned if the dog's tail hadn't been waving so hard she looked like she was about to spin right off the ground. Rachel bent down and tried to calm the mass of tongue, fur, and wagging tail, finally identifying her as a rough-coated border collie, pure white except for a patch of black fur extending over her right eye and ear, like a jaunty beret.

"Feathers! Pipe down and come back here."

Rachel recognized Cal's voice before she even stepped out of the barn. Strong and confident, with a layer of laughter under every word. The few times she had played against Cal's college team, Rachel had heard Cal call out encouragement and directions to her teammates. The throaty sound had given her goose bumps when she was a young starstruck college kid. Now, as she faced the very adult, very beautiful Callan Lanford, Rachel felt her reaction travel further than skin-deep. Everything about Cal seemed to glow, from her thick gold hair, pulled into a high ponytail, to her eyes so blue-gray they flashed like silver in the sunlight. Her skin was flushed and faintly shiny and she had a red mark across her forehead. She must have been riding, wearing a helmet and sweating in the late spring heat. Rachel clenched her teeth to make sure her jaw didn't gape open. This was not good at all.

"Feathers, get over here," Cal ordered. The white dog finally, and with seeming reluctance, obeyed, and Cal grabbed hold of her collar. "Hi. Sorry about that. She gets kind of excited when we have visitors. Hey, I remember you from college polo, don't I? WSU?"

Rachel had been prepared to identify herself, explain how she knew Cal. She certainly had never expected Cal to remember her. She reached out and shook Cal's hand, feeling the ridge of small calluses on Cal's palm, at the base of her fingers. Where her polo mallet would rest. Rachel's had softened over time, after a few years of not playing. She imagined Cal's polo-roughened hand brushing over her body, and her nipples hardened in an involuntary response. Damn. Definitely not good at all. "Um…yes. We've met. I'm Rachel Bryce."

Cal smiled at Rachel's firm handshake. Exactly as solid and impersonal as she'd expect from a woman in uniform. A very sexy woman in uniform. With handcuffs. Tasty. Cal assumed the visit was about the training job, and even though she was still adamant about refusing it, she was willing to entertain the envoy for a few hours.

"This is Feathers. I can see you've met, because you have white hair all over your pants." Cal nodded at the white dog she still held tightly by the collar. Her other border collie, a smooth-coated black dog with a white chest and nose, sat quietly and obediently by her side. "And this is—"

"Don't tell me," Rachel said, holding up her hand. "I really hope his name is Tar."

Cal laughed. Sexy and smart. She silently thanked Lieutenant Hargrove for dropping this woman on her doorstep. Rachel Bryce. All grown up, with her duty belt full of whoop-ass. A gun, handcuffs, a nightstick. Cal could easily think of some fun they could have with the latter two items. And a Taser strapped to her thigh. Cal didn't have any use for the Taser, but she had a good idea what she wanted to do while Rachel's thigh wrapped around her waist and drew her closer.

"Very good," she said. "You're right. Tar and Feathers. And you're a little overdressed for a polo reunion. Sorry about the dog hair."

Cal gave in to her desires and brushed over Rachel's legs, prolonging the contact as she wiped off the white hairs that had attached to Rachel's dark uniform.

Rachel stepped back, out of reach. "Don't worry about it. I don't mind a little dog hair. Anyway, I'm here to ask for your help."

Whatever you need, darling. Cal's resolve to decline the job suffered a minor setback. She remembered every opponent she'd ever had. During college, after college, she studied team rosters. Memorized faces. But, more important than that, she watched the opposing team as they rode onto the field and played the first minutes of the first chukker. She knew Rachel from her games against WSU. Rachel had been young, two years behind her. And rough. She obviously didn't have much formal training and she looked more prepared to ride out with a herd of cattle than to play a refined game of polo. But she was a natural rider. And she had clearly understood the rules of polo and followed them to the letter. She wasn't team captain, but her team turned to her time and again as their true leader.

"You scored against me in our first game together," Cal said. "It would have been a shutout if you hadn't gotten past me in the third chukker."

Yes, she noticed every opponent. Evaluated them, studied them. But some women had stood out more than others, and Rachel Bryce was one of the more memorable players. Something about her Cal couldn't quite put her finger on. But she wanted to get her hands on Rachel and find out every detail about her.

"Yeah, well, you left your near side open," Rachel said. She looked unfazed by Cal. "Totally unguarded. A Pony Clubber playing broom polo could have scored against you."

"Is that a challenge?" Cal asked. She stepped closer to Rachel. She had played this game before. Start it on the field, end it in bed. Rachel would be a worthy adversary on horseback and more than satisfying in the bedroom. She was beautiful, like a fir tree in a nighttime forest. Straight and tall and unyielding. With those dark evergreen eyes and near-black hair that glowed with golden brown highlights in the sun. Cal had worked hard today. She deserved a reward.

But Rachel moved another step away. "I'm not here for a grudge match," she said. She shut Cal off with her distance. With her crossed arms. "I need to ask a favor."

"Shoot," Cal said. She knelt down and ruffled Feathers's ears. She took a deep breath and grounded herself in the smell of dog fur, dirt, her own sweat. She had been driving herself like mad since she had returned from her East Coast tryouts, getting herself and her six horses in top shape for the polo season ahead. Her aggressive attitude had carried through to her recreational activities, as usual, but Rachel didn't seem inclined to bite at Cal's overtures. She needed to slow down, give Rachel some space. Cal wasn't about to give up, of course, but she had to change her tactics.

"We have a new mounted division in Tacoma," Rachel said. She squatted down so she was eye level with Cal and scratched Tar's chin when he walked over to her. Her rigid posture and tense voice seemed to relax as Cal backed off her attack.

Cal had watched the memorial service, paying special attention to the horses and riders even though she was uninterested in working with them. The antics of the obviously poorly trained mounted unit would have been funny if she hadn't realized how dangerous the situation actually was. Rachel hadn't been one of the riders and she was too good a horsewoman to have sent the unprepared squad out among the public. She must have been chosen to recruit Cal because of their past acquaintance. "Yes, I saw them on TV. Who's responsible for that disaster waiting to happen?"

"I am."

Cal stopped petting her dog and stood up again. Oops. "Well, I didn't see you on…So, um, congratulations. You seem to be doing a good job so far."

Rachel stood as well. Cal was a lousy liar. And any person with even an ounce of horse sense would have been shocked by the unit's lack of training. "Save it. I'm the unit sergeant as of today. That's the favor. I don't have any experience with this kind of training and I could use your help. We need to be ready to ride by the Fourth of July. We'll be patrolling during the celebration on the waterfront."

And my boss told me to ask you. Rachel left that part out.

Cal laughed and shook her head. "Are you planning to lead your horses from the ground like the officers did at the service? You can call yourselves the Dismounties."

Rachel fervently hoped no one else would think of that nickname. She could see it splashed across the newspaper headlines. "We'll ride on the Fourth. We have to."

"If you had more time…"

"We don't." The unit didn't have more time. Rachel didn't have more time. "Special units like this one are funded by grants, and our main function is to help with crowd control at big events. We can't sit around for months, training until New Year's Eve."

"Do you realize how dangerous this is?"

Cal sounded almost angry, but Rachel wasn't sure why. Probably because she cared about the welfare of the horses. It would be so easy for one of them to get seriously injured if it freaked out and got loose. Rachel figured Cal didn't care one way or the other about her or the other riders.

"Look," Rachel said. She felt a strange stirring of panic. Cal thought the idea was crazy and she was going to refuse to train them. Rachel had dreaded coming here, asking for Cal's assistance, but she needed it. Desperately. And as she pictured the fiasco when the unit trotted out to meet the public, she realized it wasn't only about her. About her reputation at work and this last ditch effort to fix it. These horses and riders were under her command, and like it or not, it was her responsibility to keep them safe. The burden was overwhelming and unwanted, and the concern in her voice sounded like anger when she spoke. "Either you'll help or you won't. Either way, we ride on the Fourth."

Cal raised her hands in a gesture of surrender. The sunny smile she had worn when she first saw Rachel was gone, replaced by an angry-looking frown. "Do what you want. It's your funeral."

Cal's gaze moved from the shocked and sad expression on Rachel's face to the black tape crossing her badge. Cal rubbed her hand over her forehead. She could still feel the indentation from her tight-fitting safety helmet and the growing headache from wearing it in the sun all morning. "Jesus, I'm sorry. Bad choice of words."

"It's okay," Rachel said. Her voice was quiet, with no hint of her earlier intensity. "I'll see you around."

She walked toward her patrol car, and Cal trailed slowly behind. She had been surprised and happy to see Rachel. Hopeful she could be seduced. Simple emotions. Why did she have to feel concerned about her now? She barely knew Rachel Bryce, beyond her sexy exterior and the leadership qualities she had shown on the field almost ten years ago. Two days ago Cal had watched a cop's memorial service with sadness and empathy, had watched the antics of the mounted police with humor and disapproval. In a detached way, without any of the raging indignation she felt now. Rachel was going to accept her department's insane insistence on sending the unit out among the public. And she was going to ride with them. Cal had no intention of being involved in this foolish plan, but she couldn't let Rachel walk away. She didn't have any reason to feel guilty if something happened to Rachel, but she would.

"Wait, cowgirl," she said. She held onto the door frame to keep Rachel from slamming it after she got in the car. "Say I agreed to help. What would I get out of this?"

"You'd get paid," Rachel said, tugging on the door handle.

Cal shifted her body so Rachel couldn't shut the door. She didn't doubt Rachel would slam it on her hand if given the chance. "Money? Not enough. I was thinking of a more personal form of payment."

Cal reached out and gently brushed her fingers through Rachel's short hair. Soft as a well-groomed horse. In such contrast with her coarse uniform and stiff posture. Rachel swatted her hand away.

"Is everything a game with you?"

A game. "Yes," Cal said honestly. Her life revolved around polo. Drills, practice, matches. She was serious about that game. The little time she had left over was dedicated to play. Fun. She'd much rather spend her free time having sex—with Rachel or someone else—than working with an inept bunch of riders, but she wanted to stall, to see Rachel at least once more and try to either talk her out of her promise to ride on the Fourth or talk her into bed. Preferably both, but Cal would be fine with the latter.

"So why don't we play for it?" Cal asked. She couldn't read the expression in Rachel's eyes. Contempt? Irritation? "Tomorrow morning at six. A little friendly stick-and-ball play. If you can outscore me, I'll help."

"And if I can't?" Rachel asked.

Cal smiled. "A kiss. I decide when and where. What do you say?"

She watched Rachel wage some sort of battle within herself. Rachel didn't have a chance against her on the field, but she seemed determined to get Cal's help with her team. Cal wondered how far she'd go to get it.

"Deal," Rachel said, not meeting Cal's eyes. "See you tomorrow."

Cal barely moved in time before Rachel pulled her door shut. She started the engine and let it idle while Cal rounded up her dogs and moved to the edge of the parking area. Cal watched Rachel drive away. She felt tense, agitated by their conversation. Yes, some of it was sexual tension. She had felt a spark of attraction for Rachel when she had first seen her on the USC polo field. The spark was only brighter now. The police uniform seemed designed to mask the female body, flattening it in the wrong places and adding bulk where none was wanted. But even in the unflattering uniform and thick bulletproof vest, Rachel had looked damn good. And she smelled good. Starch and polyester on the surface, but woodsy and vibrant underneath.

Cal started toward the barn but changed her mind and went to the polo team's clubhouse. She needed to work off some of her excess energy, and she didn't want to risk her horses' careful training by subjecting any of them to her emotional turmoil. Yes, she wanted Rachel. But sex couldn't come with commitment. Cal was married to polo, and she didn't have room for any other serious relationships in her life. An occasional mistress was acceptable, necessary. But nothing more than that.

Rachel came with a whole ball of strings. Cal avoided women who expected too much from her. Usually, they wanted relationships—time and attention that Cal could barely afford to give. Love that she rarely felt. But Rachel wanted even more. Cal could manage to squeak out enough time to help her with the mounted unit, and she didn't doubt that she had the skill to train them. But she would have to invest too much of herself in the project. Her rare recreational hours would be devoted to planning their training schedule. And, even more dangerous, she would be emotionally committed as well. She wasn't unaffected by Rachel and her clear devotion to her division of misfit riders. And Rachel obviously wasn't an easy lay. She hadn't seemed moved by Cal's overtures, and she didn't seem inclined to stick around unless she secured Cal's help. Training the unit merely to have more time with Rachel was too much effort to put into sex, although she had a feeling Rachel would be more than worth it.

Cal grabbed a spare mallet from the clubhouse and walked out the back door. She let herself into the large cage made of chain-link fencing. She tossed some hard polo balls into the cage one at a time, listening as they rolled down the sloped plank floor and into the trough next to the dummy horse with a loud clatter. She climbed into the wooden horse's saddle and took a few easy practice swings. She had to be able to untangle herself after a fling, but she couldn't back out if she promised to train the unit. All or nothing. And nothing but polo ever got Cal's all. She leaned over and nudged one of the loose balls into place before swinging the mallet in a wide arc and sending the ball dead center against the wooden target in front of her. She caught the ball with the edge of her mallet as it bounced back to her, and lined up for another shot.

She got into a steady rhythm, accompanied by the loud thwack of ball against target. Forehand, backhand. Lean over and hit. She'd make one last play for Rachel in the morning, and then she'd let her go. And concentrate on polo.

"You're breaking your wrist in the offside backhand shot."

"The ball's going straight, Mother," Cal said without turning around. She could feel the slight twist in her wrist where the muscles were sore and tired. But she wasn't in here to perfect her form. She was here to work Rachel out of her system.

"The ball is going straight because the wall is a few feet in front of you. If you were on the field, your trajectory would be off. Do the shot again."

Cal pushed another ball to her off side and tried again. Her irritation didn't help her concentration, and the ball hit the wire fence on the right side of the target.

She could hear her mother's sigh. "Again. How do you expect to play on a high-goal team if you can't control your swing?"

Cal sent the ball toward the target again, wishing she could hit it hard enough to shatter the thick wood. She looked back at her mom. Cecilia Calvert Lanford looked like she was about to pose for the cover of a polo magazine, not take her horse out for a schooling session. Every hair, every piece of clothing was perfect. "I did great in tryouts, so I expect I'll do fine when I play on their team."

"Not for long if you miss a pass or a goal because your mallet arm is weak."

Cal turned away from her and struck at the ball again, sending it to the target with perfect accuracy.

"Better," Cecilia said. "Keep practicing until you hit it straight every time. Remember, consistency will make you a champion. It's not enough to be brilliant on occasion, when it suits you."

Cal stayed in the practice cage long after her mother walked away, hitting shot after shot until her right arm was shaky with fatigue. By the time she dropped off the wooden horse she had corrected her breaking wrist and was hitting straight. More important, she had managed to drive her mother's criticisms to the back of her mind. Leaving plenty of room for Rachel's soft, throaty voice to take its place.

Chapter Four

After leaving Cal's farm, Rachel went back to her apartment to change into riding clothes. She wanted a chance to sit on all of the horses before her first meeting with her new team. She'd be better able to help the riders and reassign horses if necessary if she understood what each horse was like to ride, plus she needed to get in at least a little riding before tomorrow's match against Cal. She didn't have a mallet or a big enough arena for practicing actual polo, but she should be able to hold her own in a friendly stick-and-ball session. She didn't have a choice. She had to beat Cal because she needed her help and she wanted to avoid the penalty for losing. A kiss? She'd sooner kiss a…

Okay, she wouldn't mind kissing Cal. Rachel hadn't been blind to Cal's tactics today. She had come on strong and obviously was interested in more than a skirmish on the polo field. But Rachel had seen enough of Cal in her polo magazines. She had read enough articles about her to know that Cal was someone who regularly moved on. To a new team, a new horse, a new girlfriend. Rachel wanted to stay in place. To find her place. She thought she had, here in Tacoma with the police department and with Christy, but she had lost her footing with both of them. This post with the mounted unit was the one last chance she could grab on to. The one opportunity to either reestablish her place with TPD or lose it for good.

Lieutenant Hargrove had ordered a uniform for Rachel, but until it arrived she'd have to make do with her usual riding clothes. Jeans and a T-shirt. Faded and water-stained cowboy boots and chaps so worn the suede was smooth as leather. She had barely ridden over the past seven years, besides helping with ranch work when she was home on vacations, but as soon as she zipped on her chaps she felt at home. Like a second skin, and one that fit better than her first.

She left her patrol car parked by her apartment and walked down the hill to the police stables. Her building was seedy, but she had a beautiful view of Puget Sound and she was within walking distance to the park. So she paid the ridiculously high rent because she needed the smell of trees and water and exhaust from the Vashon Island ferry. She could live without new clothes and gourmet meals, but not without her nightly runs. In less than five minutes of leaving her door, she could be swallowed up by the dark and empty park.

Rachel had been tempted by the new condos springing up along Tacoma's waterfront, but the growing community was so far out of her reach she had no hope of qualifying for a loan. There were beautiful high rises, with panoramic views of Mount Rainier and Commencement Bay. Shopping and restaurants were part of the projected development of the area. Stunning, and with a stunning price tag. So Rachel had settled for a cheap facsimile. Off the water, but with a peekaboo view. Still pricey, but barely manageable. Close to being condemned, but still habitable.

And she couldn't beat the commute to her new job. Three minutes, and she was letting herself into the stabling area. The small, newly formed unit didn't have a full-time stablehand, so Rachel knew all the riders took turns feeding the horses and cleaning the stalls. She'd have to volunteer for extra shifts since she lived so close. The smell of shavings and horse and hay was intoxicating. She'd be spending all her free time here anyway, so she might as well be useful—and maybe ingratiate herself to her teammates at the same time.

Rachel's initial impression of the tack room during her nighttime visit had been correct. Saddles, bridles, and brushes were all neatly labeled and in place. She gathered the equipment for Ranger, Alex's big chestnut gelding. He was handsome and tall, with excellent conformation, and Rachel had a feeling Alex had kept the best horse for himself. After putting Ranger through his paces in the small arena, she was certain of it. The horse was well-trained and responsive, but unperturbed by the traffic and people beyond the yard's fence where the busy road leading to the ferry dock and the marina bordered the police stables. People wandered past, stopping to watch her ride as they waited for the ferry. Cars drove by with loud music blaring out the windows, and some drivers were helpful enough to honk or yell at Rachel as they passed by. Ranger obediently followed her signals without fuss. He seemed to be an ideal police horse. She dismounted and led him over to the fence so a little girl who was standing there with her father could pet him. Rachel knew mounted units were helpful not only for patrol, but also for PR. The horses needed to be friendly and approachable for even the tiniest citizens.

Unfortunately, the other three weren't anywhere near Ranger's standard. After her first ride, Rachel had been pleasantly surprised and very hopeful. Maybe the horses' behavior at the service had been a fluke, caused by the riders' grief and nerves. But by the time Rachel got to her fourth horse, Billie's gray mare Corona, she was back to her original pessimistic outlook. How could Alex have turned out one perfect horse and three poorly trained ones? Corona shied at the sound of a car starting its engine, and she skittered sideways halfway across the ring before Rachel could bring her to a halt. She tipped herself back into the saddle, waving in embarrassed acknowledgment as her small crowd of spectators clapped. The mare was a ball of nerves, hypersensitive to every sound from the environment and every signal from Rachel.

The other two hadn't been as excitable, but they needed consistent riding by someone more experienced than Rachel's officers. Clark's bay, Sitka, had potential. A couple weeks of solid schooling and he'd be as nice as Alex's Ranger. Don's mare Fancy was anything but. Ornery and dull, Rachel had been worn out by the effort of trying to get her into any gait faster than a walk. She had slid off the horse, hot and cranky, and barely evaded being bit on the arm for her troubles. Rachel had reviewed the officers' riding backgrounds, and Don was the least experienced of the three so he should have been given the easiest horse to ride. She wished that somewhere in his plentiful notes Alex had mentioned his reasoning behind the assignment of horse and rider teams because they didn't make any sense to her.

Rachel asked Corona to canter and nearly slid off her back when the mare bolted forward. Rachel managed to slow her down using her hands and voice, but she felt barely in control of the horse. Her gait was smooth but too fast, and the mare erupted into a series of bucks when the three officers emerged from the barn area and startled her.

"You're riding my horse," Billie said when Rachel finally brought the mare to a halt near the fence.

Rachel couldn't read Billie's voice. Was she angry, or just stating the obvious in her matter-of-fact way? She had known Billie the longest of any of their fellow officers, having met her on their first morning at the academy, but Rachel knew her the least. Very pretty, with black hair brushing her shoulders and eyes so dark brown they looked black as well. But very private. She had been in the military before joining the force and she looked like she had plenty of secrets hidden behind those intense eyes. Secrets she wasn't willing to share with anyone.

"I wanted to get a feel for all the horses," Rachel said. She dismounted and Billie took the reins out of her hand without another word, leading the mare toward the barn. The two men followed. Rachel ran a hand through her short hair. She had hoped to find an ally, not an enemy, in Billie, but she might have blown her chance already. She had been assigned to work with Billie in their first hand-to-hand combat training class at the academy. She had assumed she'd have an easy time since she had five inches and twenty pounds on Billie, but she had been dead wrong. Billie had shown an unerring sense of her opponent's weak areas. Rachel had gone home that night and cut off her long ponytail, never wanting to be thrown to the ground by it again. She had underestimated Billie back then, but she wouldn't make the same mistake twice.

She trailed after her team. Don and Clark sat on upturned buckets while Billie untacked Corona. Rachel felt at a disadvantage, as usual. She wished she had been finished riding before everyone arrived. She wished she hadn't spent the morning begging for Cal's help. She wished…

She could go on and on with wishes, but it wouldn't do any good. She needed to move forward, take control of her team. She was their sergeant and she needed to act the part.

"When you're done here, I want to have a team meeting in… my office," she said. She caught herself before she called it Alex's office.

Don leaned back against the wall. "We're all here. Why don't you just say what you have to say."

Rachel clenched her jaw. She could insist they walk the few yards to her office, but the battle didn't seem worth waging. Compromise. "Fine. First, I want to make some changes to our horse-and-rider teams based on your experience levels and my evaluation of the horses."

Judging by the looks exchanged by the three officers, Rachel was about to face another battle. She hoped she'd win at least one today. "Corona is out of the program. There's no way we can get her ready in time for the Fourth. She's too temperamental for police work. Sorry, Billie."

Billie shrugged, but Rachel thought she saw a glimpse of relief on her face. Billie had to realize, especially after the mare's performance at the memorial, that Corona would be dangerous on the streets. All of the horses were leased by the department, and Rachel had carefully read through the contracts that morning. She had the right to back out of any lease and return the horse to its owner, and she wondered why Alex hadn't taken the same opportunity to send Corona home. She hesitated before her next pronouncement, tempted to do what Alex had done and keep the best horse for herself. At least if disaster struck and the unit failed, she'd appear competent on the good-looking chestnut. And no one would question her right to ride Alex's mount. But she couldn't do it.

"Don, you've only been riding for a few months, so you should have the most trained horse. You'll ride Ranger, and Billie will ride Fancy."

"No," Don said. He crossed his arms and glared at her. Was he so desperate to defy her that he'd rather struggle with the difficult mare than ride Ranger? "I ride Fancy."

Apparently so. Rachel hadn't expected him to fight her on that particular change, believing he'd be relieved with the switch. She knew the officers didn't like her, but she hadn't realized they hated her so much. She rubbed a hand over her eyes. There was no way she'd be able to make this work.

"I'll ride Ranger," Billie said. She shrugged in Don's direction and looked back at Rachel. "Hey, I'm not going to get myself killed to prove a point. Corona is a beauty, and I'm sure she'd be fun to ride in a quiet arena, but she'd implode if I tried to chase a perp down a busy street. I even told Alex—"

Clark cleared his throat loudly, and Billie didn't finish her sentence. Rachel saw a small scrap of hope in the admission that at least Billie hadn't been completely sold on Alex's decisions. Maybe, just maybe, if she could convince her team that she knew something about horses, Rachel would be able to gain a little of their respect. She was making another compromise by not fighting Don on his decision, but he'd be the one to pay by sticking with Fancy. At least she was so sluggish, she'd be unlikely to run off with him.

"Good," she said, as if everything had gone her way. "Then it's settled. All the horses need more training, so I'll be riding each of them a few times a week. That part isn't negotiable," she added when Don opened his mouth as if he was about to protest. "We'll have lessons weekday afternoons."

"*You* are going to teach *us*?"

Don's voice challenged her as surely as if he had slapped her with a gauntlet. She wanted to protest, to fight. These officers were older than her and, except for Billie, they outranked her, but she was the most experienced rider. She was angry with their constant questioning, but mostly she was angry with her reluctance to defend herself. She couldn't convince them she was capable of leading the team and preparing them for their debut on the Fourth because she didn't believe it herself. She took the easy out Lieutenant Hargrove had given her.

"An old college friend of mine is one of the top polo trainers in the state. I've asked her to work with us and our horses until the Fourth." But Cal wasn't really a friend, Hargrove had been the one to choose her as the team's trainer, and Cal hadn't even accepted the role. Lots of lies. Rachel had grown up with them, telling them, believing them. She thought she had grown beyond the dishonesty, but the truth was too difficult to admit. She'd find a way to make at least some of her statements come true.

"What horse will you ride if I'm on Ranger?" Billie asked.

Rachel sighed. She had called the meeting, but her team had turned it into an interrogation. Although Billie's question was a good one, Rachel didn't have an answer yet. Almost a dozen horses had been volunteered by their owners as potential mounts, but Alex's notes said he had evaluated them all and had chosen the most promising four. Rachel didn't want to risk her life by riding a horse that hadn't even reached the low standard set by Fancy and Corona. "I don't know," she said honestly. "I'll figure out something soon so we can start riding outside the yard. Have you done much riding on the park trails?"

"Except for the service, we haven't been out of the yard," Clark said. "Alex said we weren't ready."

Rachel agreed with Alex's assessment for once, but the team *had* to be ready. "I'm sure we'll be fine."

What was one more lie?

❖

"Hi, Dad," Rachel said when her foster dad answered the phone.

"Hey, Rachel. I'm glad you called." Nelson Bryce's voice, even over the phone line, sounded warm with sympathy. "We've been thinking of you. We watched the memorial service. I'm so sorry."

Rachel sat down in her worn blue recliner. She propped the phone against her shoulder and reached for the lever to open the footrest.

"Thank you. Did you happen to see the mounted unit?"

"Well, I saw a bunch of inept officers leading some horses around. Is that what you meant?"

Rachel didn't laugh because he wasn't joking. Nelson took horses and their care very seriously, and she had quickly learned not to fool around where the animals were concerned. She had spent hours doing unpleasant and menial chores around the ranch the few times she had erred by putting a horse away without cooling him down properly or doing a half-assed job cleaning her tack or horse. She had worked off her anger and excess energy scrubbing bridles and water buckets and stable floors until she learned to respect not only the horses, but her new foster dad as well.

"Well, as of yesterday, I'm their inept new sergeant."

There was a pause before Nelson spoke. "I'm sure you can ride rings around them, Rachel, but you don't have the qualifications necessary for training an inexperienced group of people who will be facing life-and-death situations on horseback."

Warmth and honesty. Two things Rachel had missed so much over the past weeks. "I know. But I was assigned, so I don't have a choice."

"Then I'm sure you'll make it work. What's your plan?"

Rachel smiled. If you can't change a situation, stop moaning about it and figure out a way to make it better. Nelson had taught her that, but she was having trouble following the advice these days. "I've been researching training methods for mounted horses, and the previous sergeant, Alex Mayer, left behind a ton of notes. And my lieutenant suggested I ask Callan Lanford for help. I played against her in college."

"Yes, the polo player. Good plan. The horses will have to be very responsive and maneuverable, and the riders will need to stick on them no matter what. A lot like polo. But I'm guessing she's no more experienced than you when it comes to the real-life situations a mounted officer will face. You'll ultimately have to be the one in charge because you understand what it means to be a cop."

Rachel hesitated. She hadn't mentioned her disgrace during any of her previous calls. She hated lying—even by omission—to her foster parents, but she had hated to admit her failure even more. "That might be a problem," she said. She fiddled with the TV remote that was on the small table next to her chair. "I'm not exactly…popular at the moment."

"Leah and I thought something was wrong. You've sounded different for the past few months, but she said you'd talk about it when you were ready."

"Not much to talk about," Rachel said. Her throat felt tight, as if she might cry, but her eyes were dry. "I made a choice on a call and another officer was arrested because of it."

"And you believe you made the right decision?"

"Yes." At least, she'd been certain she was right. Now, after spending so much time alone and replaying the call over and over in her mind, she wasn't so sure. Should she have compromised?

"Then I'm proud of you. We both are. Standing firm with your values doesn't always make friends, but it will earn you respect from the people who matter. Don't let anyone convince you otherwise."

"I won't." Rachel spun the remote in her free hand. She should have confided to her family sooner. For a brief moment, she felt a little less alone, but she couldn't bring her parents with her every day. And she had lost respect as well as friends because she had stood for what she believed. But she didn't want to argue with the one person who was on her side. "Anyway, I'm calling because I need a horse to ride. Three of the four horses are acceptable, but I have to send one back."

"The gray?"

"Yes," Rachel said. No surprise that Nelson had been able to thoroughly evaluate the horses even after a quick glimpse of them on television. "I'm putting her rider on the chestnut, so I need a horse for me."

"Hmm…I have some decent horses, but most of them are too small. They'd be strong enough to carry you, but I assume you don't want to look like a long-legged teenager who's outgrown her pony."

"Yeah, I don't want the bad guys laughing at me while I'm chasing them," Rachel said. She smiled, thinking of the prints by Thelwell hanging in her old room. Funny cartoons of little kids on fat ponies and leggy adults on skinny ones. "I need to look tough."

"I do have one horse in mind. Big enough, and long on stamina. He's not spooky at all, but he's sensitive to the aids. Racing quarter horse bloodlines, so I'd bet on him against any fleeing criminal. I can haul him over this weekend. Needs a bit of a tune-up, and he'll be perfect."

Rachel didn't delve into the meaning behind the last sentence. But she had to tune-up the rest of the squad's horses, so what was one more? Besides, she trusted Nelson's assessment of a horse more than anyone else's.

"Great. And thank you." Rachel hung up the phone after chatting about the family for a few more minutes. The tension in her shoulders eased a fraction. She had a horse to ride. One hurdle down, and only a million to go.

Chapter Five

Cal left her bungalow before dawn and walked through the darkness of early morning, guided by the glowing windows of the main barn. Tar and Feathers gamboled through the adjacent fields, occasionally returning to her side only to dash off again after a rabbit or some other small creature that Cal could only hear as it rustled through the brush. She pulled her brown chamois shirt tighter around her body and walked a little faster through the predawn chill. She needed coffee, and she hoped Jack had been the groom in charge of brewing it this morning. Dana's was strong enough to erode her teeth right out of her head, and Craig never seemed to put the filter in correctly, allowing half the grounds to drip into the pot.

She slid open the heavy barn door and closed it again once the dogs had followed her through. She paused a moment and listened to the rhythmic morning sounds, the rumble of the feed cart and the steady chewing of contented horses munching their hay. This was Cal's favorite time of day, and it was worth sacrificing an extra hour or two of sleep so she didn't miss it. She walked down the aisle to the feed room where Craig was measuring out the horses' rations of grain.

"Good morning," she said.

"Morning, Cal." Craig added scoops of vitamins and a joint supplement to the blue buckets and handed them to her.

She carried the feed to the stalls at the far end of the aisle, accompanied by a chorus of neighs, before returning for the next buckets. Except for the initial greetings, she and the three grooms worked silently and efficiently as they fed the impatient animals. Once every horse had its breakfast and the humans had their coffee, there would be more gossip and chatter, but Cal loved the wordless teamwork of feeding time.

While the horses ate, she joined the grooms in the barn's lounge area. Dana had brought doughnuts, and Cal took a jelly-filled one and her coffee and sat on the arm of the couch. Jack, the Lanfords' head groom, wrote the day's activities on a whiteboard that hung on the wall next to the door. Black electrical tape divided the board into columns, and he filled each one with the names of horses that were to be trained or turned out during the day. Cal licked a blob of tangy raspberry jelly that had dripped on the base of her thumb and watched Jack add to the growing list of horses she needed to ride before nightfall. She'd need another doughnut.

"Excelsior has some swelling in his tendon again," Jack said to Dana. "He'll need an hour of handwalking this morning. He can go in the small paddock this afternoon, so he doesn't have room to run around and injure it more. Cal, what horses are you using for this morning's practice with your friend?"

Friend? Cal wouldn't call Rachel her friend, yet. Acquaintance sounded too cold. Potential lover? Just right. She took a drink of coffee and felt the grounds coat her tongue. "Damn it, Craig, your coffee is chewy. You're fired," she said with a mock scowl before she answered Jack. "We'll ride Raven and Roman."

"You should make her ride Grumpy," Dana said.

Cal joined in the grooms' laughter. The old gray gelding had been Cal's first polo pony, bought because her parents believed she would learn more if she had to work for every step of progress than if she had an easy horse to ride. They had been right. After frustrating hours on the hard-mouthed and dull-sided Grumpy, Cal had developed strong muscles in her arms and legs and an even stronger stubborn streak. Every horse since had been simple in comparison.

"I should," Cal said, smiling at the image of poor Rachel trying to maneuver the gray around the polo field. "Once she finally got him to canter, she'd be three farms down the road before she could make him turn around again."

The idea of putting Rachel at such a disadvantage that Cal would be able to outscore her without breaking a sweat was tempting, but after the meeting finished, Cal brought Raven and Roman out of their stalls and cross-tied them in the aisle. Both horses were clean from regular grooming, but she took her time brushing them until every hair was in place. She combed Raven's black tail and separated it into sections, leaving a few long strands dangling as she braided the rest into a tight plait. She had chosen the mare for Rachel because she was handy and responsive. Cal wanted to earn her kiss fairly, so Rachel couldn't complain about cheating and try to renege.

Cal wrapped the loose sections of hair around the mare's tail bone and made a few more plaits. The glossy black of Raven's coat would be a perfect match to Rachel's dark beauty, but whereas Raven's tail was coarse, Cal knew from her brief touch that Rachel's hair was downy soft. She definitely would get her hands back in Rachel's hair during the promised kiss. Cal shook her head and concentrated on her work. She brought the long hairs that she had left out of the original braid and twisted them around the rest of the tail until a small knot formed. She looped the last twist around the knot and tugged downward, locking the tied-up tail in place so it wouldn't interfere with their mallets during the game.

Once both horses were clean and tacked, Cal jogged back to her bungalow and changed out of her work jeans and into riding clothes. She returned to the barn well before six and untied Roman. She wasn't going to handicap Rachel with a bad horse, but she wanted her kiss enough to take advantage of a few extra minutes of warm-up time before Rachel arrived.

Rachel had to cut her run short in order to make it to Cal's farm by six on Thursday morning. She felt more and more relaxed as she left the city and drove across the expansive prairies that were part of Joint Base Lewis-McChord. A few horse trailers were parked on the side of the road, and she could see the occasional horse and rider through the fog. There were miles of open space, dotted with scotch broom and sage and bordered by cool green forests. She rolled her shoulders back and let the last of her city-induced anxiety fade away. Once she had a horse, she'd get a permit to ride out here. Maybe bring the whole team, if she ever managed to earn back their friendship.

A long trail ride would be ideal, but a friendly game of polo came in a close second. On a normal day, Cal could easily outplay her, but Rachel *had* to win. She hoped her desperation would give her the edge she needed. Cal would just be playing around, but this little stick-and-ball match was more important than any game Rachel had played in college.

She parked her Dodge pickup near the Lanford barn and got out. The stables seemed deserted, but she could hear a flurry of barks coming from the barn. No dogs appeared, so they must be contained in there somehow. Rachel headed toward the sound and met a young man at the entrance. He was leading a glossy black mare. She was groomed and tacked to spotless perfection, and her mane and tail were braided to keep them from interfering with either the ball or the rider's hands.

"You must be Rachel," he said. "I'm Cal's groom, Jack, and this is Raven. You'll be riding her this morning."

"Thanks, Jack," Rachel said. She stepped up to the horse and double-checked the tightness of the saddle's girth out of habit. She was about to mount, but Jack reached down and gave her a leg up onto the mare. From Rachel's first ride at Nelson and Leah's ranch, she had always taken care of her own horse. She cleaned her stalls, groomed and tacked her horses, even got on the animals by herself. She wondered if Jack was planning to walk beside the horse all morning and steer for her.

"Cal is already at the practice field," he said. He gestured to his left. "There's a path behind the barn. The field is behind those paddocks."

"Got it. Thanks again," she said as he walked back into the barn. Apparently, she was on her own from this point. She gave the mare a pat and walked around the huge barn. She was wearing the same clothes from yesterday's rides, but even though she had changed into a clean polo shirt, her horse was much better dressed than she was. A black saddle—with the burnished look of much-used, well-cared-for leather—sat on top of a deep blue saddle pad with maroon trim. Matching maroon wraps protected the mare's legs and her braided tail. Raven was delicate and fine boned, with small ears and wide, intelligent eyes. Rachel had to laugh. The damned horse made her feel like a dusty oaf by comparison.

Once she was past the barn, Rachel eased the mare into a trot on the grassy lane. She rode in a few circles when the path widened and then halted the mare and backed a few steps before asking for a canter. After her experiences with the unit's horses, Raven was a dream to ride. Rachel had been slightly suspicious Cal might have given her a horse with good looks but a hard mouth or dead sides, but the mare proved to be even better than her beauty promised.

Rachel came to the last paddock and saw a group of mares and foals grazing. One of the babies took off in an awkward, leggy canter when she appeared, and Rachel stopped to watch the little one's antics. Raven stood at attention with her ears pricked toward the frolicking colt, as still as a statue except for the gentle puff of her breath that moved Rachel's legs against her sides.

"Hey, cowgirl."

Rachel twisted in her saddle at the sound of Callan's voice behind her. She was riding a tall, rangy bay with a white blaze and four white socks. Lots of chrome. The gelding was as neatly turned out as Raven, with the same color scheme and tidy braids. Cal looked even better than the horses. She was wearing a royal blue polo shirt with maroon sleeves and the PNW Polo logo emblazoned in gold letters on a diagonal maroon stripe across her chest. Her breeches and tall leather boots were competition quality. Rachel, in jeans and chaps, had dressed for an informal morning practice, not a high-goal tournament. Cal's nickname for her only pointed out the difference between their appearances, but Rachel tried to shake off the implied insult as she followed Cal onto the field.

Cal casually tossed a small white ball in her left hand as they walked to the center of the field. "I wasn't sure you'd show up," she said. "You must really want me to win that kiss."

"You can try," Rachel said. The kiss was damned tempting, but Rachel had more important matters on her mind. Her team, her department, her city. She was fighting for a cause while Cal was simply playing a game. Rachel couldn't help but win.

"Just a little stick-and-ball play," Cal said. "Nothing fancy. Best of seven."

Rachel nodded. Let Cal picture a leisurely canter up and down the field as they passed the ball—and flirtatious comments—easily between them. Meanwhile, Rachel would ride like a knight going into battle, armed with her pride and her—

Cal flicked the ball onto the ground. "Go," she said without preamble as she and her horse surged forward. Cal struck the ball with her mallet and sent it sailing toward the goal line before Rachel realized the game had started without her. Shit. All images of her victorious crusade faded away as Rachel chased after Cal's bay. She spurred her horse in a late attempt at pursuit, but Cal knocked the ball between her goalposts before Rachel got close enough to challenge her. She pulled Raven to a walk as Cal trotted back to center field, her mallet tapping the ball alongside her on the ground.

"Excellent job, cowgirl," she said. "I'd love to recommend you for any of my opponents' teams."

Rachel ignored that comment and tightened her grip on the reins. This time, she kicked Raven into a canter before Cal finished saying *go* and swung her mallet as she approached the ball. Instead of trying to beat her to the shot, Cal crowded onto Rachel's path and pulled her mount's shoulders to the left so they bumped against Rachel's horse. The collision blocked Rachel's mallet between the two animals and nearly knocked her out of the saddle. She was forced to brace her rein hand on her horse's neck while she scrambled to regain her balance after the aggressive hit. Her horse's stride faltered, and Cal took advantage of it and turned the ball toward her own goal.

Cal whacked the ball between the uprights and brought it back to center. "I'll give you a head start this time," she said as she scooped the ball with her mallet and lobbed it in Rachel's direction from several yards away. Rachel wanted to refuse any pity shots, but she decided to get at least one goal before she got too choosy. She spun her horse around and ran after the ball, connecting with her mallet two times as she carried the ball up the field. She heard Cal's horse close behind her, but she had only one easy shot to make before she scored. She held Raven steady with her left hand on the reins as she leaned to the right and sliced through the air with her mallet. She anticipated the satisfying crack of contact with the ball, but at the last second Cal's mallet hooked hers with a sharp tug and spoiled her shot. Rachel's shoulder wrenched back at the impact, and she loosened her grip on the mallet so Cal didn't pull her right off her horse. Cal twisted her own stick to disentangle it from Rachel's as she cantered by, and Rachel had to take a few precious seconds to rewrap the mallet's strap around her wrist. By that time, Cal had yet again taken the ball down the field to score.

Rachel jogged back to center, rolling her shoulder to relax the muscles after the jarring blow. Without jeopardizing their mounts' safety, Cal had pushed the legal limits of both her ride-off and her hook. Any umpire would have given her at least a warning by now. Cal's suggestion that they get together for a casual one-on-one session hadn't hinted at this kind of rough play. "Stick-and-ball, my ass," she muttered as they met midfield.

"It'd be my pleasure," Cal said with a wicked grin. "Maybe after I make this match point. Go!"

Rachel didn't have time to wonder whether Cal was flirting with her or wanted to throw her off balance mentally as well as physically. She sent her horse into a gallop only a moment behind Cal. Rachel had expected Cal to play a clean game of polo, but so far she seemed as intent on unseating Rachel as scoring goals. She decided she could either complain or fight back, so rather than try for a shot at the ball, Rachel played defensively and used her horse's weight to shove Cal to one side. Cal tried to turn back in the opposite direction, but Rachel pivoted a hoofbeat more quickly and again forced Cal away from the ball.

After that, play deteriorated into a series of skirmishes as the two women swarmed around and over the ball, making less contact with it than with each other. Rachel's earlier timidity disappeared, and she wanted to cheer when her elbow connected with Cal's rib cage hard enough to make her grunt. The move would have drawn a foul in regulation play, but this match had its own rules—or lack of them. Cal had Rachel beat in physical strength and experience, since she'd probably played polo every day since she learned to walk, but Rachel used her horse's speed and agility to counteract Cal's advantage. The evenly matched battles continued as they wove up and down the field.

The intense play stopped briefly when Rachel brought her horse to a halt after a fierce collision that left Cal draped against her side, one hand on the cantle of Rachel's saddle where it barely brushed against her ass. In such close contact, Rachel could smell the muskiness of their combined sweat and see the challenge in Cal's eyes. Rachel had come here to battle Cal and overcome her reluctance to help, but now she had a new opponent. Her own libido. Her attraction to Cal was distracting in a normal situation, but here on the field it grew in direct proportion to the aggressiveness of their play. She had come with such high ideals, prepared to win for her city and community, but now all she wanted to do was pull Cal even tighter against her and fuck her right here on the open polo field.

"Do you mind sitting in your own saddle?" Rachel asked as she shoved Cal away, refusing to linger much longer with Cal's amused smile only inches from her own lips. She hoped Cal would attribute her breathlessness to physical exhaustion, not arousal. She was irritated with herself for succumbing to Cal's gorgeous looks and demonic play, like every female on the West Coast had done before her. Her only hope of escaping with some dignity was to hide her attraction from Cal.

Cal lifted her hand and wiped at a bead of perspiration that slid down Rachel's cheek. "But I'd rather ride with you."

Cal smiled as Rachel shook her head and wheeled away from her attempts at distraction. At least, Cal had intended to distract Rachel. Instead, she seemed to be driving herself mad with an attraction so strong she was unprepared to manage it. She had nearly been in Rachel's lap, and she had wanted nothing more than to stay there. Rachel had smelled so fucking good. Sweat and cedar and—Cal wasn't sure if she had been imagining this scent or not—arousal. Cal had used polo to seduce before, but she had always been in control, always been the seducer. Some of Rachel's natural intensity was rubbing off on her as their play grew more physical. Cal gave chase after a brief hesitation, but Rachel beat her to the ball and carried it down the field for a score.

"You didn't even try," Rachel said when she brought the ball back to midfield.

"I thought I'd give you a chance to catch up," Cal said with a shrug. She *had* tried, but she'd been too busy imagining what Rachel would look like naked based on the information she'd gathered from her hasty touches while they'd been pressed together. "Seemed the sporting thing to do."

"Well, don't," Rachel said. She sent the ball flying and set off after it. Cal galloped toward her at an angle, prepared to ride across her line and cut her off. Not exactly legal, but if Rachel wanted a real battle, she'd give her one. Unfortunately, Rachel seemed prepared for her move and she swung Raven onto her path. The impact with Rachel's shoulder jarred Cal in the saddle, nearly knocking the wind right out of her. She recovered quickly, shoving her feet back into her stirrups and giving chase.

Cal asked Roman to open up and gallop full speed toward Rachel. The move had been a good one, and Cal felt strangely proud of Rachel's tactic. Cal was fighting with every trick she had at her disposal, but she was even more satisfied when Rachel bested her than when she got the upper hand. Maybe Cal was ready for a change. Her female companions were always so shallow—or at least Cal hadn't taken the time to explore their depths—but Rachel was something else. Fiery and strong and deep. So intense when she talked about the mounted unit or when she played polo. So intense when she stared right into Cal's eyes, her breasts rising and falling from exertion, and licked her lips in such a hungry way. Cal had been turned on by Rachel's appearance, but now she was aroused by her passion. An affair with Rachel would be consuming and a little frightening, but Cal never shied away from a challenge. She'd do whatever it took to wear Rachel down.

Rachel sensed Cal and her horse bearing down on her as she neared her goal. She raised her arm in preparation for a full swing, but at the last moment she contracted her biceps and turned the mallet so she merely tapped the ball to the right. Cal, obviously anticipating the trajectory of the ball after a hard hit, swept several strides down the field before she could turn back. Rachel pivoted and batted the ball toward her goal. Again she could hear Cal close on her heels, and she leaned low over Raven's neck as she urged her on. She extended her arm up and around in a strong swing, expecting to feel the hook of Cal's mallet at any moment, but instead she connected solidly with the ball and sent it straight and true through her goalposts.

"Well played," Cal said as she pulled up next to Rachel, her face red from exertion. Rachel searched for a hint of sarcasm in her voice but didn't hear one.

Cal glanced at her watch. Her mother would be out soon to watch Cal school her two young horses. She'd much rather continue playing with Rachel, maybe spend some more time in her lap, but she needed to finish the game. She closed her mind to everything but polo. There'd be plenty of time to fantasize about Rachel after she had finished her schooling for the day. With her focus intact, she made short work of her fourth and final goal.

"Four to two," she said. "I have a few more horses to school, so go cool off Raven and I'll see you at the police stables on Monday. I'll let you know when I'm ready to collect my kiss."

Rachel came to a halt, her breath rasping, as her body, unaccustomed to casual riding let alone this grueling kind of match, struggled to recover. She frowned in confusion as Cal rode off the field. She had lost, so why was Cal coming to the stables? "Wait," she called. Cal halted and looked over her shoulder. "Does this mean you're going to help us?"

Cal laughed. "Of course I am, cowgirl," she said. "This game was just for fun."

❖

Rachel waved when she saw Nelson's blue Ford pickup drive through the park's entrance. She hurried to push open the gate leading to the stable yard, wincing as her muscles protested her quick movements. She still hurt from her grueling match with Cal two days earlier and from the unaccustomed exercise of riding three horses a day. Hours in the saddle would eventually get her riding muscles back in shape, and until then she had to suffer through with the help of aspirin and beer. Another benefit of living in the fancy waterfront condos—she would have had access to a hot tub to soothe her whimpering body. Soaking in the tiny tub in her apartment, with her feet dangling over the edge, was a poor substitute.

She slid the chain-link fence shut after her dad drove the trailer into the yard. She locked the gate and gave a sharp gasp as the metal lock rubbed over her palm. Where she'd once had small calluses like Cal's to protect her hand from her mallet, she now had a row of tiny but ferocious blisters. Yet another souvenir from her time at the Lanford farm. As if the near-constant state of arousal she had felt after their very physical polo game wasn't enough, Rachel's hand and thighs throbbed with pain every time she moved or touched anything. Her body seemed determined to remind her of Cal at every turn.

She heard the bang of a horse hoof striking the side of the steel stock trailer. Dark brown ears were visible above the solid metal panel. Her horse had arrived—her new partner, as much as any human could be. Someday their lives might depend on the bond they'd form together. She watched Nelson hop out of the truck's cab and walk toward her, feeling somehow connected to all the comforts of home when she saw him in his usual worn jeans, old flannel shirt, and dusty cowboy hat. He grabbed her in a hug and spun her around before setting her back on her feet.

"Hi, Dad," she said, feeling the familiar tickle of his long moustache when he gave her a kiss on the cheek.

"It's good to see you, Rachel," he said before patting her on the back and letting her go. He looked her up and down as if he were evaluating a horse. "You've lost weight. And you have dark circles under your eyes. Aren't you sleeping?"

Rachel tried to shrug off his concern with a joke. "Some. I guess I'm just worn out from riding so much. I feel as out of shape as a tenderfoot at a dude ranch."

"Well, Leah figured you'd be too skinny, so she sent a cooler full of food for you."

"Chicken pot pie?" Rachel asked hopefully. The frozen versions never measured up to her mom's home cooking, but most nights they were all Rachel felt capable of making.

Nelson laughed. "Of course. And you remember the best cure for saddle sores, don't you?"

"A sweaty saddle pad," Rachel grimaced as she quoted her dad's favorite saying. His answer to most problems was to tell her to ride until she and her horse had broken a sweat. They had traveled for miles across the sagebrush-strewn pastures and pine forests around Cheney, alongside crystal-clear, ice-cold lakes. And he had been correct every time. Her bad memories, her teenaged angst, her inexplicable anger, they had all faded as she jogged and loped for hours. Working out her tension, her emotions that were too intense for her young self to handle. She had substituted long runs in the park since moving to Tacoma, and now she had horses to ride again. But she didn't think her current problems could simply be trotted away.

"Let's get this fellow out," Nelson said as another impatient bang from the horse's hoof echoed through the yard. He walked to the back of the trailer and unlatched the door. "His name's Bandit."

Rachel grabbed one side of the ramp and helped her dad lower it to the ground. Nelson whistled softly as he approached the horse and rubbed the gelding's neck before untying him and leading him out of the trailer. Rachel stood back and appraised the horse. Very nice. His liver chestnut coat, dappled from good care and careful grooming, shone in the sun. He was muscular and tall enough to accommodate Rachel's legs, but he had a lightness about him that promised speed. Long forearms, short cannon bones, a good slope to the shoulder. She stepped forward to run her hands over his legs and check for bumps or old injuries like Nelson had taught her, but the gelding pinned his ears flat against his head and tried to bite her.

Her dad reprimanded the horse with a short tug on the lead rope. "No!"

Rachel raised her eyebrows in surprise. Nelson never accepted anything but respectful behavior from his foster kids or his animals. He was never cruel, but he was very clear about the rules on his ranch. Rachel hadn't expected any horse he brought her to have behavioral problems.

"So, when you said he needed a tune-up…"

"He's had a tough go in life," Nelson said with a shrug. He clucked to the horse and started walking him around the arena to work out his kinks after the long trailer ride. Rachel followed after them.

"And?" Rachel prompted. The gelding barged into Nelson's space, but he calmly elbowed the horse back into line.

"Don't really know what happened, but I recognize the signs of abuse when I see them. He changed hands a few times that I know of over the past year, and his last owner called Doc Grady. Wanted him to put the horse down, but you know what a softy Doc is. He wanted to give this big guy one more chance, so he called me."

Yes, Doc Grady was a softy, but Nelson was worse. Rachel felt her chest tighten at the story. She felt sorry for the horse, but she also recognized the similarities with her own history. If Nelson hadn't been such a sucker for hard-luck cases, who knew where she'd be now.

"So you're pawning him off on me?" she asked, but with a smile. Bandit might have been out of place in his previous homes, but here he'd be just one more misfit in a whole group of them.

"Thought you two might understand each other," Nelson said. He patted the horse's well-muscled neck, and Bandit pinned his ears again. "It'll take some doing to gain his trust, but once you do you'll have a hell of a partner. Bet he'll take a bullet for you."

"Let's hope it doesn't come to that," Rachel said. She sighed. A unit that hated her, an emotionally challenged horse, and forced contact with Cal. Great. At least Cal seemed to like her—although too much for Rachel's comfort—but every relationship in Rachel's life had grown far too complex. Nelson seemed to think she and Bandit would be good for each other, but Rachel wanted easy. Simple. Fate seemed to have other plans.

She got an armful of hay out of the feed room while Nelson settled Bandit in his new stall. They leaned on the door and watched the horse alternate between eating and glaring at them.

"I think he might be happier if we leave him alone while he eats," Rachel said. "And I could use some lunch, too. If you don't mind a short walk, there's a place next to the ferry landing that serves a great salmon."

"Perfect," Nelson said. He hung Bandit's halter and lead rope next to his stall.

"See you soon, buddy," Rachel said to the gelding. He pinned his ears and bared his teeth at her. *Yeah. Love you, too.*

CHAPTER SIX

Cal parked by three police vehicles and got out of her car. The morning was cool, with a misting summer rain, and Cal reached into her backseat and pulled out a yellow umbrella before walking toward the arena. The officers were already there, watching her. Rachel stood a little apart from the others, and her horse looked as grouchy as she did. Cal paused to catch her breath before she joined the group. She had seen Cop Rachel and Cowgirl Rachel, and both were sexy. Mountie Rachel was incredible. Dark blue breeches with a gold stripe down the side, emphasizing her long legs. Tall black boots so shiny Cal could probably see her reflection in them. A fitted navy top that enhanced everything Rachel's regular uniform had tried to hide. Cal had wanted to get Rachel out of the other outfits she'd worn. She wanted to rip off this one with her teeth.

Cal hadn't been able to get Rachel out of her mind since their polo match. She hadn't had so much fun on the practice field for ages. At times, she worried her obsession with Rachel might be a detriment to her focus on polo, but after a long schooling session with her mother on Sunday, Cal had changed her mind. Thinking of Rachel, planning exercises for her unit, planning various seduction scenarios, had helped her keep her cool while she performed drill after drill under Cecilia's critical eye. The confirmation of Cal's acceptance on the East Coast team had only made her mother more determined to whip Cal into shape. Playing with Rachel and the mounted version of the Keystone Kops should prove to be exactly the sort of stress relief Cal needed.

As long as she kept her cool and didn't drool all over Rachel's nice new uniform.

Cal forced her attention to the other officers. She had already seen the other horses and riders on TV, but then she had been torn between laughter and disbelief. Now they were her students, and she sized them up quickly. One Thoroughbred, a pinto, and two quarter horses. All reasonably athletic looking, except for the heavy, spotted mare with the sullen expression. It'd probably take a firecracker under her tail just to get her into a trot. And judging by the straight line of her shoulder and her long pasterns, her trot would be hell to sit. The riders didn't look any easier to handle as they sat watching her with stubborn expressions that were easy for Cal to read. They expected her to prove herself before they'd listen to anything she said. But she wasn't about to defend herself or her credentials to them. All she needed to do was prove how little they knew, and they'd be damned sure to listen to her, then.

She tapped the umbrella on the ground like a cane as she walked into the center of the arena. Rachel's short dark hair was curling in the light rain. She sat relaxed in her saddle, with one hand on the reins and the other resting on her thigh. Cal turned away from her and faced the other three. She wasn't sure she'd make it through the lesson without needing to stop and hose herself down.

"I'm Cal Lanford," she said with an easy smile. No one returned it. She leaned on her umbrella. "Rachel asked me to help out for the next month, getting you ready for the Fourth of July celebration."

She saw fleeting changes in the expressions of the officers when she mentioned Rachel's name. Cal paused. She had thought everyone was irritated by *her* presence. Maybe they were angry with Rachel instead. For replacing the sergeant they had recently lost?

"From what I saw of the horses during the service, we have a lot of work to do. At least you're actually on the horses now. I want to help you learn how to stay on."

"We already know how to stay on," the man on the pinto said with obvious contempt in his voice.

"Oh, really?" Cal asked. She lifted the umbrella and opened it in one fluid motion, aiming it at Rachel because she was the one most likely to be able to survive Cal's demonstration. All four horses spooked as the large yellow monster sprang to life right before their eyes, but Rachel's mount reacted most violently since Cal opened the umbrella right in front of his face. He spun away and ran a few strides with Rachel clinging to his side. She managed to pull herself back into the saddle and bring him to a halt.

"Jesus!" she yelled as she turned back to face Cal. "What the fuck are you doing?"

Cal didn't answer, but she spun the umbrella in her hand and waited calmly while the four officers recovered. No one had fallen off, but the horses had scattered to the edges of the arena with their officers barely managing to stay in their saddles, let alone control their mounts. The pinto had headed back to the barn at a lumbering trot, and her rider was ineffectively pulling on the reins trying to get her to stop. He ducked as she went under the overhang and into a stall. Cal could hear him swearing before he finally reemerged and walked back to the arena.

"Hey, you were right," Cal said when he made it back to the group. "You *were* able to stay on. But barely."

"What the hell are you trying to prove?" Rachel asked, her face flushed and angry.

Cal dropped her friendly tone. "I'm trying to prove how fucking dangerous the four of you are. To yourselves, your horses, and the people who will be in your way on the Fourth." She looked at each officer in turn, not surprised to see the change in their expressions. They had been stubborn at first, and then angry after Cal's umbrella stunt. Now the surge of adrenaline was wearing off, and they were all a bit pale and shaky. Except Rachel. She still looked pissed.

"I'm one person with an umbrella. What if it rains on the Fourth? You'll have thousands of these, opening unexpectedly. There'll be baby strollers and running children. Fireworks and an air show. Smart-ass kids who think it's funny to throw things at you or your horses." She lifted the still-open umbrella, and the horses startled slightly at the sudden movement. "If you can't handle this, how will you survive the night?"

Cal closed the umbrella. Point made, point taken. "I'm sure you focused on defensive driving when you learned about high speed pursuits. Well, today we're going to start learning defensive riding. Tricks to help you stay on the horse no matter what happens. You don't need to look pretty up there or have perfect form. You just need to stay on. You, on the bay, what's your name?"

"Clark."

"Okay, Clark, I'm going to shorten your stirrups a few inches so you'll have a more secure base. The rest of you, start trotting on the rail."

Rachel took a few deep breaths as she nudged Bandit into a trot. She could feel his tension through her legs and seat, and she knew her own fury wasn't helping. She reached forward and rubbed his shoulder, murmuring quietly not only to calm him but herself, as well. She had spent the past couple of days working with the gelding, trying to establish some sort of rapport with him. She had soon noticed the signs of abuse Nelson had mentioned. Bandit was aggressive, but she was starting to see the fear behind his cantankerous exterior. He was honestly afraid of what she was going to do to him, and now Cal had come along and scared him even more. She was angry with Cal for her stupid umbrella trick, but she needed to control her emotions if she wanted to help her horse.

Once her breathing settled into a rhythm, she felt Bandit settle as well. He had been startled by the umbrella, but not hurt by it. And Cal was right—he would be exposed to scary new objects and unpredictable citizens every day. He needed to get accustomed to movement and color and sound, but more important, he needed to trust Rachel to take care of him no matter what happened.

Knowing Cal was right didn't help. Part of her anger was because Cal had sauntered into the arena and gained the trust and respect of the officers within minutes, something Rachel hadn't been able to do no matter how much she knew about horses, and no matter how many times she had tried to explain how unprepared the unit was.

Rachel tried to concentrate on Bandit as she ran through Cal's drills. Twisting and contorting in the saddle. Learning to counterbalance and brace, like she had done when she'd first taken hold of a polo mallet and leaned so far to the side in order to swing it without hitting the horse's legs. Rachel was grateful to have help and relieved that the other officers were so intently listening to Cal's instructions, but she couldn't fight off her hurt feelings. She had wanted to be the one to teach her squad. To earn their respect and attention.

When the lesson was over, she took Bandit to his stall at the end of the barn and tied him to the wall where she'd be able to groom him without getting bitten. The other riders kept their horses under the overhang, and Rachel could hear them asking Cal questions and enthusiastically thanking her for the lesson. It had taken Cal ten minutes to gain their trust and admiration. It had taken Rachel about as long to lose both things when she made the decision to have Sheehan arrested. She swiped the brush a little too roughly over Bandit's back, and he raised his head and rolled his eye back to stare at her. She apologized and fished a smushed piece of apple out of the pocket of her breeches. He accepted the offering, nearly taking a finger as well, and she started grooming him again, but more gently this time.

"He'd make a great polo pony," Cal said. She was standing in Bandit's doorway, leaning against the jamb with her arms crossed. "Strong, but not as bulky as a stock-type quarter horse."

Bandit pinned his ears and snorted at the sound of her voice, giving his usual equine version of a scowl.

Rachel laughed. "Yeah, he's got the looks. But not the attitude to match."

"You suit each other," Cal said with a smile. "You usually have your ears back when I'm around, too."

Rachel was starting to recognize when Cal's expression grew more intimate. The sexy way she'd look right before she'd initiate some sort of physical contact. Like a golden lion on the prowl. Rachel moved to the other side of Bandit.

Cal watched Rachel not-so-subtly put the crotchety horse between them. Cal liked a challenge. And Rachel seemed determined to be one. The only reason Cal was doing this mounted training was to get closer to her and to have a little fun in the process. She wasn't going to get dragged into the mounted police drama unfolding in the stable yard, but she was too curious not to dig around a bit. She glanced behind her to make sure the other riders were out of earshot.

"So what's up with you and your team? You're their boss, and you're obviously the most qualified rider here, but there seems to be a barrier between you and the rest of the squad. Is it because you replaced their old sergeant?"

Cal watched the tense lines form on Rachel's forehead. She had seen them before. When Rachel had first asked her for help, when she had lost the polo match, when Cal had nearly gotten her tossed on her butt with the umbrella. Obvious signs of an unhappy Rachel. Cal didn't want her to be unhappy, if only because Rachel wouldn't be as easy to seduce if she was. "What is it, Rach?"

Rachel drew her brush over Bandit's side in a long, sweeping stroke. She shrugged but didn't meet Cal's eyes. "I guess you'll eventually hear about it anyway, so you might as well get my side. The whole department sees me as a sort of pariah these days. I've only been a sergeant for a few months, and on one of my first nights I made a decision that got another cop arrested."

"Had he done something wrong?"

"It was a domestic abuse call," Rachel said. She had shown up to assist the two officers on the scene because another cop was involved. If she only had been on any other shift, in any other sector, her life would be so different right now. "He shoved his wife. She didn't have any marks and she said she didn't want him to be charged, but the law says the physical aggressor is always arrested whether the victim wants it or not. She and the other officers wanted to let him off with a warning."

"Sounds like you made the right call," Cal said. She wanted to touch Rachel. Take away the loneliness echoing through her voice as she spoke. "So why is everyone blaming you?"

Rachel took off Bandit's halter, and he moved to the back corner of the stall. "He spread a rumor that I made the decision without enough evidence. That I shouldn't have ruined his family's reputation by letting this be made public instead of handling it quietly within the department. He's from a long line of cops and he's popular. Everyone had to choose a side, choose me or him, and I guess I lost. It's not fair to use family connections that way. To think you're better than other people, or above the law, just because you belong to some fucking dynasty."

Rachel's words stung, even though Cal knew they weren't aimed at her. She was all too aware of how difficult it could be to live up to a family's reputation. To be responsible for maintaining it. She had spent a few hours yesterday—in fact, she had spent her whole life—being told she was riding not for herself but for the Calvert and Lanford clans. If one shot sailed wide of the goal, she threatened the accomplishments of all her ancestors.

"It's not always easy to live up to a family name," Cal said. It was difficult, but it had to be done. Especially since she had been raised to believe it was her destiny to carry on, or surpass, her family's fame in the polo world.

"Really? You're taking his side?"

Cal started at Rachel's furious voice. She had gotten lost in her own world and forgotten where she was for a moment. Rachel's face was flushed and angry looking.

"Poor guy. He got everything handed to him. A career, promotions, friends. I'm supposed to feel sorry for him? Look the other way when he pushes his wife around? Sweep it under the rug like other officers had done over the years?"

Cal grabbed Rachel's arm as she stormed past on her way out of the stall. She had been thinking out loud, reacting to the subject of families, not to Rachel's story. "Hey, I didn't say you were wrong. I just—"

"Just made an excuse for him, like all his friends. The well-bred have to stick together, don't they? I didn't even know what a real family *was* until I was fifteen, but I don't use that as an excuse. I make my own way wherever I go. I didn't have the advantage of climbing my family tree to get where I am."

Cal let go of Rachel's arm and stepped back. That one felt personal.

Chapter Seven

Rachel left Bandit's stall and saw her three teammates staring at her. Her voice had been raised enough for them to have heard every word, and they weren't even trying to look like they hadn't. Fucking great. And no chance of a graceful exit since she'd have to push past them, rummage in her desk drawer for her apartment keys, and let herself out the locked yard gate. Instead, she turned the opposite direction and walked around to the back of the barn. She slid to the ground and leaned back against the wood siding. She was going to get dirt on the seat of her brand-new uniform pants by sitting on the ground like this, but she didn't give a shit. She took a small bit of comfort from the knowledge that Bandit was on the other side of the wall from her.

The view before her helped ease her anger. She could see the marina and yacht club below her. Mount Rainier was still hidden by clouds, but she knew exactly where it was to her right. A line of cars drove off the ferry and up the hill toward her. She took a deep breath, imagining healing and salty ocean air from Puget Sound filling her lungs.

Cal came around the corner and sank down beside her. They sat in silence for a few minutes. Rachel could hear the officers' cars starting up, and the clang of the gate as the last one left.

"I guess I ruined what scraps were left of my reputation," she said. She picked up a stray piece of hay and shredded it with her fingers.

Cal shrugged. She was sitting so close, Rachel could feel the movement. She wanted to lean toward Cal, get even closer, but she held her body rigid.

"You made a pretty spectacular scene," Cal said. "But maybe it was good for them to hear you speaking so passionately about what happened. I'm guessing you're usually very stoic about everything."

"Sometimes it feels like it's all I have left," Rachel said quietly. She attributed her sudden spate of honesty to the acute embarrassment of being overheard. "Acting like I don't care if no one likes me or if they think I was wrong."

"Maybe they need to protect themselves. If he's as popular as you say, maybe they're trying to keep from being shunned, as well. It's cowardly, but understandable. And I'm sure plenty of people in the department believe he should have been arrested for what he did. They're probably relieved they didn't have to be the ones to do it," Cal said. She shrugged again, but this time the action felt more like a rub, an intimate touch, than a simple gesture. "And I really wasn't trying to defend him, or to criticize you. For what it's worth, I think you were very brave to stand up for your beliefs and not give in to pressure from him or anyone else."

Cal sounded almost sad when she said the last sentence, like she had when she was talking about families before Rachel's outburst. Rachel had no idea what Cal could possibly be sad about. She had everything money could buy, plus a living dynasty to pave her way in the polo world. When Rachel had been tossed from foster home to foster home, with short sojourns in juvie along the way, she had fantasized about her real family coming to find her. Not the actual parents she had known in her first few years of life, but the imagined ones she knew must be out there somewhere. They'd have been like Cal's family. Offering her acres of space, horses to ride, foals to train, grooms to hand her tacked and polished mounts. Clean and wonderful things to replace the pain and grime and rage she lived with every day. Nelson and Leah had saved her life by giving her all of that—minus the grooms, of course—but Rachel had waited fifteen years to find them. Had gone through hell before she found peace. She was about to ask what Cal could possibly find wrong with her family when she spotted a flash of movement at the edge of the lot.

Rachel pushed to her feet and walked along the back wall of the barn. The back of the lot, outside the police fencing, was still used by the park as a temporary dumping ground. She saw someone sitting next to a pile of broken cement barriers, most likely removed for some renovation project. As Rachel got closer she could see it was a woman, somewhere in her twenties. Crying.

Rachel hooked her fingers through the chain link fence. "Hey. Are you okay? What are you doing back here?"

Cal had followed along, curious about the woman as well, but her attention shifted back to Rachel at the sound of her voice. A cop's voice. Authoritative and no-nonsense, but with a note of compassion behind it. Even her bearing was different—she seemed taller, somehow. This must be what Rachel was like on the job, and Cal was intrigued. And very turned on. She wondered if this Rachel would carry over to the bedroom as well. Cal had assumed she'd be the top in their relationship, but now she wasn't so sure. Maybe Rachel would want to fight her for the position.

"Very sexy," she murmured.

Rachel frowned, but didn't turn away from the woman who was now approaching them. "What?" she asked.

"Nothing," Cal said. The woman clutched a bundle of clothing close to her chest, and Cal noticed Rachel had her right hand resting on her gun.

"Stop there," Rachel said. "Put that down and let me see your hands."

"It's just his coat," the woman said in a high-pitched whine, but she did what Rachel asked, putting the jacket on the ground and raising her hands as if she were being held at gunpoint.

"It's all right," Rachel said. "You can put your hands down. But keep them where I can see them. What's your name?"

"Clare Ames."

"Okay, Clare. Why don't you tell me what you're doing back here?"

"I had to see where it happened. Where he was killed."

Rachel felt her whole body stiffen. Prepared. For what, she wasn't sure. She wished the other officers hadn't left. "You're talking about Alex Mayer?"

"The cop? Yeah." Clare wiped her hand over her cheek and nose.

"Whose coat is that?" Rachel asked, fishing in her breast pocket. She pulled out a small notebook and pen. "And how do you spell your name?"

"C-l-a-r-e. And it's my boyfriend's coat."

"And his name is…?" Rachel prompted. Why didn't people ever tell cops the whole story at once? It always had to be dragged out of them sentence by sentence. She glanced at Cal when Clare hesitated. The last thing she needed was a civilian involved in this. "Why don't you wait for me by the arena."

"No, thanks," Cal said.

Rachel sighed. She needed to find out what information Clare might have about Alex's murder, so she couldn't take the time to drag Cal away from the area. Maybe she could use her Taser? Tempting, but too much paperwork. "What's your boyfriend's name, Clare?"

"Randy. Randy Brown."

Clare's voice was barely audible, but Rachel heard the words. This wasn't a name she needed to write down to remember. Clare's boyfriend was Alex's killer. Alleged killer, but looking guilty as sin.

"He didn't do it," Clare said, as if reading Rachel's mind. "No one will listen to me, but I swear he didn't do it."

Of course, he didn't. Rachel had heard the refrain before. From every person she'd ever arrested. Still, something about Clare's shrill voice, the desperation in her eyes, spoke to Rachel.

"I'll listen," she said. "Tell me what happened that night."

Clare sniffed and wrapped her arms around herself. "Randy, he was in bed and he got a call from…his cousin. His car had broke down and he needed Randy to come pick him up—"

Rachel flipped her notebook shut. "See ya," she said as she started to walk away, grabbing Cal's sleeve and dragging her along.

"Wait, wait," Clare called.

Rachel paused. "Are you going to tell me the truth?"

"Yes. Please, just listen to me. He didn't do it."

"So tell me what he *did* do."

"He got a text. Some guy wanted to do a deal, here in the park. I told Randy, don't you go out in the middle of the night, but he went anyway."

"What time was this?" Rachel asked.

"'Round three. I remember because I had to get up and feed the baby about an hour before."

Rachel opened her notebook and jotted down the time to give herself a moment to think. Alex had been shot at one thirty in the morning. Someone was lying, and right now Rachel would bet all her savings on it being Clare.

"When did he get home again?"

"Four or so. Then the cops come breaking down our door an hour later. They say he killed some officer. But he didn't…"

"He didn't do it," Rachel finished for Clare when a sob kept her from finishing the sentence. "So how do you explain the murder weapon found in his car? Or his footprints all around the crime scene?"

"I told you, he did a deal here. But he didn't see a dead guy or nothing. He wouldn't have stuck around if he had."

"And the gun?" Rachel could feel Cal's focused gaze flipping back and forth between her and Clare, as if she were watching a tennis match.

"It was stolen only a few days before. I don't know how it got back in his car."

"How convenient," Rachel said. "Anything else? Any proof that he's innocent?"

Clare shook her head, her crying quieter now. Rachel wrote her number on a page in her notebook and tore it out. She handed it to Clare through the fence.

"Call me if you have more information. Now you need to go. You shouldn't be hanging around back here."

"Can I take his coat?" Clare asked, pointing at the jacket she had dropped on the ground.

"Of course," Rachel said.

Clare picked it up and held it tight against her, like a security blanket. She started to walk around the pile of rubble.

"Wait," Rachel called. "Where's the cell? You said Randy got a text."

"It's not at home," Clare said. "He must've had it on him when he got arrested. Or it was in his car."

"Look for it, will you? And give me a call if you find it."

Rachel made sure Clare left the lot before she turned back to Cal. "Let's get out of here."

"Do you think she's lying?" Cal asked.

"Chances are."

"But the stolen gun. Wouldn't he have filed a police report?"

Rachel laughed. She walked back toward the barn. "Yeah, right. Hi, I'm a convicted felon and I'd like to report the theft of my illegal handgun. For insurance purposes, I'm sure."

"But you listened to her. Like you might believe what she was saying."

Rachel moved along the barn aisle, double-checking the latches on the stall doors like she did before leaving every afternoon. "I'm not big on conspiracies. Usually the guy holding the smoking gun is the one who pulled the trigger. And why would someone bother to frame a small-time criminal?"

"So why did you listen?"

Rachel shrugged. "I was being polite. Why are you so interested?"

Cal laughed. "It's fun. Like watching a crime show, but in person."

"Listen, Cal, this isn't a joke. Alex came here to check the horses, and he stumbled on a drug deal. Randy Brown panicked and shot him. End of story. Now would you please give the horses some hay while I lock the office?"

Cal rolled her eyes and went into the feed room, muttering something about spoilsports. Rachel ignored her, going into the office for her keys before shutting out the lights and locking the door. The only discrepancy in Clare's story was the time. But Randy could have killed Alex at one thirty, and then gone back to the park at three. Or—much more likely—Clare knew when Alex had been shot, and she was trying to give Randy an alibi. Either way, the cell records would prove her right or wrong.

Rachel shut and locked the gate to the stable yard after Cal drove away. She walked a few yards up the hill and then turned around and came back to recheck the lock. She had learned this lesson the hard way soon after she had arrived at Nelson and Leah's ranch. She had carelessly left a gate open behind her, letting a herd of cows roam onto a hay field. She had spent hours trudging over sunbaked dirt and hay stubble trying to herd the reluctant cows back to their pasture. The job could have been finished in minutes if she'd been allowed to be on horseback, but the lesson would have been forgotten just as quickly. Instead, it was burned into her brain as she stomped through the shadeless field. When you go through a gate, make damned sure it's shut behind you.

But, more important, she had learned to pay careful attention to the rules. When she followed them, life was good. When she didn't, she had to rage—swearing and fuming—through her private hell full of slippery cowpies and ornery cattle until she emerged, sunburned and exhausted, on the other side.

Once she was sure she had secured the stable yard, Rachel hiked the quarter mile to her apartment and let herself into the tiny place with a sigh of relief. She eased out of her tall boots, the leather still new and stiff even though she had spent a couple of days oiling them. They needed hours of break-in time before they'd be comfortable. She sat on the edge of her tub and poured rubbing alcohol over the blisters on her ankles and toes. She was turning into one big blister, rubbed raw over the past few days. All she wanted to do was crash in her recliner with a cold beer and a hot microwave meal. Turn on the television and forget about the rest of the world.

So why did she turn on her work computer? And why did she search through the twenty or so reports from Alex's case? Feeling sorry for Clare had nothing to do with it. Nor did recognizing Randy as a petty criminal, a throwaway kind of guy most people wouldn't find worth fighting for. All that mattered were the facts of the case.

Facts like cell records that were easily checked. Unfortunately, Rachel couldn't find the cell phone listed as property on any of the reports. But she did find the name of the guy who supposedly sent the text. The man Randy Brown met in the park the night Alex was murdered.

CHAPTER EIGHT

Rachel made the long drive out to Cal's farm after her jog the next morning. She wanted to borrow some poles and jump standards because she planned to school the police horses over them and then have the officers attempt it. They might have to jump over a small fence or some other obstacle while on-duty, and they needed to practice in the soft arena before they tried it on the pavement somewhere.

Of course, she could have asked Cal to bring them when she came for their afternoon lesson, but Rachel really wanted to start jumping later this morning. And she enjoyed the drive outside the city limits. Her mind was freer out here, better able to think and process the troubling questions racing through it. The missing cell phone, the confusing timeline. And her ethically questionable plan for finding out the truth. She wanted open spaces around her while she made her decision. And she wanted to talk to Cal about her plan because Cal seemed to be the only person who had any faith in her besides Nelson and Leah. And Rachel knew exactly what they'd have to say about her idea.

The view of Mount Rainier was clear today. The snowy mountain and the bare Cascade foothills were starkly outlined against the blue sky. No city haze out here, blurring the horizon. Rachel tapped her fingers on her truck's steering wheel. She had to admit, she wanted to tell Cal about her scheme because Cal would be thrilled with it. She'd see it as a lark, a living reenactment of the game Clue or some unrealistic cop show. Nothing was serious to Cal, and this one time Rachel wanted some of that devil-may-care attitude to rub off on her. She lived by the rules, but look where they'd gotten her. Maybe it was time to do a little bending of her own. And Cal was the one person she could count on to wholeheartedly encourage her.

Rachel parked in the now-familiar lot and walked into the barn. As her eyes adjusted to the darkness after being in the sun, she saw that the stables were as beautifully turned out as Cal's horses had been. The rich wood stall doors looked freshly stained, and each had a bronze nameplate on it, announcing the name of its probably impeccably bred occupant. Dark leather halters with miniature versions of the stall nameplates hung next to each stall, above folded maroon and blue blankets. Everything matched, including the large tack trunks lining the aisle.

Rachel walked slowly past the stalls, admiring the horses and petting the ones that came to greet her. It was lovely, but she still preferred the ranch in Cheney. With its mismatched nylon halters and straw-covered dirt floors and horses whose coats were scruffy and furry in the winter, sun-bleached in the summer.

She nearly ran into Jack when he walked out of the tack room. "Hello, Rachel," he said formally. "I wasn't expecting you."

"I stopped by to speak with Cal. Is she around?"

"She's schooling one of her young horses on the practice field. Where you rode last week."

"Thanks. I'll find her."

Rachel enjoyed the walk to the practice field more than she had the other day. Then she had been nervous, determined, desperate to earn Cal's help. Now she had it, and as much as Cal frustrated her—and as much as she was jealous of Cal's popularity with her unit—Rachel was relieved to have found an ally, of sorts. She stopped at the last paddock when one of the foals came over to the fence. Rachel could see Cal through the trees, cantering on a small gray gelding. Rachel leaned her arm over the fence and scratched the filly's soft neck while she watched Cal ride.

For all of Rachel's criticisms of Cal as flighty and unserious, she had to admit she saw nothing but focus and intensity today.

Cal rode her horse through a series of figures designed to supple and soften him, setting the groundwork that would make her play seem effortless when she was riding in a real game. Rachel had seen firsthand how easily Cal moved over the polo field, and she knew the hours and hours of training required to make a difficult sport seem so simple. And Cal had to train at least six horses to the highest level in order to have enough polo ponies for a full season of high-goal tournaments. Rachel was exhausted teaching the basics to her four charges, so she couldn't imagine how Cal felt by the end of the day. Of course, she probably had a Jacuzzi for soaking her sore muscles.

The thought of Cal's lean, toned body lounging in a hot tub, preferably naked, was too distracting. Rachel gave the foal one last pat and walked toward the trees that lined the field. She was about to step beyond them and wave at Cal when she saw another rider canter into sight.

Cal's mother? A few inches shorter than Cal, but with the same sharp cheekbones and straight nose. Graying blond hair caught in a tight bun, and the same match-ready riding clothes as Cal was wearing. The two women looked prepared to shoot a Ralph Lauren ad, not ride around in the isolated privacy of their own farm.

Rachel stood out of sight next to a fir tree, her hand braced on its scratchy bark, and watched the mother and daughter duo run through some practice drills. Yesterday's conversation with Cal had reminded Rachel of her old long-lost-but-loving mother fantasies, and now she had a chance to witness the real-life version of it. After a few minutes, however, she realized Cal's relationship with her mother bore little resemblance to Rachel's imaginary one. The constant stream of corrections and criticisms made Rachel grit her teeth in sympathy for Cal. She wouldn't have lasted five minutes before she whacked the woman over the head with her polo mallet or, at least, stormed off the field in a rage, but Cal seemed completely unperturbed. She rode through the drills, correcting her barely discernible mistakes with no change in her calm expression. She was either a candidate for a best actress award, or she was so accustomed to her mother's critique that she wasn't bothered by it.

Rachel had played polo for herself, because she loved the sport. But Cal didn't have the same luxury. Rachel understood a little better what Cal had been talking about yesterday, when she said it was difficult to be responsible for a family name. Calverts and Lanfords dotted every polo magazine, spanning the country and the history of polo in the States. Callan had to live up to both sides of her illustrious family, merging them into a single polo superstar. Did she even like to play?

Cal cantered after a missed pass and spotted Rachel as she rode toward the sideline. Her face lit up in the first smile Rachel had seen from her since she had been watching the practice. She had seen the same smile on Cal when they had played their "friendly" stick-and-ball match last week. Yes, Cal seemed to love the game, but maybe only when she was allowed to play as herself, not as a branch from her family tree.

"What's up, cowgirl?" Cal asked as she trotted over to the line of trees.

"I came to borrow a few jumps, if you can spare some. I want to see if the horses can handle them." Rachel stroked the gray's neck. His coat was barely wet with sweat, even after a strenuous practice, a testament to slow and careful conditioning.

"Sure. And I wish I could be there to watch you try to convince poor Fancy to haul all four feet off the ground. Ask Jack, and he'll load them into your truck." Cal glanced over her shoulder at her mother who looked pointedly at her watch. Cal laughed. She dropped her reins on the gelding's neck and pulled off her leather riding gloves, running her hands through her damp hair. "I'd help, but this is our mother-daughter bonding time."

"Well, try not to bean her with the ball. I'd have to take you to jail, you know."

Cal laughed again, with less strain this time as her nose and the corners of her eyes crinkled. Rachel couldn't help but smile in response. Maybe she had helped make Cal's practice session a tiny bit easier to bear. She wasn't sure why the thought made her feel good, but she wanted to prolong it.

"Can you stick around after the unit's lesson tonight?" she asked. Why merely tell Cal about her plan to figure out Randy's timeline on the night of Alex's murder? Why not include her in the unofficial sleuthing?

"Sure, gorgeous," Cal said, clearly—and most likely deliberately—misinterpreting Rachel's intentions. She leaned against the pommel of her saddle and brushed her hand over Rachel's cheek before she could move away. Before she could decide whether she wanted to move. "What do you have in mind?"

"Not the same thing you do," Rachel said. She took a step back even though Cal had withdrawn her hand and was sitting upright again. "Clare said Randy got a text to go to the park at three, but Alex was shot around one thirty. I have an idea how we can find out whether she was telling the truth."

"I knew you believed what she was saying," Cal said, slapping her gloves against her thigh.

"I'm not saying I believe her. But I need to know for sure. Do you want to come along?"

"Of course I do," Cal said. She put her gloves on again. "Which one do I get to be? Good cop or bad cop?"

Rachel shook her head at Cal's eager expression. "You get to be the civilian who has to stay in the car unless she promises to behave herself and not say a word."

"Fine, I won't talk," Cal said. She picked up her reins and turned her horse away from Rachel. She looked back over her shoulder. "But I'm definitely not promising to behave myself."

Good. Rachel tried to stop her response before it fully formed in her mind, but she couldn't. She was enjoying Cal's flirting more than she wanted to admit. Maybe because she had so little contact with people in her life right now. Few conversations, no friendly coffee klatches, definitely no physical contact. Loneliness, that's all it was. Certainly not an attraction to Cal. Rachel walked back to the barn, working hard to convince herself that was true. Some hard work would help her forget Cal's touch, her beckoning smile. Haul some jumps around, ride some horses. Then Rachel would be back to normal, all shields in place.

CHAPTER NINE

Cal stood in her walk-in closet wearing only a black sports bra and matching hipster briefs. She rifled through the hangers, examining and dismissing each of her shirts. She had riding and dress clothes, but no outfits suitable for a stakeout. She didn't even know what *was* suitable for a stakeout. She felt out of her element with Rachel, entering uncharted territory with nothing to wear.

Her life was exciting but predictable. Long hours of work interrupted by high-speed polo matches and equally turbulent affairs. But the games and the women had started to blend together in her mind. Working with the mounted team was fun because it was so different. Being with Rachel was exciting and more of an adrenaline rush than Cal had experienced for a long time. She pulled out a dark blue silk blouse and hung it up again with a shake of her head. Even her non-riding clothes were in her team colors.

Maybe it was because Rachel had rejected her advances. So far. Cal had been forced to stick around and get to know the unique facets of her, all the details and depth Cal usually missed as she hurried from women's beds and back to the field. She loved to win every time she played polo, more for her team and her family than for herself, but no matter how much importance her parents put on her success, she was still playing a game. Her relationships were a game, too. Fun, and over the minute she scored. Rachel had so much more at stake in her life, and Cal saw the way her responsibilities had shaped her character. She was loyal to so many people and ideals. To her foster family and her team. To her convictions and her demanding fight for what she believed to be right.

Cal lifted the sleeve of one of her polo jerseys and let it drop again. The blue and maroon uniforms defined her identity. Rachel had talked about not having a family to give her advantages in life, but Cal thought she was wrong. Rachel had the advantage because she had created herself. She had been shaped by her foster parents and by her experiences as a child, but she had single-handedly formed her own character. Cal felt as if she had been made by her parents, not raised by them. Pieced together from the Calvert and Lanford sides of her family, just like the name Callan had been coined. She worked hard to live up to expectations, but she rarely set them herself.

Every time she rode or taught a lesson, she wore the colors of her polo club. Every time she went out or had dinner with her family she wore clothes designed to represent her name well on the pages of a glossy polo magazine. Always surrounded by other people, and always dressing for them.

Cal grabbed a clean outfit out of the pile of clothes she wore when she fed and cleaned stalls in the early mornings. She'd wear her usual riding clothes for the lesson and change into her old and worn ones for her night with Rachel. She had noticed a loneliness in Rachel, an emptiness because she had spent too many years without a family and because her teammates and fellow officers seemed determined to shun her.

But Cal saw the loneliness reflected in her own heart. Family and lovers were close physically, but distant emotionally. Even the grooms—although they welcomed her help and company—never seemed to forget that she was the Lanford daughter and, therefore, their boss. Cal pulled a navy long-sleeved T-shirt over her head, and then she slipped into a pair of stretchy maroon breeches. She felt her anticipation increasing as she thought about the evening ahead. Maybe, after they kept each other company while they tracked down the perp, she and Rachel could find a way to ease each other's loneliness.

❖

Rachel moved the two little jumps out of the arena before the unit's lesson. She had managed to get all four horses over the foot-high obstacles, although Fancy had technically gone through the jumps more than over them. Still, Rachel counted any forward movement from the mare as a small victory. Sitka had been willing but clumsy, and Bandit and Ranger trotted and cantered over the poles with minimal fuss. Rachel's muscles were adjusting to the new work, and she enjoyed her time alone with the horses. She dragged the last pole to the edge of the makeshift arena as Billie drove through the gate. People. Here to spoil her solitude.

Cal came soon after, and she greeted Rachel with nothing but a friendly, casual hello. Rachel was relieved since she hadn't told Cal to keep their meeting with Clare—and the proposed meeting tonight—a secret. There'd be a record proving she had used her computer to search through Alex's murder reports, but she was sure plenty of other officers had read through them as well. She wasn't doing anything wrong, but she was too accustomed to staying under the radar if at all possible. If she discovered anything significant, she'd go straight to homicide and tell them.

Rachel pushed all her worries aside as she rode Bandit through Cal's drills. He was working well for her, and she found him much more pleasant when she was on his back and not within range of his teeth. But she kept part of her focus on Cal. Not because she looked so striking in her team colors, but because Rachel didn't want to be caught unaware again. Who knew what Cal was hiding in her pockets and when she'd pull it out to scare the horses again. Snakes, plastic bags, explosive devices?

She needn't have worried. Cal had apparently decided she'd proved her point with yesterday's umbrella stunt, and she concentrated on correcting the riders and offering suggestions. Halfway through the lesson, she told them to untack their horses and come back to the arena with halters and lead ropes.

"Hey, Bryce." Clark's voice stopped Rachel as she was leading Bandit toward his stall, her usual hiding place.

"What?" she asked. Only a hint of challenge in her tone. She was improving.

"Sitka's been different since you've been riding him. More… bendy."

Rachel had been working the bay through a series of suppling exercises. He'd never be as flexible and light as Bandit or Ranger, but he had been coming along nicely. She was surprised Clark had noticed. And even more surprised he'd brought it up in front of everyone.

"Just doing my job," she said. She kept Bandit outside of his stall while she unbuckled his girth and removed her saddle, instead of ducking inside as usual.

"Fancy, too," Don added before he turned away from her. Billie caught Rachel's eye behind his back and gave her a wink. Rachel smiled. Small victories, but they felt very good.

Cal watched the brief interchange between Rachel and her team. She was proud of her. Rachel had put aside her own pride and managed to finagle Cal into assisting her. She had ignored the spite and sullenness of her unit and continued to train the horses. She was working for something bigger than herself, in spite of the obstacles. Cal didn't do that. She played polo for her family, but out of guilt and habit, not conviction. And she hated to ask for help. She knew Rachel did, too, but she had done it anyway.

Cal got an armful of crinkly raincoats out of her car and met the dismounted officers in the arena. She kept one clear plastic coat over her arm and hung the rest on one of the orange pylons. No need to wave them around since she had everyone's complete attention.

"We're going to start desensitizing the horses, so they'll be ready to face anything the public throws at them," Cal said. She took Sitka's rope from Clark and led him in front of the group. "We obviously can't anticipate every single thing they'll encounter, but we can teach them two important lessons. One, scary objects are not necessarily going to eat them." Cal paused while the officers laughed at her little joke. They seemed so different from the angry and defiant people she'd met only yesterday. Much more at ease, and ready to learn.

"And two," she continued, "they can rely on us to keep them safe. We'll use different methods to introduce new things over the next few weeks. It's up to you as the horse handler to figure out what method your horse responds to best. I'm going to use an approach called flooding with Sitka now. My goal is for him to stand still while I flap this raincoat at him, but I'm not going to force it. Try to pay attention to my timing—when I push for more and when I back off."

Cal walked Sitka to the far end of the arena. She kept his rope in one hand and waved the coat at him with the other. He snorted and skittered away from the rustling plastic, but she calmly followed him as he danced in a circle. Every time his hooves stopped moving, even for a fraction of a second, she stopped flapping the coat and praised him. As she had expected, it was only a matter of minutes before she could wave the coat right in his face and he barely flinched. She eventually tossed the coat over his back and he stood as calmly as if she were putting on his saddle pad. She rubbed his neck and led him back to the rest of the officers.

Cal waved off their applause. To the more inexperienced riders, the display looked like a success. To her and Rachel, the demonstration only pointed out how far the horses had to go before they'd be ready for the Fourth. One umbrella had nearly unseated the whole unit. And one raincoat had taken up half their lesson.

"Everyone grab a coat and try the same exercise. Spread out in the arena so your horses are free to move without hurting each other. Clark, why don't you find something new to use with Sitka. Maybe an empty grain bag."

Cal looked over to where Rachel was standing with Bandit. She let him sniff the coat before she gently waved it in his direction. Cal wanted to hang out at her end of the arena, watching Rachel's gentle movements when she was working with her mount—so different from her prickly demeanor when she had to deal with people. Staring at Rachel's ass and long, muscular legs in her skintight breeches.

Cal sighed and walked over to Don. He was a poor substitute for Rachel, but he obviously needed more help than his sergeant did. He was trying, though, gamely continuing to flap the raincoat even when Fancy stood on his booted foot and refused to budge. Cal shoved the mare's shoulder until she moved, and then she took Fancy's rope from Don. Her gaze skimmed over the other officers even as she showed him where to stand so he was safe from the heavy mare's hooves. Clark's movements were awkward, but the patient Sitka was more interested in sniffing the grain bag than in shying away from it. Billie was gently tossing the raincoat over Ranger's back and around his legs while he stood at the end of his lead rope with an unconcerned expression on his face.

Once Don seemed more comfortable and able to keep his feet safely out of harm's way, Cal went back to Rachel's corner of the arena. Bandit was quiet, one hind hoof cocked in a relaxed posture, as Rachel slid the coat over his back and neck.

"The two of you seem to be bonding," Cal said. She rubbed the horse's forehead and kept all her fingers intact. "And his attitude sure is improving."

Rachel shrugged. "We understand each other, I guess. He likes having a job to do every day." She glanced around the arena. "Good lesson today. Everyone seems to be doing well."

"Especially Ranger," Cal said. "Did he have more training than the others when he came?"

Rachel put the raincoat over Bandit's head. It rustled when he pricked his ears forward, but he didn't move. She slid the coat off and rubbed his nose. "Actually, no. He and Sitka were donated by the same woman. She used to compete with them, but she got pregnant and leased them to the department. Ranger is younger and a Thoroughbred, so I would have expected Sitka to be the quieter of the two."

"Must be his temperament, then," Cal said. She took the raincoat from Rachel, taking advantage of the chance to slide her hand over Rachel's, their fingers briefly tangling together. Long and sensitive, weathered and strong from working outdoors. Cal had a good idea what else those fingers could do. She noticed the slight flush where the open neck of Rachel's uniform shirt left her throat exposed. Maybe she wasn't the only one thinking about putting Rachel's hands to use.

"Seems to be," Rachel said. She moved her hand away but stayed still and didn't put the horse in between them, for once. "To be honest, I think that's why Alex chose to ride him."

Cal smiled. Always slightly out of reach, but never too far away. She must be wearing down Rachel's resistance. Desensitizing her to touch and closeness. Cal was the one to step away this time.

She walked to the center of the arena and called the riders over to her. "Great job, everyone. You can use this same technique as often as you want, both to teach your horses and to strengthen your connection with them. Anytime you have an hour to spare, come out here and work with your horse. Bring whatever unusual objects you can find. Bikes, strollers, plastic jugs filled with rocks. Tomorrow afternoon we'll work with the raincoats again, but while you're mounted."

Rachel lingered in Bandit's stall while Cal and the rest of her team groomed and fed the horses. She had made a little progress today, and the praise from Clark and Don made the hours she had spent on their horses seem worthwhile. But she still didn't believe they'd accept her in the joking, playful circle they'd formed around Cal.

She brushed Bandit's tail until it was silky and tangle-free, standing off to one side in case he decided to kick. He seemed to have a great work ethic, and he tolerated her leadership in the arena whether she was on foot or in the saddle, but he still seemed to resent her when she came into his stall, his private space. So she spent as much time there as possible. They were partners, and he'd have to learn to accept her presence no matter where they were. Plus, she needed a place to hide during those lonely times when she heard the unit talking and laughing, just beyond her reach.

Cal didn't come over to Bandit's stall like she had the night before, but she was sitting on an upturned bucket when Rachel finally emerged after she heard the patrol cars leave the yard. Rachel's step faltered when she saw that Cal had changed out of her more formal teaching clothes. The gray polo shirt emphasized the color of her eyes and hair, making her look silver and gold. The worn and faded jeans were snug, drawing Rachel's attention to Cal's ass—the exact area Rachel continually fought to avoid staring at whenever she was near Cal. She cleared her throat before attempting to speak.

"Give me a minute to change, and we can go find Skunk."

"Skunk?"

"It's his street name," Rachel said. She didn't know why, and she wasn't particularly anxious to find out. She had recognized his given name, Warren Albuez, on the reports she'd read the night before. Every cop in town had dealt with some member of the Albuez family at some time during their career. Usually more than one member, and more often than once. There should have been a separate chapter in the training manual to cover this one extended family. Skunk was a minor player in the clan and not the most reliable of witnesses.

Rachel took her backpack into the office and closed the door behind her. She quietly turned the lock even though she felt silly doing it. She wasn't sure whether she was worried Cal might walk in when she was changing, or worried about what she'd do if Cal *did* come in. And part of her did want Cal to walk through the door. To catch her when she had stripped down to her briefs and sports bra…

No. They were too different. Rachel was attracted to Cal, more turned on than she cared to admit by Cal's persistent and overt flirting, but she couldn't allow the relationship to move any further than where it stood. They were colleagues of a sort, united in their drive to make the mounted unit a success, although for very different reasons. Cal was there to have fun, to play at being a mounted police trainer, an undercover detective, any role she could find. Rachel was there for one reason. To salvage her reputation.

Those differences were the very reasons Rachel wouldn't sleep with Cal, no matter how hard Cal pushed. And no matter how much Rachel wanted her to push. Cal would be moving to the East Coast soon after the Fourth. She'd continue her bid to be polo champion of the world while playing with the next available woman who came along. Rachel wanted a stability Cal could never offer. A home, a family. A safe place to live surrounded by friends, and a lover she trusted to stand by her no matter what. She might not find it with TPD, and she definitely wouldn't find it with Cal. But she had to keep striving for it.

Rachel peeled off her tight uniform and pulled on her most faded, most comfortable jeans. They were frayed at the crotch and the knees, not because of a fashion statement but because they'd had a hard life on the ranch. The rest of her outfit was black. Studded belt, tight ribbed tank top, leather jacket, cowboy boots so dusty they were almost gray. She tucked her gun into her jeans at the small of her back and shoved her wallet and commission card into a pocket. She might look like a street thug, but everyone in the bars she and Cal were going to visit would make her as a cop. She'd probably arrested most of the people they were going to meet. They'd be safe enough, but she was having second thoughts about bringing Cal along. She knew it was too late to back out—there was no way Cal would go home now—and she seriously doubted she could force Cal to stay in the truck with the doors locked.

Rachel left the office and pulled the door shut behind her.

"Oh my God," Cal said.

Rachel turned around and Cal closed the distance between them with two long strides. She pushed Rachel against the door. Rachel hadn't managed to shut it all the way before Cal was on her, and they stumbled backward into the office as the door banged open again. Rachel automatically put her arms around Cal's waist to keep from falling.

Cal tangled her fingers in Rachel's short hair and pulled her forward for a kiss. She had been lecturing herself about going slow with Rachel. Being content with brief touches like the brush of their fingers today in the arena. But then Rachel had walked out of the office looking like some sort of sexy badass biker chick. Cal changed tactics in a heartbeat. Flooding. Kiss Rachel until she stopped fighting so damn hard.

Rachel's kiss was better than Cal had hoped. Her lips were soft, her teeth were rough, her tongue thrust against Cal's when she slid it into Rachel's mouth. Rachel was oh-so-definitely kissing her back. Rachel kicked the door shut and shoved Cal against it, pressing her thigh between Cal's legs. Cal moved against her, already wanting to come, but Rachel broke their contact and their kiss so suddenly Cal almost dropped to the ground.

"No, don't stop now," Cal insisted. But she could see Rachel's closed expression. She was so far away right now, she could be in a different state. Fuck. Cal had pushed too hard, too fast, but she couldn't help it. Cal was always so good at this game. Reading her potential sex partner. Understanding instinctively when to move forward, when to hang back and let the other woman do the chasing. She had been right about the need to go slow, but all of her common sense had disintegrated when she saw Rachel.

"I take it you approve of this outfit," Rachel said. Her voice was steady enough, but she could feel a tremor in her hand when she ran it through her hair.

"It'll do," Cal said. Her eyes had gone steely gray and her skin was as flushed as Rachel's felt. "I'm sorry I…"

Her voice trailed off and she raised a hand to fix her now-disheveled ponytail. Rachel made a shushing sound as she stepped closer and captured Cal's hand with her own. She tucked a strand of gold hair behind Cal's ear with her free hand, sliding it down to cup Cal's chin.

"Don't be. Please," she said as she rubbed her thumb over Cal's bruised-red lips. "We both wanted that kiss. But I don't do casual."

Cal smiled against Rachel's thumb. "And casual is all I *can* do. But if you change your mind…?"

Rachel pulled Cal forward and kissed her cheek. "You'll be the first one I call."

She kept her fingers wrapped around Cal's as she shut and locked the office door, rattling the knob to make sure it was secure. "We can leave your car here and take my truck. It's only a short walk to my apartment, and I think the fresh air will do us some good."

"And then we can work off our sexual frustration by shaking down some perps."

Rachel laughed. She kept hold of Cal's hand until they got to the yard's gate, wanting to prolong the contact. Was she insane to push Cal away? To keep her confident, breezy persona in place when inside she was trembling with desire? No. She had to keep her distance.

"We're not shaking anyone down. We're just going to have a conversation."

They were silent on the short walk to Rachel's apartment. Her hand felt ice cold without Cal's warmth. But Rachel was too familiar with loneliness. She had lived with it for her first fifteen years, when it had been all she knew, and its return had hurt like hell this year. After living with Nelson and Leah and her foster brothers, after newfound friends in high school and college and, more recently, a tightly bonded police family, she'd learned what it was like not to be lonely. But these past few months, she had been thrown back to childhood nights on strange beds, mission floors, detention cell cots. When she had lain so still under thin blankets and felt as if she were the only person on the planet, as if her breath were echoing through an empty, uninhabited world.

A night with Cal would be amazing. Based on tonight's kiss? Spectacular. Their breath joined together as they'd fought to capture a connection and release. But then Cal would go away. And Rachel would be even emptier because she had experienced a night of incredible fullness.

Rachel unlocked the passenger door of her pickup and opened it for Cal before walking around to the driver's side. She started the engine, conscious of Cal's eyes on her. *Please don't touch me. Please don't challenge my willpower because I'm not that strong.*

"So what's the plan, Sarge?" Cal asked. She clasped her hands on her lap as if she had heard Rachel's silent plea. "Are we going to troll the streets for Skunk?"

Rachel laughed. The combination of Cal's sexy, cultured voice and the goofy sayings was endearing. This might be a worthless night of investigating, but she was suddenly glad to have time with Cal. To have been shaken by her kiss, to laugh at her silliness. To have a friend.

"We're going to check out a few bars, have a beer or two, and ask some questions. Maybe we'll find Skunk, maybe not."

Cal settled back in her seat as Rachel drove through the North End streets, heading out of the more respectable residential area and toward Tacoma's downtown. She wanted to touch her again, but it was too dangerous. Rachel was right—they were looking for different types of relationships. But Cal worried about something else, something too unsettling to dwell on for long. Rachel's kiss had turned her on, exciting her more than she had expected and making her want more. That was fine. Great. The scary part was how affected she had been by Rachel's gentle touch after their kiss. The friction of her fingers against Cal's chin and lips. The comfort of Rachel's hand holding hers. Those were girlfriend moments, and Cal couldn't allow herself to want them. Her heart belonged to polo, and she didn't have time for anything more serious—and Rachel was unquestionably serious—than a casual fling.

"What are we trying to learn from this conversation? Do you really think Randy Brown is innocent?"

"I doubt it," Rachel said, checking over her shoulder before she changed lanes. "Clare said he got a text at three, but the cell phone is missing. It wasn't booked as evidence or property when he was arrested, and it was a burner, so unless Clare finds it, there's no way to find out if she's lying. Skunk's statement says he met Randy in the vacant lot by the police yard a little after one. He left after their transaction, but Randy stayed behind. The next morning, he hears that a cop was shot in the same place, at the same time. So Skunk, being an upstanding citizen, calls the cops."

"And if he really met Randy at three, like Clare said?"

"Then maybe someone else killed Alex and is trying to frame Randy. It'd have been easy to steal his gun and then stick it under the seat in his car while he was in the park with Skunk."

Rachel parked in the tiny gravel lot behind a decrepit brick building adorned with a faded painting advertising a long-gone furniture store. She tapped her fingers on the steering wheel. "This is crazy. Of course Randy did it. All the evidence points at him. And of course Clare was lying. Why wouldn't she? She's desperate to protect him."

Cal reached over and poked at Rachel's stomach until she laughed and caught Cal's hand. "So we're going with your gut and against common sense? Must be scary for you to stray from the rule books and the police reports for once."

"Very funny," Rachel said. She squeezed Cal's fingers lightly and let them go. "I can be as spontaneous as anyone."

"Given adequate time to prepare." Cal unhooked her seat belt. "So what makes you think Mr. Skunk will be hanging out in a bar on a Tuesday night?"

"Well, let's just say he doesn't have to get up tomorrow and go to work, so any night is as good as the next to be in a bar. And if he did help someone set Randy up, he'll have been paid for his trouble. From my experiences with Skunk, I think it's safe to assume he'll be drinking twenty-four/seven until the money's gone."

Cal followed Rachel into the dimly lit bar. The crowded room fell silent when they entered. "Jeez, I feel like I walked into a saloon with the bad guy in a Western," Cal said quietly to Rachel. She noticed a skinny girl next to the bar, wearing a tight skirt, a fake-fur-lined sweater, and a scowl on her face as she watched Rachel. "Miss Kitty over there looks particularly unhappy to see you."

"I'm the sheriff, not the bad guy," Rachel said. "And you always start by questioning the person who looks least inclined to talk because they usually have the most to say."

Rachel walked over to the young girl and leaned against the bar next to her. "Two Sam Adams," she said when the bartender walked over. She picked the first brand she saw that came in a bottle and wasn't on tap because she wasn't about to drink out of one of the bar's glasses. She turned toward the girl while the bartender went to get the beer. She felt Cal close by her side, not touching, but definitely close. "Hey, Lyla. How's it going?"

"I'm not working," Lyla said belligerently. "I got every right to be here."

"Oh, really? You turned twenty-one lately?"

Lyla only scowled harder in response. Rachel took that as a no. The bartender returned with the two bottles, and Rachel tried not to notice how grimy his fingernails were. She dropped a twenty on the counter. "Either of you seen Skunk lately?"

Rachel saw Lyla eying the money, so she fished another bill out of her pocket and set it in front of her. She knew what Lyla had to do to earn twenty dollars. If her own life had taken a few different turns, she might have been standing in Lyla's shoes right now. On the wrong side of the badge.

"So?" she asked.

The bartender swiped the twenty and put it in his pocket. "He was in here a couple nights ago."

"Drinking more than usual?" Rachel asked. The bartender wiped the counter with his questionably clean rag, so she dropped another twenty on the counter. Doing off-duty investigating was fucking expensive.

"Maybe. Bought a round for the whole place, and stayed 'til closing." He shrugged. "That's all I've got," he said as he walked away to serve another customer.

Rachel resisted the urge to wipe the mouth of her bottle before she took a drink. Cal's interest in playacting apparently didn't extend to germ warfare—she used the hem of her gray polo shirt to clean the bottle. Rachel laughed and turned back to Lyla.

"You got anything else for me?"

"Maybe," Lyla answered. The twenty in front of her had already disappeared.

Rachel pulled out another. She'd have emptied her pockets if she thought the money would help Lyla, but it would only get her drunk or high enough to survive the night.

Lyla took the money and tucked it in the top of her high-heeled boot. "I saw Skunk last night at the Oyster. Drinking pretty good. He even bought me some fancy gin for nothing. I mean…not that I drank it."

"Of course you didn't," Rachel said. She took another swig of her beer and set the bottle on the counter. She pulled out a card and wrote her number on the back. "You ever want out of this game, give me a call. I'll help. Come on, Cal, let's go."

"Bye, Lyla," Cal said as Rachel tugged her toward the door. "I like your sweater."

"What was that for?" Rachel asked with a laugh as she held the door open for Cal.

"I was being good cop," Cal said. "Poor girl. She looked about fourteen."

"Sixteen. Plenty of cops have tried to help her and the other young ones off the street, but we can only do so much. And I thought good cop was the one doling out money."

"No. Your voice changed when we were in there, and you sounded very intimidating. Are we going to the Oyster, whatever that is?"

"The Oyster's Cove. A dive down on the Tideflats. And yes, it's our next stop."

Cal climbed in the cab of the truck. Rachel had sounded so sure of herself in the bar, but her concern for Lyla had been clear to see. She could see the tight set of Rachel's jaw as she drove across the Puyallup River and onto the industrial Tideflats area. Cal looked away. The large cranes used to on- and offload containers from ships were silhouetted against the twilit sky. Massive tanks at the oil refinery appeared only as lurking shadows on the horizon. The normally smoggy and smelly underbelly of Tacoma appeared interesting and mysterious in this light. Cal didn't expect the next bar to be even as clean as the last one had been. She'd probably need a bucket of hand sanitizer—and not just the hem of her shirt—to make their bottles safe enough to drink from.

Rachel turned off the truck's headlights as she pulled into the lot of a tiny shack covered with neon beer signs. She squinted through the windshield before she threw the truck into park.

"Stay here," she ordered before she jumped out of the truck and ran toward the back of the building.

"Leaving so soon, Skunk?"

"Hey, I was goin' home for the night. Minding my own business." Rachel had the front of his T-shirt in her hand, pressing him into the wall so he was standing on his toes. He was still at least three inches shorter than she was.

Rachel glanced over her shoulder at the sound of footsteps on gravel. Cal. Damn it. She gave her a *get back in the truck* glare before she turned back to Skunk. "Or maybe someone tipped you off that I was looking for you. If you haven't done anything wrong, why'd you run?"

"Someone says the police are asking questions about me, seems the smart thing to do is make myself scarce."

An honest answer. Rachel eased up on his shirt and let him stand flat on the ground. She moved closer to him, emphasizing her height advantage. "You've been hitting the bars pretty good lately," she said. "Seems the smart thing to do is tell me how you're suddenly able to afford to buy drinks for everyone you meet."

"I earned that money," he said, suddenly unable to look her in the eye. "I got a job."

Not so honest. "I know all about this job of yours," she said. "Who paid you to lie to the police about the night you met Randy Brown in the park?"

"Me? Lie to the police? Why would I—"

"Shut it," Rachel said. "We have Randy's cell phone. With a text on it from you, telling him to meet you in the park at three. So I'm going to ask again. Who paid you to lie and say you met him around one?"

Rachel saw his expression change when she mentioned the phone. From cocky to terrified in a heartbeat. Damn. Her ridiculous scenario was right. And Clare had been telling the truth. Rachel hadn't truly believed either until she observed Skunk's reaction.

"I don't know what you're talking about," he said in a whisper, his gaze darting from side to side as if he expected someone to emerge from the shadows. "I told the truth. Are you going to arrest me for telling the truth?"

Rachel released her hold and he disappeared into the very shadows he had been so suspicious of only moments before. She braced her hand on the side of the building and tried to deepen her shallow breaths. She felt an arm slipping around her shoulders. Cal. Rachel needed to get her out of here.

"Are you okay?" Cal asked.

"Yeah, fine," Rachel said. She took hold of Cal's hand and walked quickly to her truck. "Get in the truck—where I told you to stay, by the way. We're getting out of here."

Rachel drove quickly through the dark streets, hardly able to breathe until she and Cal were across the bridge and off the Tideflats. Jesus. She had been playing a game, no different from Cal. Moved beyond reason by Clare's high-pitched voice, her conflicting timelines. Rachel had been feeling so isolated on the department, so alone, that she hadn't even considered bringing her suspicions to one of the detectives working Alex's case. Instead, she had run off on her own—with a civilian along, for God's sake—like some renegade cop in a movie. She had expected to visit a few bars, have a few beers with Cal. Maybe find Skunk, maybe not. Mention the alleged three a.m. text and watch him deny it without any signs of dishonesty.

"You were supposed to stay in the truck," she said as she sped along the downtown streets, snapping at Cal because she suddenly felt responsible for her. Foolish for bringing her to these hellholes. "Why didn't you?"

"I was your backup," Cal said quietly. She reached over and took Rachel's hand in hers. "Rach, what does this mean? He looked very scared when you said you had Randy's phone."

"It means someone framed Randy. And whoever it was paid Skunk to set him up. Premeditated. Alex's murder wasn't an accident."

Rachel drove up the windy road from the waterfront to the park entrance and braked to an abrupt halt by the stable yard. She got out of the cab and strode over to the gate with Cal close behind her.

"What do we do now?" Cal asked as Rachel swiped her card and opened the gate.

"Now *you* get in your car and drive home. Forget any of this happened. And I go home and call my superiors. The detectives will take it from here. And I'll probably be fired."

Cal didn't obey. Big surprise. Instead, she traced her fingertips along Rachel's forehead where Rachel was certain her tension was visible. Cal's touch relaxed her a bit. Enough to make her remember their earlier kiss. Why the hell had she stopped it? Why hadn't she taken Cal back to her apartment rather than taking her on this insane mission? She caught Cal's hand and brushed her lips against it.

"Go home, Cal. I'll see you tomorrow."

Cal leaned forward and kissed Rachel on the lips. Even with her mind in turmoil, with her job possibly on the line, Rachel couldn't help but respond to Cal. To the strength in her kiss, the heat when her tongue slipped into Rachel's mouth. Cal broke their kiss and leaned her forehead against Rachel's.

"You did the right thing," she said. "Everyone deserves to know the truth."

Rachel used to believe that, but now she wasn't so sure. Exposing the truth had gotten her in trouble before, and she wasn't under the illusion this time would be any different. She stood in place long after Cal drove away, long after she had locked the gate. She eventually felt herself shivering in the cool evening air, so she got in her truck and drove the short distance to her home. Fifteen minutes later, she hung up after spilling the entire story to Lieutenant Hargrove's answering machine. She stripped out of her clothes, leaving a messy trail on the way to her bedroom, and slid naked between the sheets. She had done her part. Whatever happened next was out of her hands.

CHAPTER TEN

Rachel still hadn't heard from Hargrove by the next afternoon. She went through her day mechanically. Jogging in the early hours, feeding horses and cleaning stalls, riding her four charges. She even cleaned everyone's tack and rearranged the office while she waited for Cal and the other officers to arrive for their lesson.

Cal was early. She tapped on the door to Bandit's stall where Rachel was grooming him for the fourth time that day. He was going to be bald, but at least he was accepting her touch without trying to bite her arm off.

"Heard anything?" Cal asked.

"You were supposed to forget last night," Rachel said. She couldn't hide her smile, though. She felt too relieved to have someone to talk to, someone who would understand how worried she was about what she had done. She knew her reputation couldn't get any worse, and she hadn't done anything bad enough to be fired, but she had a nagging suspicion that somehow her life was about to get even more miserable.

"I did," Cal said. She winked at Rachel. "But I keep having flashbacks. Something about a bar, and a badass cop roughing up a hoodlum. Oh, and I remember an incredible kiss. You wouldn't know anything about *that*, would you?"

Rachel laughed. She picked up the saddle she had draped over Bandit's stall door and set it gently on his back. "Let's count the kiss as payment for our polo match. I owed you one."

"Sounds fair. So, you didn't answer me. Have you heard anything from the detectives?"

"No, and I probably won't." Rachel buckled Bandit's girth loosely around his belly and reached for his bridle. "They'll question Skunk. Get phone records. Whatever. No reason for me to be in the loop since I only had a hunch, but no hard evidence. I'll find out what's going on when everyone else in the department does."

"So that's it? You don't—"

The sound of cars driving over gravel interrupted Cal's question. She looked behind her. "Clark and Billie are here," she said, "and someone I don't recognize."

Rachel stepped to the doorway. Lieutenant Hargrove. Making a barn call. That couldn't be good. She handed Bandit's reins to Cal and went out to face whatever was about to fly her way.

Abby Hargrove's face looked furious, but the rest of her was as put together and polished as usual. Rachel walked toward her and couldn't help but wonder how she managed to look so beautiful yet so ready to explode, at the same time. Hargrove started yelling before Rachel made it across the parking lot.

"I knew you were going to fuck this up somehow, Bryce. I didn't realize you'd do such a spectacular job of it."

Rachel saw Billie and Clark standing near the tack room, watching the show. Don was pulling into the lot. Great. Wouldn't want anyone to miss *this*.

"I'm sorry, but I—"

"No. I'm talking now. I spent the past three hours getting my ass handed to me by two captains, the assistant chief, and half the dicks from homicide. So now it's your turn. Really, how hard would it have been for you to do what I asked? Finish what Alex started. Let Callan Lanford do the training while you kept your mouth shut and your nose clean. But no. I come in this morning and find out you decided to promote yourself to detective and start interrogating witnesses. You got an assignment every other sergeant wanted, but it wasn't enough for you, was it? I didn't want you here, but I set it up so a child could run this program. All you had to do was come out here and ride a horse around for an hour a day. Then go home. What do you have to say for yourself? Well?"

Rachel kept silent until Hargrove's last word was delivered with plenty of venom and followed by a long pause. Apparently it was her turn to talk now. "Randy Brown's girlfriend just showed up the other day. I didn't go looking for her. And as soon as I found out Skunk—I mean Warren Albuez—was lying, I called you."

"You *think* he was lying," Hargrove said, correcting her. "Don't you think he might have been reacting to the false information you gave him?"

Rachel felt her anger rising. She trusted her instincts and she knew Skunk had been paid to lie about his meeting with Randy. Maybe Hargrove and the rest of the detectives should give her a break and go find out who really killed Alex. "So bring him in and ask him yourself."

"He's gone, Bryce. Our key witness has disappeared thanks to your inept investigation. What do you have to say for yourself now?"

Nothing. Rachel kept silent. Damn, she knew Skunk had been spooked last night, but she hadn't expected him to vanish. She'd figured he'd go home to his family, or head to the next bar.

"I didn't think—"

"That's right, Bryce. You didn't think. I would love to fire you right now, or at least kick you out of this unit, but I can't. For some reason, the brass wants you to stay. God knows why. The only thing that would make me happy right now is your letter of resignation on my desk."

Abby marched back to her car, her posture stiff. Rachel wanted to let her go, to be finished with the scene at least for the moment, but she needed to be sure her mistake hadn't been in vain. She had done something stupid, yes. But the information she had uncovered was still valid.

"Wait, Lieutenant." Hargrove stopped but didn't turn around. Rachel pushed on. "Albuez was lying, I'd swear to it. Someone planned Alex's murder. Paid Albuez to lie about Randy. I shouldn't have talked to him last night, but it doesn't change the facts. You have to look at Alex, find out why he was targeted—"

Hargrove spun around. "Watch it, Bryce. Think long and hard before you start insinuating anything about Alex Mayer's character.

He was loyal to his family, his community, and this department. That's more than I can say about you."

Abby got in her car and spun out of the lot. Rachel could feel her officers and Cal watching her. Waiting for…Rachel didn't know what. Was she supposed to defend herself now? Try to explain when no one ever seemed to listen? Ignore Hargrove's visit and go on with the lesson? Rachel was out of answers, out of options. Hargrove was right. She had had her chance to be a silent part of the mounted unit. An unwanted but harmless parasite. But she had blown it.

Rachel walked over to Cal and took Bandit's reins without making eye contact with her. She brushed off Cal's hand and tightened Bandit's girth before swinging into the saddle and aiming him toward the gate Hargrove had left open. Aiming for the familiar trails that would lead her deep into the park.

Cal had tried to stop Rachel, to make her stay, but Rachel was out of her reach and crossing the paved road leading to the ferry. She spun around and faced the unit's officers, who were staring after Rachel with the same stunned look she herself must be wearing.

"I've got to go after her. Can you guys…?"

"We'll be fine. Take Ranger," Billie said. "I'll help you tack him."

Don ducked into the tack room for Ranger's saddle, and Billie led him out of his stall. Cal fumbled with his bridle while she fumed at the three people who had watched without helping while Rachel had gotten chewed out. "I can't believe that bitch. Rachel was trying to help, trying to find the truth. Isn't that your fucking job? To make sure the people you arrest are actually guilty?"

Billie took the bridle from Cal's hands and calmly slipped the bit into her horse's mouth. "Look, I don't know what happened last night, but our lieutenant has every right to be upset if Rachel did anything to jeopardize this team. Hargrove is the one who fought for us. She spent months trying to get approval from the city manager and the chief. She got our grant and picked our team. If we fail, her reputation is on the line even more than ours."

Cal jerked the reins out of Billie's hand. "Does Rachel know about that?"

The three officers exchanged glances. "I don't know," Billie said. She shrugged and stepped out of the way as Cal swung herself onto the chestnut's back. "She wasn't part of the unit during the planning stages, so probably not."

"Well, maybe if you actually spoke to her, you could have told her about this. Warned her about how to deal with Lieutenant Bitch." Cal stared at each of the officers in turn. "She's out here every day working to make your unit a success. Training *your* horses. Ignoring her own pride and asking me for help. And you won't even talk to her, won't bother to find out if the rumors you've heard about her are true. Rachel and I should step out of the picture and let the three of you fuck up this city's Fourth of July celebration. And believe me, without Rachel's help, you'd do a damn fine job of it. Now, where do you think she is?"

"Go past the zoo," Clark said, pointing in the direction Rachel had taken. He looked a little shaken, whether by his superior's unexpected visit or by Cal's speech. She hoped it was the latter. "There are lots of trails off the Five Mile Drive, so you'll have to look for hoofprints to find the one she's taken. I can get Sitka and—"

"No," Cal said. "You'll probably fall off, and then I'll be searching for two riders, not one. Stay here and clean something."

Cal wheeled the gelding and trotted over the gravel and out the gate. She had to keep him at a walk as she crossed the busy road to the ferry, dodging between cars as they waited in line to board. She didn't dare trot him across the pavement since he still wasn't shod for such a slick surface. The thought of him slipping and falling on the pavement—probably on top of her since she wasn't wearing a helmet—made her keep her cool. She only hoped Rachel would do the same thing, even in her hurt and angry condition. She pictured Rachel lying on one of the paved roads, bleeding and pale, and the image made her push Ranger into a canter as soon as she was on the grassy hill leading to the park.

She had no idea what it was like to be judged and found guilty by coworkers. All her life, she'd been the captain, the instructor, the trainer. Commanding respect because of her last name and her polo skills. But she knew exactly how it felt to be judged and found wanting by her family, to always feel like her best efforts were not quite good enough. To aim for approval—or love?—and have it dangled just out of reach.

Cal dodged around the surprised-looking parents and children dotting the park. She was thankful the weather was still typical for the Northwest's climate. Misty and overcast, still unseasonably chilly. Summer wouldn't really arrive until July, and so the park wasn't as crowded as it would be a month from now. Ranger cantered along as if he had done this a thousand times, ignoring the honks and encouraging shouts as people drove past him. Cal brought him to a trot on the pine-needle-strewn shoulder of the road leading to the Five Mile Drive. She hadn't seen any sign of a horse since leaving the damp grass of the picnic areas. There, Bandit's prints had been easy to see and follow, but now that she was entering the woods, they'd be harder to spot.

Cal turned off the main road when she noticed some churned-up dirt on a trail leading into the woods. She was watching the ground, searching for some confirmation that Rachel had come this way, when Ranger came to an abrupt halt. Cal pushed off his neck and back into the saddle.

"Sorry about that." The young man she had nearly run over paused beside her, running in place. He was wearing jogging shorts and a sweaty T-shirt. "Are you okay?"

"I'm fine, thanks. Sorry I almost took you out," Cal said as she put her feet back in her stirrups, glad the rest of the mounted unit hadn't seen her near dismount.

"Not a problem," he said. He gave Ranger an awkward pat on the nose. "I jog out here all the time, but I've never seen horses on these trails until today. You're the second."

"I'm looking for the other one. Is she back that way?" Cal pointed in the direction he had come from.

"Yep. Go left when the trail forks."

Cal was trotting off before he finished speaking. "Thanks," she called over her shoulder. She took the path to the left and emerged into an open area. The tall bleached-wood fence around the Fort Nisqually exhibit was directly in front of her, and she veered left again and passed behind it. The living museum wasn't open yet for the season, but there were lots of families in her way. Some of them called out to her, wanting to pet her horse, but she ignored them and kept trotting. Let the officers deal with them once they were ready to ride in public. Cal had only one objective right now. She finally made it to the back wall of the fort and saw Rachel ahead of her, heading toward the woods again.

"Rach? Stop!"

Rachel waved Cal off without turning around, but a few seconds later she had to pull Bandit to a halt as a toddler ran in front of her horse. Rachel dismounted and picked up the little boy as he lunged forward to pet the horse's front legs. Cal rode up beside them as a breathless man arrived.

"Jimmy, you can't run away like that," he said, his voice obviously laced with worry. "I'm sorry. He saw the horse and took off."

"It's okay," Rachel said. She held the boy up so he could pat Bandit's neck, while she kept one hand tight on the reins so the horse couldn't reach Jimmy with his teeth. Bandit stood quietly, however. "I was explaining to him that he shouldn't run in front of a horse, like he wouldn't run in front of a car."

"Thank you," the man said, taking his squirming son from Rachel. "I saw the new barn out by the ferry landing. So we'll be seeing horses in the park from now on?"

"Yes," Rachel said. Cal recognized her cop voice. Strong and assured. Approachable, but in charge. She was relieved not to hear any trace of hesitation or self-doubt even after Rachel had been berated by her superior. Cal exhaled in relief. Rachel would be okay. "We'll be patrolling in the park and along the waterfront this summer."

"Glad to hear it. My dad told me stories about how he used to ride out here when they had a livery stable. Years ago," the man said. He carried Jimmy over so he could pet Ranger as well. The horse nosed the boy gently.

"We'll have to plan an open house some weekend this month," Rachel said as she mounted Bandit again. "So everyone can meet the horses and their riders."

"We'll be there, won't we, Jimmy? And I'm sure my dad would be thrilled to come, too. Thanks again, Officer."

Rachel waved and then turned to Cal. "It's bigger than I am," she said. Cal frowned, not quite sure what she meant.

Rachel struggled to explain what had been racing through her mind since she had run away from the stable yard. "When Hargrove assigned me to this unit, all I could think about was how it would affect me and my career. My reputation. I've wanted the team to succeed and be safe, partly for them, but mostly because I thought it'd make me look good. Maybe help me be part of this department again."

Rachel squeezed her calves to ask Bandit to walk, aiming him toward the trails on the far side of the fort. She let her reins hang loose, and Bandit ambled along with his head low. Rachel noticed Cal wasn't quite as relaxed on Ranger even though the horse was quiet. She probably expected Rachel to run off again at any moment.

"When she was yelling at me today, all I could think about was my career again," Rachel continued. "It's as good as over, although someone seems determined to prolong its demise. I don't know why I'm still in charge of this unit when I seem to be the one person best suited to destroy it. No one wants to listen to me, I don't have enough knowledge to train them, and no one above or under me has any faith I'll succeed."

"I do," Cal said. "You're doing an excellent job training those horses, and—"

Rachel stopped her with another wave of her free hand. She used the other to guide Bandit onto a path leading down the bluff and toward the Sound. The carefully maintained trail was wide enough for the two horses to walk side by side. "But don't you see? It doesn't matter. I can do the impossible and get these officers trained enough to patrol on the Fourth without killing themselves or anyone else, but it won't make a difference. My lieutenant will still hate me. My team will still disrespect me. Everyone on the force who knows I got this job without the right qualifications will still resent me."

"I'm sorry," Cal said. She leaned over and squeezed Rachel's hand. "I wish those jerks had stood up for you today. Or that you had pulled out your Taser and zapped that bitch."

"I was tempted," Rachel said with a smile. She kept her hand loosely twined with Cal's for a few moments, soothed by her touch. Relieved to have at least one person seek contact with her when everyone else seemed determined to push her away. She finally let go and gestured down the hill.

"The livery was down there. And sometime I'll show you where the old mounted police stables were. We're part of the history of this park now. The history of this city."

The trail ended at the pebbly stretch of Owen Beach. Rachel steered Bandit along the water's edge, where the footing wasn't as deep, and headed toward the marina. She looked around and sighed. The two bridges spanning the Narrows were behind her and Mount Rainier was barely visible in front. She loved it here. The green hills of Vashon Island and Brown's Point across the Sound. Huge tankers edging slowly toward the Tideflats. The murky half circle where the Puyallup River emptied into Commencement Bay. And, even more, she liked having Cal here beside her. The only person who stood by her side. Not for long, since she'd be leaving soon. Moving away. But for now she was here, and Rachel had to enjoy her while she had the chance.

"So what changed?" Cal asked when Rachel had been silent for several minutes. "You sound so calm now, but you were so upset when you ran away. I didn't know what you were going to do."

Rachel shrugged, unable to explain how her mind had changed as she had ridden deeper into the park. She always thought more clearly out here. "I realized it's bigger than I am," she repeated. "That little kid, his dad, his grandfather. This unit is important to them and to the rest of the city. We'll be able to keep people safe in places like the park where it's not easy to have officers on foot or in cars. And we'll be a liaison between the department and citizens. People love seeing horses around their town. Talking to us, visiting the animals. For kids like Jimmy, this might be the only opportunity to touch animals besides dogs and cats. And what I did last night. Maybe it was stupid, and maybe Hargrove had every right to yell at me in front of everyone, but it doesn't matter. What matters is that Alex Mayer's killer is found. And Randy might not be citizen of the year, but he and Clare sure don't deserve to be punished for someone else's crime."

"So what are you going to do?" Cal asked as she steered Ranger around a pile of driftwood. "Give Hard-ass Hargrove your resignation? Or tough it out because the city needs you?"

Rachel turned away from the beach and skirted the parking lot, avoiding the more crowded areas. "I'll stay until the Fourth. Do my best to get everyone through the night alive. Then I'll try to lateral to another department. Maybe Spokane or Cheney so I can be closer to my parents. I can't spend the rest of my career alternating between being invisible and being used for target practice."

"They'll miss you," Cal said. "They might not say it out loud, but I really think they will."

Rachel gave her a halfhearted smile. She didn't think Cal was right, but she didn't care enough to argue. The only person she would miss—and the only person she wanted to be missed by—was Cal herself. And there wasn't much chance of that happening. She turned at the ferry landing and headed Bandit up the steep hill toward the police yard. He slipped on the pavement, and she turned to more practical matters with a sense of relief. "I called your farrier, and he's coming out next week," she said. "He'll take care of the horses' shoes so we can start riding out as a team."

Chapter Eleven

Cal was surprised to see the unit's officers actually doing constructive work when she and Rachel rode through the gate. Clark and Don were trotting around the arena while Billie struggled to ride a bicycle through the deep tanbark. She circled the horses and rode up behind them, ringing the bike's little bell. Cal had to admit, she was impressed. Bikes were definitely something a police horse would face on the Tacoma streets. Sitka and Fancy seemed relaxed even when Billie rode directly in front of their faces.

Cal wanted to call them over, force them to apologize to Rachel. She didn't know why she felt so protective of her, but it was not a feeling she was accustomed to having. Rachel was certainly strong enough to take care of herself, but Cal had been allowed to see her softer side. The part of Rachel that felt hurt when she was treated so badly. Cal hurt, too, for Rachel. Because Rachel stood alone, with no one else by her side. Cal was rooting for the underdog, that was all. It didn't mean she cared for Rachel.

Okay, maybe she did. But after listening to her talk during their impromptu trail ride, seeing and hearing the quiet conviction in Rachel's voice, Cal felt shallow in comparison. Rachel might have been looking out for herself when she was first assigned to the mounted unit, but now she was on a mission. Protector of the city. Defender of the innocent. Cal admired her and would do anything she could to help her, but Rachel's attitude adjustment only highlighted the differences between them.

Everyone was watching Cal, as if waiting for her to set the tone for the rest of the afternoon. Rachel sat perfectly still on Bandit next to her, and the rest of the team—Don and Clark on their horses and Billie straddling her bike—hovered near the arena fence. Cal decided the best thing she could do for Rachel was to proceed with the lesson as planned. Business as usual, with no mention of Rachel's chastisement or her subsequent flight.

"Billie, come get Ranger," she called. "And the rest of you make a big circle here on the gravel. Clark, did you bring those flares?"

"Sure did. They're in a box in the tack room."

Cal brought four flares out to the parking lot. "We need to get the horses used to these in case you work an accident scene. Horses are instinctively afraid of fire, so they'll really need to trust you if they're going to override those instincts and not run away. Once I light this, start walking in a big circle around it. Gradually move closer if you feel them relax."

"I think Alex might have done this with the horses when we weren't around," Don said. "A couple mornings I noticed scorch marks here in the parking lot."

If Alex had worked any of the horses around flares, Cal had a feeling it'd be Ranger. He apparently hadn't skipped any steps in the handsome Thoroughbred's training. Ranger had been easy to ride in the park today, he was comfortable around people and traffic, and he hadn't batted an eye at any of the desensitizing objects Cal and Billie had put in front of him. She couldn't understand why Alex hadn't even seemed to bother with the other three. He had spent hours giving the officers riding lessons, so time hadn't been an issue. And they were willing to learn. Yes, he'd have looked good on Ranger in comparison with his bungling unit, but his reputation as the team's sergeant and leader would have suffered at the same time.

Cal lit the flare and set it in the center of the circle of riders. Sitka and Bandit snorted loudly and backed away from the smelly red flame. Fancy's entire body stiffened as she stared at the flare. And Ranger walked quietly forward when Billie nudged him with her heel. Completely unconcerned, of course.

"Turn Fancy to the right, Don," Cal said, forcing her attention off Rachel who was stroking Bandit's neck and cooing softly to him. "It's best to keep her moving."

"Good, Don," she said when he finally coaxed Fancy into a walk. Soon all of the horses were calmly circling the flare. "Let's reverse and walk the other way. Remember, horses process visual information through each eye separately, not together like we do. When we're desensitizing them to any object, it's important for them to see it from both sides."

Billie was able to walk Ranger close to the flare, and the other horses, as was typical for herd animals, followed his lead and relaxed. Maybe Alex had been planning this all along—train Ranger thoroughly, and then use him as a steadying influence on the others. Unlikely. Cal figured it had more to do with ego than with a grand training scheme.

Completely the opposite of Rachel's approach. Cal watched her inch Bandit closer to the fire-breathing demon. He arched his neck and flared his nostrils, but he didn't fight Rachel's control. Cal could see that most of Rachel's attention was on her own horse, but she was also aware of the other riders. Cal knew Rachel would be out here tomorrow morning, working each horse through whatever issues she had noticed in them the night before. She wouldn't let her team suffer even though she was suffering in her exile from the police community. Because, as she had said on their trail ride, she really believed the unit and its duties mattered more than her personal misery.

Cal, on the other hand, lived only for another championship, another shiny trophy, another one-night stand. Rachel had stopped their kiss last night, had refused to have sex with Cal, because they were so different. Cal had agreed. She wanted fun and the freedom to move on when it suited her. Rachel wanted love and loyalty. But now Cal could see the gulf between them was much deeper. It had nothing to do with what they wanted, but everything to do with who they *were*. Deep inside, where it counted. And Cal was more discomfited by the comparison than she cared to admit.

Dusk was settling over the park as Cal set out another two flares. The lesson had started later than usual, but she was glad to have the deepening gloom during this exercise because the flares stood in sharp contrast to the dark shadows outside the circle of light. The acrid smell of smoke and the hiss of the flames coupled with the scary nighttime world gave the horses and riders a very small taste of what they'd encounter on the Fourth of July. Very small. The gulf between where the unit was and where it had to be was frighteningly huge, but by the time she told the riders to dismount, they were able to weave among the three flares, walking within several feet of them. Cal decided to consider the small bit of progress a success.

"Great job, everyone," she said as they led their horses back to the barn. Rachel, of course, disappeared with Bandit into his stall while the others clustered together under the overhang. Cal doused the flares with water before covering them with dirt in a corner of the parking lot, as far from the barn as she could get them.

"I'll be playing polo for the next few days, but we'll have another lesson on Monday," she said when she returned to the barn. "Try to work with as many desensitization objects as you can before then. Once the horses are shod properly, we'll start working them on the roads."

Rachel half listened to the drone of talk outside Bandit's stall while she brushed her horse and mentally reviewed their lesson. Don was still having trouble getting Fancy to move forward. No surprise, since Rachel figured the heavy mare would prefer to stand in one place for the rest of her life, as long as someone brought her food and water. Maybe a change of scenery would help. She'd take the horse out of the yard this weekend. A long gallop in the open spaces of the park might be enough to pique the horse's interest and ease her ring-sour attitude. Clark was still having some flexibility issues with Sitka, especially when they were turning to the right. She'd do some extra suppling exercises before their next lesson.

Rachel was planning her next ride on Ranger when a burst of laughter from Cal made her turn her attention back to the foursome's conversation. Yesterday, she had listened with a sense of longing, a desire to be included, and a deep feeling of loss because she *had* been part of this community not so long ago. But Hargrove's visit had convinced Rachel her dreams of restoring her reputation were futile ones. She wasn't home yet. Until she got a fresh start in a new city, with a new department, she wouldn't find the peace of having a family and community that she craved. She'd stay long enough to finish what she had started—or what she had been forced to start. She would give the mounted unit a fighting chance, and then she'd go.

She focused on Cal's voice, tuning out the others. So deep and sexy, the sound wrapped around Rachel like a soft comforter. Rachel was focused on what her unit needed—how to train the horses and riders, and how to keep them safe. But why couldn't she devote a little time to her own needs and desires? One simple kiss with Cal was enough to prove she'd be able to distract Rachel from her troubles for a few hours. No, she'd do more than distract Rachel. Cal would be able to render her so fucking out of her mind she wouldn't give a damn what Hargrove had said or how her unit treated her. Cal wanted her, had been open about her interest from the first moment they were reunited at her farm. Why not grab at this connection, short-term or not?

She'd wait until the other officers left. Ask Cal to come over to her apartment, stay for dinner, discuss the upcoming training schedule for the team. Not that she needed to make excuses. Cal wanted her, had pushed for this night, so all Rachel had to do was say yes. She could picture them on her couch. She'd kiss Cal and tug on her thigh until Cal straddled her. Slide her hands up Cal's ribs, over her beautifully toned torso, rub her thumbs over nipples so hard she'd—

"I'm taking off," Cal said. She was leaning against Bandit's stall door. "I'll see you Monday."

Cal had been standing there for several moments, watching Rachel. Watching her absently groom her horse while her green eyes—as dark and shadowed as the night beyond the stable's lights—gazed into some distance Cal couldn't see. Cal was surprised her own voice, when she finally spoke, didn't betray any of the lustful thoughts she experienced as images of Rachel rapidly shifted through her mind. Rachel over her, under her, on her knees. A repeat of last night's kiss, but with no stopping, no second thoughts.

Rachel looked at her, her eyes inviting Cal into the shadows. "It's late. Why don't you come over to my place? We can order pizza. Hang out."

Yes. Cal wanted to. She'd wanted Rachel from the moment she had seen her in her uniform. So poised and strong, her polished demeanor dissolving into smiles as she played with Feathers. Last night, after their kiss, Cal would have jumped at the invitation she saw in Rachel's expression. But now she was the one having second thoughts.

"It's late," she echoed. "And I have to be up at dawn tomorrow. But thanks for the invite. Maybe some other time."

"Sure, maybe," Rachel said shortly, turning her back to Cal and resuming her work on Bandit's coat. "See you Monday."

Damn. Cal walked out to the parking lot, fighting with every step against the urge to go back and jump at the offer Rachel had made. She got into her car and slammed the door. This was crazy. She had only taken this job as trainer to spend time with Rachel. Seduce her. Now she had the chance she had been looking for, and she had said no. And had probably confused and hurt Rachel in the process.

Cal drove through the streets of the city. The lights and traffic slowly fell behind as she got deeper into the countryside. Dark expanses of prairie land opened up on either side of the road, making Cal feel isolated in the protective bubble of her car. She had been hoping to convince Rachel to play. To put aside her naturally serious nature and accept the terms of a fun sexual tryst. And she apparently had. Today Rachel had been chewed out in front of her team, and she had told Cal she was only sticking around until she finished this job. Then she'd move on. Tonight Rachel had wanted a chance to forget. Wasn't that exactly the opening she'd hoped for? Why hadn't she accepted Rachel's invitation?

Cal had expected to eventually overcome Rachel's resistance, but what she hadn't anticipated was Rachel's influence on *her*. She had finally convinced Rachel to accept a no-strings relationship, but now Cal knew she wouldn't be satisfied by one. Last week Cal had known exactly what she wanted. Polo. Freedom. Rachel. Now she wasn't so sure.

Chapter Twelve

Rachel skipped her morning run. And when sunlight streamed through her open curtains, she rolled onto her stomach and pulled the covers over her head. Don was scheduled to feed the horses this morning, and Billie would be there in the afternoon. The animals had been training hard for a week and they deserved a break. *She* deserved a break. A day with nothing better to do than watch television and eat junk food. A day alone, without the rejection and pain and frustration other people caused.

She was exhausted from the previous week, too. She had been so aroused by the thought of spending the night with Cal, so turned on by the imagined exploration of each other's bodies. Unfortunately, Cal's refusal hadn't been enough to douse any lingering remnants of desire. Even though Rachel had fallen asleep that night without dinner, without doing more than pulling off her riding uniform and tossing it on the ground, she had spent a restless night plagued by dreams of Cal. And two more, since.

Her cell phone vibrated its way along the top of the dresser across the room. Rachel growled and tucked a pillow against her ears, but the phone wouldn't stop, even after it thumped onto the floor. She dragged herself out of bed and got on her knees to rummage under the dresser until she found the cell. Even though she cleared her throat a few times before answering, her voice came out in a hoarse croak.

"Hello?"

"Rachel, I need you at the barn. Hurry. Something's wrong with Fancy."

"Be right there," she said, suddenly wide awake and alert. She didn't bother asking what was wrong since the use of her given name combined with the panic in Don's voice was enough to make her move. The veteran police officer had seen his share of emergencies and trauma over the years. If he was this worried, then so was she.

Rachel hopped across the room as she pulled up her jeans and crammed her wallet and gate card in a pocket. She grabbed the closest T-shirt she could find and tugged it on before jamming her feet in her running shoes. She didn't bother tying them but ran out the door and down the hill with her laces flapping against her bare ankles.

Thank God she lived so close. Within seconds of Don's call, she was letting herself in the gate and running over to where he stood outside Fancy's stall. He waved her over and pointed into the stall while she took a deep breath and prepared herself for whatever she was about to see. A broken leg, a dead horse, stuff oozing out of parts that shouldn't ooze.

She blinked a couple of times and ran her hand over her eyes. Fancy was standing in her stall and eating hay, looking as unconcerned about life as she usually did. She rested the tip of one forefoot on the ground. A little lame. No big deal. Rachel felt shaky with relief.

"What happened, Don?" She tried to keep her voice calm, and to keep from throttling him for scaring her.

"I don't know. I took her into the arena after I fed breakfast. I was going to get her used to that baby stroller I brought," he said. He gestured into the arena where a child's toy stroller sat, abandoned, with a doll hanging over the side. Rachel wondered where this big tough cop had gotten the stroller. "She seemed fine at first, but then she started limping when I asked her to trot. I don't know what I did wrong."

"You probably didn't do anything," Rachel said. "Put her halter on and bring her out of the stall. I'll be right there."

"Is it all right to move her? We won't need to—"

"She'll be fine," Rachel said. She put her hand on his shoulder, finally realizing how upset he was. For her, with years of horse experience, the sign of a sore foot wasn't anything to panic over. Don probably only had vague references from movies and books to guide him. If the horse is lame, shoot it. "I need better light so I can check her hoof."

Rachel hurried into the tack room where she had stored the farrier tools Nelson had brought when he delivered Bandit. She wasn't skilled enough to shoe the horses, but he had taught her the basics so she could handle any emergencies at the ranch. She ran her hand down Fancy's leg, feeling some heat in her pastern before she lifted the mare's hoof off the ground. She straddled the horse's leg and used a pair of hoof testers to press against the sole and walls of the hoof. She inched around until the pressure she applied made the mare jerk her leg in response.

"She probably has a stone bruise. Turned into an abscess. I'm going to take this shoe off, and we can soak her hoof until we get the farrier to come take care of her."

"She'll be okay?" Don asked, stroking Fancy's neck.

"She'll be back to normal in a week or so," Rachel said. She didn't think it was much of a reassurance since Fancy's normal wasn't the epitome of equine behavior, but Don seemed relieved by the news.

Rachel loosened the clinched nails and gently eased the metal shoe off Fancy's hoof. She used her hoof knife to scrape at the sore area, but the abscess wasn't close to the surface yet. She'd let the professional Cal had recommended dig a little deeper and relieve the pressure in Fancy's hoof. She stepped away and placed the horse's hoof back on the ground. "Take her back to her stall, and I'll be right there."

Rachel put a bucket under the hot tap in the tack room. While it was filling, she got a carton of Epsom salts and poured a few handfuls into the bucket, stirring with her hand to help them dissolve. She had bought the salts, along with bandages and ointment and other first aid items, the day after she had taken over for Alex. He had been very organized and had bought the highest quality bridles and saddles the unit's grant would allow, but he had overlooked key items. Rachel had been surprised to see the lack of basic health care and training supplies. But the mounted division had still been fairly new, so maybe he hadn't gotten them yet.

She turned off the water and hauled the heavy bucket into Fancy's stall. She let the mare sniff suspiciously at it before she set it on the ground. "The heat and salts should help draw the abscess closer to the surface. Then it'll either burst on its own, or the farrier will be able to cut into it and drain the pus. She'll feel a lot better once that happens. We can soak her for about twenty minutes or so, a few times a day."

Rachel kept chatting in a low voice as she eased the mare's leg into the bucket, interspersing her instructions with words of encouragement for Fancy. The mare jerked her leg free a couple of times, but Rachel kept putting it back in place, pressing on the horse's shoulder to shift her weight. Eventually Fancy seemed to decide she liked the warm water, and she stood quietly. Rachel stayed close to her side, rubbing the mare's withers.

"You said she had a stone bruise. Is that common?" Don asked, speaking for the first time since he had brought Fancy back to her stall.

"Happens all the time," Rachel said with a shrug. "Since our horses will be going over all sorts of terrain and won't spend their time in soft arena footing, I'm going to have the farrier put pads under their front shoes. They'll protect the soles in case they step on a rock or something sharp. He'll also weld some Borium on their shoes. It's a metal alloy, and it'll give them better traction on slick surfaces like pavement."

"They were slipping all over the place when we were at the service. Scared the hell out of me." He paused and seemed to consider his next words carefully. "Hargrove said you'd never worked with a mounted unit before, so how do you know all this?"

For once, his questions seemed to be triggered by genuine interest and not angry defiance. Rachel brushed her fingers through Fancy's mane, untangling a small knot. "My parents had a ranch in eastern Washington. In Cheney, near Spokane. My dad did all the shoeing since we had so many horses, and he taught me a lot about the anatomy of horses' hooves."

"What about this Borium stuff? Not much pavement on a ranch."

Rachel made a show of looking out of Fancy's stall as if to check for eavesdroppers before she answered. "I was a junior rodeo princess when I was in high school. I led the Founder's Day parade. And if you tell *anyone* about that, I will shoot you."

Don gave a snort of laughter. "Hard to imagine you a princess of anything. Did you have to wear some sort of dress and tiara in the parade?"

"Chaps and a cowboy hat," Rachel said. After a childhood spent moving from school to school, rarely having the chance to make friends and fit in, her nomination for the rodeo court had been an embarrassing but touching honor. It had been the first time she had felt accepted, and it was a confirmation of the benefits of following Nelson and Leah's rules. Proof that she had finally turned her life around. "But I'll admit, my outfit had its share of fringe and rhinestones."

Don laughed. The sound startled Fancy, and she lifted her hoof out of the bucket and leaned back, but Rachel caught her foot and moved her into place again. She automatically started murmuring softly to the mare, like Nelson had taught her, until the mare settled down again.

"Just a relaxing day at the spa," Rachel said as she rubbed the mare's shoulder. "Don, do you think you'll be okay here if I go back to my place and take a shower?" And brush her teeth. And put on some underwear. "I can come back later this afternoon and do another soak."

"Yeah, we'll be fine," he said.

Rachel brought a bucket so he had a makeshift seat while he soaked Fancy. She let herself out of the stall again, but he stopped her before she left.

"Thank you, Sarge," he said, before he leaned back against the wall and closed his eyes as if he was about to take a nap.

Rachel paused, speechless as the gruff old cop gave her his acceptance with his use of the casual title. She hadn't done anything more than put Epsom salts into a bucket, but she had managed to earn Don's approval, his acknowledgment that she was this unit's leader. She quietly latched Fancy's stall door and headed home. She ran a hand through her hair, still spiked from sleep, as she walked up the hill to her apartment. One little victory, after a mountain of defeats. She'd take it and be grateful.

❖

Cal arranged the double set of reins in her left hand and wrapped the mallet's strap around her right wrist, grasping the handle securely in her palm. Roman, usually calm and unruffled, danced onto the polo field as if he sensed Cal's seething energy. All afternoon, she had been playing even more like a fiend than usual, driving her team from her 3 position and stealing the ball time after time from their opponents. She had barely slept for days, far too conscious of what Rachel had offered and what she had refused, and with every hard smack of stick against ball she hoped to ease the pressure building inside her.

Her aggressive play wasn't giving her the release she so desperately needed—only another invitation from Rachel, accepted this time, would have been strong enough to shatter her tension—but the positive result of Cal's running about was the very one-sided score, and she and her team rode into the fifth chukker six points ahead. She wheeled and spun on Roman, breaking up the other team's scoring attempts and sending the ball downfield to her own offense. Her aim was accurate even though she could feel the anger reverberating through her arm every time she connected with the ball. She was angry at herself for insulting Rachel by turning her down, and probably for other things she really didn't want to think about. At all.

It took almost all of five chukkers, but slowly a new sort of anger filtered into Cal's consciousness. She sent the ball rocketing to her number 2, Tabitha, and watched as the less experienced player fumbled for control as the ball came in hot. Cal glanced around the field, finally breaking out of her fog of sexual frustration. She had been dominating the defense and hijacking plays that should have belonged to Crystal, and she had been overpowering her two offensive teammates with shots that were too difficult for them to handle.

Although she had initially taken the job with the police unit because she'd wanted a chance to seduce Rachel, over the past week she had gradually started to feel the same loyalty to the unit and drive to make them succeed she knew Rachel felt. She had been attempting to create partnerships between horse and rider and among the riders in the mounted division, but she had forgotten to apply the same lessons with her own team. She had been running around today like a whirlwind, and she couldn't figure out whether she was chasing something or trying to run away.

When the chukker ended, Cal rode off the field and dismounted, handing Roman's reins to Jack in exchange for Casper's. The young gray gelding reacted to her emotions just as Roman had, but instead of simply getting revved up like the more experienced horse, he was already breaking out in a nervous sweat. Cal took a deep breath and settled her thoughts before she mounted him. She was unaccustomed to having doubts, to questioning her life's path, but she couldn't deny her confusion. She had been following the steps along her career with unwavering confidence, but Rachel had her wondering what she really wanted. Last month, winning a place on the Virginia team would have been her answer. Now she wasn't sure.

But now Casper needed her to be calm and present. She was riding him in this single chukker for the experience—since her team was so far ahead—and a rough and fast ride might ruin the careful and positive months of training she'd put into him. And her team needed her, too. To be the leader they expected and deserved. She met with them on the edge of the field while they adjusted tack and drank some water before the sixth and final chukker.

"Tabitha, I'd like to keep Casper out of the rough play, so would you mind playing Three?"

Tabitha looked doubtful. "Even on Casper, you're a better—"

"Don't think about how I play the position," Cal interrupted, before Tabitha could fully voice her concerns about changing to the position usually held by the most experienced member of the team. "You've been Three plenty of times in practice, and you've done well. I'll take the Four spot, so I'll be there to help with defense. Crystal, you can take over as One, and Miranda, you'll move to Two."

Cal turned Casper and rode onto the field before she could hear any protests. She had just rearranged the entire team, essentially giving each member but herself a promotion, and yet she finally felt able to take a deep breath and let the knots inside her stomach unravel.

Because she had shaken up the roster, the first minutes of play were chaotic as each player struggled to adjust to her new position. Their opponents scored twice with little challenge. Cal kept Casper out of the worst of the melees, staying back and watching the team as a whole. She was vocal at first, encouraging and driving the team, but as Tabitha began to look more comfortable in her new position, Cal let her take charge.

Although they didn't score any more goals, they managed to hold the other team to only two goals, and Cal felt a rush of success as she rode off the field, smiling and laughing with her team. Casper had calmed down enough to make a few fast runs, and Cal felt happy with the way he had handled the bumps and jolts from other horses. Tabitha had stepped up as a leader—the position she'd need to fill once Cal left—and Crystal and Miranda had seemed to enjoy the change of pace. Most of all, Cal had felt a return of her old equilibrium. She had ridden with nothing to prove, no need to show off or impress anyone. Just playing polo for the hell of it and loving every second. She was still missing Rachel's touch and berating herself for saying no when her body was screaming yes, but she knew she'd survive. Polo had been all she'd wanted and needed until Rachel came along. Once Rachel was out of her life, polo would be enough for Cal again.

Rachel spent her day hiding out in her apartment. She walked across the street to a sandwich shop for lunch and saw Clark's car in the police yard. She brought home a huge vegetarian burrito she was sure had more calories than a greasy cheeseburger, but at least the vegetables and beans eased her guilt. Her earlier satisfaction with today's interaction with Don started to fade as she had to face the reality of her situation. One cop out of the entire department had given her a small nod of approval—and only when they were the only two people in the isolated stable yard. And she still had to work closely with Cal over the next three weeks. Cal, who had seemed interested in Rachel, but had rejected her offer of sex. Not the stuff of nightmares, but the stuff of very detailed dreams that left Rachel wet and longing when she woke up alone.

Plus she had a team of mounted riders and horses that needed to be prepared for the Fourth. No matter how hard they worked, how hard they tried, there was a chance they wouldn't be ready in time. She had wrenched some respect out of the other officers, but she couldn't perform miracles.

Rachel left her apartment in the early afternoon and walked down the hill to the police yard. The sight of the arena and parking lot helped buoy her spirits a little and assuage some of the guilt she'd been feeling after taking a morning off. When she had taken over for Alex, the stables had been neat and organized, everything in place and well documented. She might not have the organizational skills Alex did, and her lesson notes were scribbles on notepads and the backs of feed invoices, but she was proud of her yard. The arena was littered with disparate items. Tarps and banners and children's toys. Helium balloons were tied to the pylons, and Billie's bike and Don's stroller were propped against the wall, under the barn's overhang. Before, the stables had looked like a display, but now it was a working area.

Rachel walked past Don's car and over to Fancy's stall. She peeked over the door and saw Don sitting on a folding chair. Fancy had her hoof in a bucket of steaming water, and her head was low and resting next to Don's knee. He was reading out loud from a gun magazine, and Rachel recognized the low and soothing lilt she used around the horses in his voice. The pinto dozed quietly while Don read an article debating whether to use the Isosceles or Weaver stance while shooting.

Rachel backed away before Don saw her. She walked back to her place, quietly closing the yard's gate behind her. When Don had so vehemently refused to switch from Fancy to Ranger, Rachel had assumed his argument was with her. But maybe—and shockingly—Don's reluctance hadn't been about Rachel. Maybe he actually liked his horse, his crazy little mare. Rachel had heard it in his voice this morning when he thought she was seriously hurt, and it was there again as he sat near her, doing his best to help her.

Rachel glanced back toward the cluttered arena and the quiet barn before she climbed the stairs to her apartment. She and Cal were desperately trying to teach the officers how to handle the sounds and sights they'd be exposed to on the Fourth. But the bond between horse and rider—and between the members of the unit—were the only things they couldn't teach or force. But they could mean the difference between life and death when the team was on the streets.

Rachel got a beer out of her fridge and settled in her recliner. Her own situation wasn't any better than it had been this morning, but she felt a curious sense of relief. Don and Fancy, Billie and Clark and their horses. They had a chance. She had helped, but they were the ones who were creating partnerships. Suddenly her own problems seemed less stressful. She missed feeling like part of the department, and her body still ached for Cal's touch, but the unit would be okay. And that was all that mattered.

Chapter Thirteen

Rachel jogged down the road and past the barrier blocking the park's entrance. Her rubber soles made a slapping sound on the pavement, but the noise was swallowed up by the night as she veered onto the grass, and then onto a dirt path. Sunday night. She had been tossing in her bed and had finally given up on sleep. It wasn't even midnight yet, but she needed to get out of her apartment, start her run early. She'd see Cal tomorrow, at the unit's afternoon lesson, and she hoped she could get through the encounter with some dignity intact. She had offered herself to Cal and had been rejected, but she had to act as if she didn't care. Untouched and unfazed. Untroubled by constant thoughts and dreams of Cal naked and moaning and calling her name.

Rachel sped up as she passed the upper edge of the zoo parking lot. She had worked herself and her team hard, fueled not only by the desire to train them properly, but also by the need to distract herself. She had schooled the horses every morning, riding through drills designed to increase their manageability and agility. Then she had worked with the team in the afternoon as they rode the horses around flares, under tarps, and over wooden planks. Fancy was on stall rest at least until the farrier arrived on Tuesday, but Don could continue most of the desensitization exercises in her stall. They'd be heading onto the roads and trails of the park this week, riding among the families and bike riders and cars in the park. Rachel hoped she had done enough to keep them—and everyone around them—safe.

Her worry drove her to run faster than usual. She took long, deep breaths of night air. The park seemed so still, she almost felt as if she couldn't pull enough oxygen into her lungs. The usual owls and raccoons were eerily silent, and she changed routes after a short spurt through the forest. Instead of going farther along the Drive, she ran down the sloped parking lot of Owen Beach, nearly out of control as she let gravity increase her already brisk pace. She ran along the water, glad to have the liquid sound of the lapping waves as an accompaniment to her quiet footfalls. And cool, briny sea air to breathe. And…

Smoke. Rachel stopped running and wrinkled her nose as she inhaled, turning around as she tried to pinpoint the source of the smell. It was coming from the southeast. Where her apartment was. Where the horses were. She was running again, flying past the marina and the ferry dock, when she heard a shrill neigh echo along the bluff.

She could see the flames as soon as she turned onto the road leading toward the stable yard from the ferry landing. Her lungs burned from the steep road, the fast pace she had set earlier, the panic as she watched flames curl and leap across the roof of the barn. She ran along the fence line, clawing at the gate card she always wore around her neck when she was in the park, but the gate was propped slightly open when she reached it. She ran toward the stables, fighting to keep her head while the horses screamed from their stalls.

The door to the feed room was open, and Rachel could barely make out the outline of what looked like the box of flares as it burned. She knew they had been stored far from the barn, on the other side of the parking lot in a small maintenance shed. But she couldn't stop to wonder who had moved them into the room filled with dry hay and shavings. She recognized Bandit's deeper neigh among the others and wrestled with a momentary urge to rescue him first. But Ranger's stall was closest to the fire source, so she went straight to him. She grabbed his halter and lead rope from the hook outside his stall and pulled off her T-shirt. She had to protect her hands with the shirt as she opened the hot metal latch on his door.

Rachel eased into the stall and toward the tall chestnut. He cowered near the back wall, occasionally half rearing in fright. Rachel kept her voice calm but loud enough to register over the crackling of the fire. She barely had buckled his halter when the gelding reared again, tossing her against the side of the stall. She ignored the pain in her shoulder and lunged for Ranger's lead rope, quickly draping her shirt over his eyes and tucking the edges under his halter. Once he was temporarily blinded, he settled enough for her to urge him out of the stall and across the yard. She tied him to the chain-link fence and ran back to the barn.

The acrid smell of burning diesel hit her as she entered Sitka's stall. An accelerant. The flames were rolling across the roof of the barn, traveling faster than they normally would. She forced her hands and voice to stay steady as she approached the bay gelding who was shaking with fright in a corner of his stall. A section of the roof fell next to them, and she paused to stomp out the fire as it quickly spread through the clean shavings. The whole barn was a pile of kindling waiting to erupt in flames. She haltered Sitka and wrapped the shirt over his face. He almost ran her over as she trotted him out the door and over to where Ranger was tied.

Cal's three flares hadn't prepared the horses for this. They pulled against the fence, and the rattling chain link combined with their loud screams to fill the night with terror. Rachel felt as if she was pushing through quicksand to get back to the barn and into Fancy's stall. The mare, sore and reluctant to walk on a good day, planted her hooves and refused to move out from the perceived safety of her stall. Rachel used the end of her lead rope to smack the pinto's hindquarters, but she stubbornly put her ears back and locked her legs. Rachel swore and pulled, until finally a small chunk of glowing wood fell from the burning roof and landed on the mare's back. She dove through the door, nearly knocking Rachel to the ground, and limped over to the two geldings.

Rachel almost cried in relief when she finally could run to Bandit's stall, the last in the line. She could hear sirens in the distance, but she didn't have time to wait for help. Bandit's entire doorframe was on fire, but the gelding came toward her when he heard her frantic voice. Even though she could feel his tremors as she slipped on his halter and covered his eyes with her smudged shirt, he unhesitatingly followed her through the ring of flames like a circus horse.

The first fire truck pulled into the lot while Rachel was tying Bandit next to Fancy. She leaned against the fence and slid down until she was sitting on the ground, close to Bandit but safe from his restless hooves. The metal diamonds dug into her back where it was unprotected by anything but her sports bra. She had pulled her shirt off Bandit's face and tossed it aside when they got to the fence, but she was too weary to look for it.

Rachel watched numbly as the crews got organized and began to fight the fire. She was sure it had been started in the feed room, with the flares, and it had spread quickly over the stalls. The short side of the L-shaped barn, where the tack room and office were, looked fairly undamaged. Someone had wanted to hurt the horses. And if Rachel hadn't been out in the park, they probably would have succeeded. She wiped a sweaty hand across her forehead, unable to shake the sensation of heat and destructive energy from the flames even though she was too far away to feel them anymore.

One of the firemen came over and draped a blanket over her shoulders. "Hey, Rachel," he said, shining his flashlight over her singed arms, "you did good, getting all the horses out. Are you injured anywhere?"

"I'm fine, um, Mark," she said, finally recalling his name. She had been on plenty of calls with him in the past, but she was having trouble doing anything but stare at the burning barn. "I bumped my shoulder in one of the stalls, but I can move it."

She rotated her shoulder to prove it was all right and barely hid her wince as a stab of pain shot across her collarbone. She stopped moving it.

Mark laughed as he gently probed around her shoulder. "Yeah, didn't look like *that* hurt at all. It's not dislocated, and nothing seems to be broken. Probably a deep bruise, but you'll need to get to a hospital and get checked out."

"I will," she promised. Tomorrow. Or the next day. If it still hurt.

Mark went back to the fire, and suddenly Clark was standing by Rachel. He looked pale and shaken.

"I had my radio on," he said. "I heard the call and…I thought I'd get here and find all the horses were still…"

He dropped next to her with a thump. "I checked Sitka while Mark was here with you. He has a couple of singed spots, but he's okay. He's really okay." Clark repeated himself before he put a hand on Rachel's shoulder and squeezed. Then he clasped his hands between his bent knees. "I can't believe you got them all out. How'd you get here so fast? Do you know what happened?"

"I was out jogging," she said, out of habit omitting the part about being in the park after it closed, even though she doubted he'd give a damn about the broken rule. "I smelled smoke, and then I heard the horses neighing. The gate was open." She told him about the box of flares.

"Billie got a few out of the shed yesterday, but she didn't move the box. I can't believe anyone would do this on purpose."

Rachel shrugged out of the blanket, suddenly hot and agitated. She had been scared, and then numb. Now she needed to get moving. "Well, someone poured diesel in the barn. I could smell it. And the box of flares was moved into the feed room. Doesn't sound like an accident to me." She stood up. "I've got to get these horses out of here. Can you unlock the trailer while I go get my truck?"

"Of course. Where will we take them?"

"Not we." There were already a couple of patrol officers arriving on the scene, and she had a feeling Hargrove would be along any minute. "I'll take them to Cal's farm. I need you to stay here and handle the paperwork. I don't feel up to answering a ton of questions. Tell Hargrove I'll be back in the morning."

Clark nodded and moved toward the trailer. Rachel jogged across the street to get her truck. She had the key and wallet in the pockets of her shorts, so she didn't bother going upstairs. She wanted to get away from the smell of smoke. Get the horses safely to a clean barn and herself safely out of the clutches of Lieutenant Hargrove.

Chapter Fourteen

Rachel called Cal as she drove. The horses had seemed as anxious as Rachel to be on the road, and she and Clark had gotten them loaded without any trouble. Cal's voice sounded sleepy and then shocked on the phone, and she assured Rachel they'd have stalls ready by the time she arrived. Rachel ended the call and wondered if Cal had been in bed with someone when she answered. Tangled in the sheets, tangled together. Exhausted by a night of sex.

Forget it. It's not important. But Rachel would rather contemplate Cal's love life than face what *was* important. Someone had tried to kill her horses. She pulled the trailer slowly to the shoulder of the road and idled there for a few minutes, her arms wrapped around her shivering body. She still only wore her shorts and sports bra, but she wasn't cold. She was experiencing a normal physiological response, like she'd seen in so many other people she dealt with as a cop. She recognized the moment when the immediate threat had disappeared, but the reality began to settle in. She understood the stages as a victim processed an event like this, but understanding it didn't make the anxiety and tremors go away.

Rachel pulled back onto the deserted highway leading to Cal's farm. She needed to talk this out, figure out what was going on, but first she had to get the horses settled. She heard a thud as one of them kicked the trailer when she accelerated. She was so relieved to have them alive and ornery and kicking. Clark had promised to call Billie and Don in case they heard about the fire and panicked about the horses.

Rachel parked the trailer in front of the brightly lit barn, and a group of people led by two dogs came out before she had even turned off her ignition. Cal. With her mother, Jack, and two men and a woman Rachel didn't recognize.

Cal had been pacing since she got Rachel's call. A fire. The horses. Rachel was coming. She had appreciated her mother's overbearing nature for once as Cecilia calmly took charge of the situation and helped the grooms fill four empty stalls with deep beds of shavings and fresh water and hay. Cal had been sound asleep, her usual dreams of Rachel even more intense than usual because she had been excited and nervous to see her this afternoon. Rachel had been vague about the fire on the phone, and Cal had been half-asleep and unprepared to question her, but now she was wide awake and concerned. How could a fire have started in the brand-new barn?

Rachel came around the front of her truck, and Cal swore silently. Rachel's arms and face were covered with soot and nasty red welts. Her right arm was bruised from the shoulder all the way to her elbow. But her expression got to Cal more than the surface marks. She looked exhausted, haunted, and Cal stepped forward and grabbed her in a big hug, taking care to avoid her injured arm. Rachel hugged her back, burying her face in the crook of Cal's neck.

Cal rubbed her hand over Rachel's back, relieved to have her close. The sharp crack of a horse's hoof against the trailer made her step back with a laugh.

"They sound impatient. Are any of the horses injured?"

Rachel shook her head. "Only a few small burns from drifting embers. We were lucky."

Cal followed her to the back of the trailer where Jack and Craig were already lowering the ramp. Yes, lucky. What horse owner didn't dread barn fires? And Cal felt as close to these mismatched horses as she felt to her own. She would have hated losing any one of them. And Rachel. What if she had been seriously injured, or worse, as she ran into the burning barn with no regard for her own safety? Cal was sure, without a doubt, Rachel hadn't even considered herself for one moment as she pulled the horses out of the barn.

Cal's mother had set up a mini triage center in the aisle, and as each groom led a horse into the barn she inspected it from head to hoof and began treating the minor burns. Rachel stood to one side, pointing out singe marks, and Cal slipped her arm around Rachel's waist.

"Come on, Rach," she said. "You can take a shower at my place, and I'll make you something to drink."

"No," Rachel said as she pulled weakly out of Cal's grasp. "I need to take care of the horses, and then I should go home—"

"Nonsense," said Cecilia. "We'll take good care of your animals. You go with Cal. You need to wash those burns and get some ointment on them."

"But Fancy has a stone bruise, so she's lame. And she has a burn near her withers," Rachel protested, although she looked ready to drop at any moment.

"Child, I've been taking care of horses since before you were born. Go."

No one disobeyed when Cecilia gave a direct order. Not even Rachel. She went over to Bandit, where Dana was applying some cream to a scraped foreleg, and wrapped her arms around his neck in a hug. She came back to Cal, but still seemed reluctant to leave.

"Thank you for doing all this," she said. "The department will pay board for—"

"Come *on*, Rachel," Cal said.

"Go!" Cecilia ordered at the same time. "Goodness, what kind of a monster would I be if I didn't let—"

Cal left while her mother was still talking. She towed a now-unresisting Rachel around the barn and down a dark path to her little bungalow with Tar and Feathers scampering ahead of them. She had moved out of the main house when she was eighteen, and she loved the privacy of her secluded home so much she rarely even brought girlfriends there, preferring to have her separate space. The thought of Rachel showering there, sleeping there, was surprisingly okay.

Maybe a little *too* okay. Cal kept Rachel's hand in her own as she walked her through the house and into the bathroom. It was decorated in greens and browns, with horses running across the shower curtain. Cal let go of Rachel and opened a cabinet. She chose a forest-green towel for Rachel—perfect with her eyes—and draped it over the shower rod.

"I'll leave some clothes on the counter," Cal said, backing out of the bathroom and pulling Feathers with her by the collar. She lingered in the bedroom, allegedly giving Rachel some time alone to strip and get in the shower before she came back in with a pile of soft sweats and shirts. But she really needed the time to gather her willpower. She would leave the clothes and go into the kitchen. *Not* into the shower stall. Make Rachel a drink instead of making her come. She was so relieved to have her there and safe, she didn't want to let Rachel out of her sight or beyond her touch. But even more, she had missed Rachel this weekend. Had gone over and over their little scene from last week, but in her imagination she always said yes when Rachel invited her back to the apartment.

Cal busied herself in the kitchen, getting glasses and filling them with ice and whiskey, feeding the collies. Because Rachel had been in danger tonight didn't mean the differences between them had gone away. By the time Rachel appeared in the doorway—her dark hair curling damply and her pale face accented by ugly red welts—Cal had gotten her libido somewhat in check. Enough to keep from walking over to Rachel and tearing off her clothes.

"Take your shirt off," she said.

"I...what?"

"Just the sweatshirt," Cal said as she carried the drinks into her small living room. She set them on the coffee table and gestured toward the sofa. "You can leave the tank on, but I want to check your burns and put some ointment on them."

She went into the bathroom and got a jar of burn cream, hesitating for a moment when she was wrapped in the textures of Rachel. The room was warm and steamy from Rachel's shower, and the scent of rosemary and lemon lingered. Rachel had used Cal's shampoo, of course. Cal had expected she would, but she hadn't anticipated how much the thought turned her on. Rachel in *her* shower, with lather from *her* shampoo sliding over her slick skin...

Cal shook off the erotic image and returned to the living room, only to be confronted by an even sexier picture. Rachel was resting with her head on the back of the couch and her eyes closed, and Tar curled in a tight ball at her feet. Feathers was on the sofa with her head resting on Rachel's lap, and she slowly ruffled her fingers through the dog's fur. She had obediently taken off Cal's USC sweatshirt, and the gray tank showed off her beautifully toned arms. The color also emphasized Rachel's pallor, however, and Cal swallowed her desire to take Rachel right then. Hard. Instead, she squeezed into the small space on Rachel's other side and uncapped the jar of ointment. She dipped her finger in the cream and smeared some across an inch-long burn on Rachel's cheekbone.

Rachel felt Cal's presence even before she sat down, but she kept her eyes closed until the ointment touched her raw flesh. The first brush of Cal's finger had felt cool and soothing, but the cream stung. She pulled away.

"I'm fine," she insisted. "It's only a couple of scrapes."

"If you're so fine, why are you cringing?" Cal slid her fingers along Rachel's scalp as she used her other hand to attack the burns on her neck.

Rachel kept her head still as Cal's fingers curled through her hair. Cal's touch was almost enough to chase away the pain of what felt like a million paper cuts. "I'm not cringing, I'm trying to get away from the disgusting smell of that stuff. Ouch! What the hell is that crap made of? Salt?"

"This scrape on your collarbone is pretty deep," Cal said, concern apparent in her voice. "And the ointment is unscented. You're being a baby." She withdrew her hand from Rachel's hair and used it to cradle Rachel's forearm in her lap. "Tell me what happened."

Rachel stared at Cal's fingers as they gently traced the crisscross of burn marks on the inside of her wrist. She focused on the stinging pain as the ointment scalded her already burned flesh and told Cal the whole story, from her jog to her drive to the Lanford farm.

"So it was deliberate," Cal said. She reached across Rachel's lap for her other arm.

"Had to be. The gate was open when I got there, and we were always so careful with the flares. No one would have moved them to the feed room."

"Any idea who? Or why?"

"I can't imagine the horses were the target," Rachel said. She leaned back and closed her eyes again, enjoying the feeling of Cal's fingers trailing over her skin, despite the sting of the cream. "We carry full insurance policies on the leased horses, but they're not valuable enough to be worth this kind of crime. Maybe someone wants the whole unit to fail."

She shuddered as Cal lowered the neckline of her tank and rubbed cream over a burn above Rachel's left breast. Cal mumbled an apology, but Rachel knew her reaction had nothing to do with pain. Her nipples tightened in response to Cal's gentle strokes over the swell of her chest, and Rachel had to fight to keep from arching her back and pushing closer to Cal's hand.

"The gate was open, but the lock was intact," Rachel continued, focusing on the story and not on Cal's shiny gold hair as it hovered tantalizingly close to her breasts. She imagined the strands brushing across her bare nipples and she inhaled sharply. "So it must have been someone who has access. But there's only the team, Hargrove, a couple of captains."

"I can't believe any of your officers would hurt the horses," Cal said. She raised Rachel's tank top and leaned closer as she worked over the burns on Rachel's abdomen.

Rachel involuntarily contracted her abs. She wasn't going to last, not if Cal kept talking while she worked, her cool breath so comforting and arousing as it played over Rachel's skin.

"I can't, either. You should have seen Don with Fancy yesterday. He seems to really like her. And Clark was so upset when he showed up at the barn this morning. And Billie? No way."

Rachel shifted forward at Cal's urging—she didn't feel capable of denying Cal anything at the moment—and she rested her elbows on her knees as Cal lifted the tank and rubbed her hand over Rachel's bare back.

"Maybe it's not about the unit," Cal said. Was Rachel imagining things, or had her voice taken on a huskier tone? "Maybe someone wanted *you* to fail."

"That's a long list," Rachel said wryly. She sighed as Cal's hand smoothed over her back. No ointment, just a comforting gesture.

"Your lieutenant didn't seem fond of you."

"But she *is* fond of the unit. It was her idea from the start, so why would she jeopardize it? If the horses had been killed in the fire, there's no way the city would rebuild the program. She doesn't like me, but I can't believe she hates me so much she'd destroy her own project to put me out of a job."

"What about the guy you had arrested? What was his name?" Cal rubbed her thumbs along the sides of Rachel's spine, and she leaned into the relaxing pressure.

"Mm. That's nice," she said. She couldn't help herself. The touch felt so good to her sore muscles. "Sheehan. Yeah, I could see him or someone in his family doing this to get back at me. He didn't have access to the yard, but it wouldn't be impossible."

Cal massaged the tense muscles around Rachel's shoulder blades. She had run out of burns and scrapes to treat, but she didn't want to break their contact, especially given the new topic of conversation. If Rachel had really been the target, what would the attacker try next?

"I can't believe anyone would do this to get revenge," Rachel said, her voice muffled since she was now leaning on the coffee table, resting her head on her crossed arms.

"You have the most to lose if the team fails," Cal said. She pushed with the heels of her hands as she moved them up Rachel's spine again. She lightened the pressure as she swept her hands down and over Rachel's ribcage. She repeated the movement, barely tickling along the sides of Rachel's breasts.

"Me and Hargrove. But you're right. This was my last chance to redeem myself to the department. I don't know what I would have done if we had lost the horses."

Cal stilled her hands on Rachel's ribs. She could feel the rise and fall of her breath. "So the team won't be disbanded?"

"I hope not," Rachel said. She sat up and pulled the tank down again. "We have the horses, and it looked like the tack room wasn't badly burned, so we might be able to salvage our saddles. I kind of thought we could train here until the barn can be rebuilt. Or we can make other arrangements."

"No," Cal said. She took her time screwing the cap back on the jar of ointment, unwilling to meet Rachel's eyes. She was worried about her. Worried about what might happen next. She could so easily picture Rachel rushing into the fire. Maybe she wouldn't be so lucky next time. "You're welcome to keep the horses here as long as necessary."

"Hey," Rachel said. She took the jar away from Cal and set it on the table before she wrapped her hands around Cal's. "Most likely the inspectors will find this was a simple act of arson. Horrible, yes, but not personal. If I really thought someone was after me or the team, I wouldn't keep them here and put you and your family in danger."

"I know. I just…" Cal paused. She wasn't sure what she was trying to say. How relieved she was to have Rachel and the horses safe. How she kept replaying the imagined spectacle of Rachel, the burning barn, the panicked horses until she felt as if her own lungs were filling with smoke, making it impossible to breathe.

Rachel finished the sentence for her by leaning over and brushing her mouth against Cal's. Cal inhaled and felt Rachel do the same. They needed each other in order to keep breathing tonight. To get past the fear and the shaky relief and the what-ifs. Cal stood and held out her hand, feeling calmed and excited at the same time as Rachel took hold of it with her firm grasp.

Chapter Fifteen

Rachel followed Cal down the short hall and into a bedroom decorated in dark shades of blue. She shut the door firmly behind them, barring entrance to Cal's dogs, and then wrapped her arms around Cal's waist. She held her tight, pressing every inch of her body against Cal's. Cal gently nuzzled her neck while Rachel stared out the window behind them. The curtains were open, and the night sky was the kind of dark only found in the country. Rachel hadn't seen so many stars since leaving Cheney. They seemed so bright and clean, drowning out the smoke and flames still dancing in front of her eyes, opening up her world that had only hours ago shrunk down to a series of burning twelve-by-twelve-foot stalls.

Cal sighed against her neck, and Rachel felt the tingle of goose bumps rising where Cal's breath touched her. Rachel knew what was happening. Over her years as a police officer, she had seen so many people who had been touched by trauma, by a rush of danger and violence so uncommon in daily life. Heightened emotions, heightened need. The desperate attempt to grab on to another solid human being, to reorient oneself in a world suddenly gone chaotic. She and Cal were turning to each other for comfort and companionship, like other victims turned to the police or loved ones or medical staff. Grounding. Wiping away the negative emotions and replacing them with positive ones.

Cal softly kissed Rachel's bruise, leaving a slightly damp trail from her shoulder to her elbow. Night air eased the throbbing ache of the injury as it brushed against the moisture from Cal's tongue. Rachel could let Cal take care of her. Over the past two weeks, she had turned to Cal for help with her team, for friendship when no one else would talk to her, as an ally in a world suddenly devoid of them. Tonight she would take what Cal offered, but without guilt or remorse because she would give as much comfort as she received. And because they both understood the terms of their alliance. They'd come together out of mutual need, and then they'd both head east without regrets or complications. She'd go back home to Cheney, to her adoptive family, and Cal would go even farther, to play with the Virginia-based team.

Rachel lifted her arms when Cal pulled the tank top up her torso. Cal threw it onto the floor and cupped Rachel's breasts. Her nipples were already so hard they ached, since Cal had been teasing around them during her burn ministrations and her massage. When Cal finally touched them directly, brushing her riding-callused thumbs over the tight peaks, Rachel thought her knees would give out. She backed up until she bumped into the bed, and Cal reached behind her to tug the blue comforter out of the way. Cal pulled the sweatpants off Rachel's legs and pressed on her good shoulder until Rachel dropped onto the bed. She gave a half sob, half sigh as she slid between the cool sheets, the smooth cotton so comforting to her raw body.

Cal stripped quickly and got into bed beside Rachel. "Do you hurt, Rach?" she whispered against Rachel's ear in between licks. "Will you tell me if I hurt you?"

"I want you," Rachel said, shivering with pleasure at the feel of Cal's tongue tracing her earlobe. "Please don't worry, don't hold back."

Cal shifted so she was straddling Rachel, supporting her weight so only their breasts brushed. She bent her head and kissed Rachel on the mouth, her tongue teasing Rachel's lips and dipping into her mouth for fleeting moments. Rachel gripped Cal's arms, trying to pull her closer and deeper, but she could feel the tension in Cal's strong muscles as she resisted.

"Slow down, cowgirl," she said. Rachel could feel the puff of breath as Cal laughed against her mouth. "I'm not in a rush."

Rachel struggled with her need to control the pace, to rush headlong toward the release Cal's mouth and hands offered. But she was sore and tired, and the lazy circles Cal's tongue was making around her nipples felt so good. She relaxed her head onto the pillow, loosening her grip on Cal's biceps and rubbing her hands over the toned muscles.

"Mm, much better," Cal said as her cool, rough teeth gently bit a nipple.

Rachel arched toward Cal's mouth, stretching her aching muscles and making a sound deep in her throat that sounded like a purr. Cal came back for another kiss, and this time she didn't tease. Her tongue moved into Rachel's mouth in long, deep strokes until Rachel was unable to keep from moaning and pressing her hips toward Cal's. She felt Cal move so her knees were between Rachel's, pushing her legs wide. Cal's hand was on her abdomen, then tangling in Rachel's wet curls.

Sighing and gasping as Cal's tongue continued its onslaught, Rachel gave Cal such complete control she surprised herself. Everything she had experienced so far with Cal—from her overt sexual come-on during their first meeting and their polo match, to the fiery kiss they'd shared only days before—had made Rachel expect sex between them to be explosive and fast. But Cal moved so slowly, taking her time as she entered Rachel with one finger, then two. Fighting shy of speed as she found a steady rhythm with tongue and fingers that was intense and oh, so deep. Rachel moved with Cal, relishing the sensations without rushing toward a goal, letting Cal fuck her senseless. Her orgasm hit without warning, shattering her like a river's ice after a thaw.

Cal continued her relentless stroking as Rachel shuddered beneath her. When Rachel finally grew still, Cal rested her forehead against Rachel's good shoulder and gently eased out of her before she rolled to one side and pulled Rachel into her arms. She could have brought Rachel to climax much more quickly, giving her a satisfying release of the tension and fear she'd experienced during the night. But Cal hadn't wanted to hurry. She had savored the connection, the feeling of reaching into the deepest parts of Rachel and wringing out the stress of the past few months. Cal had always felt a sense of smug satisfaction after bringing a partner to orgasm, but she had never been so present. She hadn't come with Rachel, but she might as well have. The tremors rocking through Rachel's body had reached to Cal's core.

Cal lifted her hand to her lips and licked her fingers, inhaling the scent of Rachel. "I wanted to taste you," she said, brushing her lips against Rachel's temple. "But I didn't want to stop kissing you. Next time."

"Okay, but give me a minute," Rachel said with a weak laugh. She shivered in Cal's arms.

"Are you cold?" Cal asked, reaching for the comforter. Rachel stopped her with a hand on her arm.

"No, I'm fine," she said. Her hand slipped off Cal's forearm and slid between her thighs. "But I think we have some unfinished business."

"Not if you're too sore. I'll be okay," Cal said, even though her body was telling her otherwise. She spread her legs as Rachel's hand stroked her thigh, barely tickling her curls.

"I feel a little weak," Rachel said. She pushed herself a few inches lower on the bed. "You might have to do most of the heavy lifting, but I get to take care of the good parts. Come here, and that's an order."

Rachel tugged on Cal's leg until she got on her knees, carefully straddling Rachel's head. Rachel wrapped her arms around Cal's thighs and used her thumbs to spread her lips wide as Cal clasped the headboard, supporting her weight. She looked down, and Rachel smiled at her before raising her head and lapping her tongue through Cal's folds. Cal tried to smile in return, but she wasn't sure what expression was on her face. She had been in this position before, had watched another woman tongue her, so why was this so different? She should be feeling pleasure, fun, arousal. Not the intense and unnamable emotions coursing through her as Rachel's firm tongue entered her.

Cal gasped. She knew she was dripping wet. She shuddered as Rachel explored every millimeter of her. But she was too much in her head to let go. She had turned Rachel down last week because Rachel was more than she could handle. She had thought it would be fun to play with someone so intense—in her job, her relationships, her sexuality. A nice change from the women Cal was used to dating. But she hadn't anticipated the dangerous side of chasing a complex, intelligent, interesting, strong woman. They were much harder to leave.

At least Rachel would be. Cal heard herself whimper as Rachel's tongue slid around her clit, not touching it. Her head and her body still seemed disconnected as she responded to Rachel's touch and, at the same time, felt the gaping emptiness from her eventual inevitable departure.

Rachel didn't seem to be in any hurry as she licked slowly through Cal's wetness, occasionally sighing or moaning so Cal felt the vibrations move deep into her belly. She had spent her life avoiding relationships, avoiding anyone like Rachel. She had thought these feelings would make her weak, make her lose focus. But she had played better polo than ever this weekend. As sharp and disciplined as always, even though Rachel had haunted her dreams, her early morning schooling sessions, her daily drills in the practice cage. And she felt anything but weak around Rachel. She wanted to take care of her, protect her. She wanted to kill the bastard who had dared put Rachel and her horses in danger. She felt strong.

And connected. Rachel slid one hand along Cal's waist, her ribcage, up to her breast. She rubbed her palm over Cal's nipple until it grew hard. Cal tried to keep thinking about her relationship with Rachel and their future and the risk of caring about her. But when Rachel pinched her nipple more roughly than Cal had expected and moved her lips to cover Cal's clit, Cal felt her thoughts and reasons and worries fade away. Until she was left with her body, and with Rachel. With Rachel's tongue darting over her stiffened clit. With her own hips moving over Rachel's face. With the shuddering orgasm that started where Rachel was touching her and spread like an electric charge through her whole body.

Cal somehow managed to keep her grip on the headboard, holding herself up until the deepest tremors of her orgasm ebbed enough for her to move back to her place by Rachel's side. She kissed Rachel's cheek, her lips, tasting herself and growing hungry for Rachel once more.

"Wow," Cal said, drawing the word out for several syllables. "Very nice."

Rachel laughed, twining her fingers through Cal's hair as Cal kissed along her collarbone and along the top of her breast. "I'm a perfectionist. I'm sure I'll improve on my next try."

"You have to let me rest first," Cal said as she dipped her tongue in Rachel's navel, feeling Rachel's grip on her hair tightening as she moved lower.

❖

Rachel got less than an hour of restless sleep before the morning sun woke her. Cal was lying on her stomach, the sheets tangled around her legs and a pillow tucked over her head. Rachel was tempted to sift her hands through the gold hair peeking out from under the pillow, reflecting the sun's light. Or to run her hand over Cal's toned, sexy ass. But Cal needed her sleep, and Rachel needed to use the bathroom and walk off some of her stiffness. She eased out of bed and gathered her discarded clothing before she quietly opened the bedroom door.

And almost stepped on the black and white pile of dogs lying in the hall. Rachel stumbled over them and hurried to shut the bedroom door again, before Feathers could explode into the room and onto the bed. She got dressed in the bathroom and slipped her feet into her ash-marked running shoes and then let herself and the dogs out the front door. The dogs took off into the adjoining field, and Rachel sat on the stairs and waited for her head to stop pounding.

She felt like she had a serious hangover. Her shoulder and head throbbed, and her brain felt fuzzy from lack of sleep. When she took a deep breath, her throat still burned like it had when she was straining for breath and coaxing the horses from their burning stalls.

The memory was enough to get her back to her feet. She walked toward the main barn, the dogs running a zigzag pattern ahead of her, and squinted in the bright sunlight. She hadn't checked a clock, but it looked to be about eight. Even in her half-asleep and muddled state, she could appreciate the setting of Cal's little bungalow. Big leaf maples and silver birch surrounded the small white house and gave it a sense of privacy on the big farm. Large pastures provided a buffer between the house and the polo fields. Rachel hadn't been able to see much when they had walked here last night, but she had felt a sense of space and peace she usually could only find in the park late at night.

She was greeted by a few nickers as she walked into the barn. One of the grooms from the night before, a woman Rachel hadn't yet met, popped her head out of a stall at the noise.

"Oh, good morning, Rachel," she said. "I'm Dana. Your horses are in the next aisle, to your left. They were doing fine when I fed breakfast."

"Great, thank you," Rachel said. "I appreciated your help last night."

"You're welcome," Dana said. "Glad to do it. Let me know if you need anything."

She disappeared into the stall again, and Rachel hurried down the aisle. Bandit must have recognized her voice or footsteps because he had his head out the door and was neighing loudly before she got to his stall. Rachel opened his stall and stepped inside, wrapping her arms around his neck and leaning her head on his shoulder. She felt the pressure of tears as his greeting—and the awareness of how close she had come to losing him—overwhelmed her exhausted mind. She stood next to him for several minutes before letting go. He went back to eating his hay, and she checked every inch of his body for wounds. He had a few scrapes and singe marks on his dark chestnut coat, but they had been carefully treated and none of them was serious enough for a vet call. She moved through the next few stalls, examining each of her horses in turn. She came to Fancy last. The mare had the worst of the injuries, a burn near her withers, but it looked like it would heal fine. Rachel squatted next to her and ran her hands over Fancy's leg. She had some swelling in the joint above her hoof. Trotting across the gravel and fretting while tied to the fence hadn't done the mare any good.

"I'll call Tim and let him know to come out here to shoe the horses instead of going to Tacoma," Cal said. Rachel looked up and saw her standing in the doorway with a mug in each hand. "Coffee?"

"Sure," Rachel said. She shut Fancy's door and followed Cal to a bench outside the barn door. Cal looked as if she had had a full night's sleep, not a mere two hours. Her hair was smooth and sleek in a low ponytail, and she was wearing her breeches and polished tall boots. Instead of the maroon and blue polo shirt she had worn during their match, she had on a snug black T-shirt. Rachel took the mug of coffee and made a valiant effort to stop staring at Cal's chest.

"Some night, huh?" Cal said. She stretched her long legs in front of her and crossed them at the ankles. Her dogs settled in a patch of sunlight close by.

"Yeah," Rachel said. She wondered if Cal meant the fire or the sex. She took a sip of the strong coffee. "I'm exhausted."

Cal laughed. She wanted to touch Rachel. Hug her, rub her stiff-looking shoulders, kiss her until the rest of the world melted away again, like it had last night. "You should be. I'll bet you'd sleep for a week if you could."

"Unfortunately, I need to get back to the station. Hargrove will want to talk to me, and I need to get some answers about the fire."

"Of course." And Cal needed some space, some time to think. She had woken up and reached for Rachel before she realized she was gone. Cal hadn't wanted sex, but she had wanted to hold Rachel. Cal was usually the one who disappeared, not the one who woke up alone. She didn't like being on the other side of the sheets. "Jack unhitched your trailer last night. You might as well keep it here until you're ready to move the horses again. Do you need me to drive you to Tacoma?"

"No, thanks. I'll be okay to drive. Look, about…" Rachel's voice trailed off and she stared off toward the arena. "About today's lesson. I think the horses need a day off, and I don't know how long I'll be at the station…"

"Sure," Cal said. She figured Rachel had been about to bring up their night together but changed her mind. Cal was relieved. She needed time, too, to gather her thoughts before they talked. And maybe, if they each took long enough to think about it, so much time would pass that they could get by without having the talk. Getting back to business as usual with the team's training would be a good start on the road to forgetting the night had even happened. "We can start tomorrow. I'll make sure the horses get turned out in the paddocks after they finish breakfast. It'll be a little vacation for them."

Rachel handed Cal her half-drunk cup of coffee. "Thank you. And keep track of what we owe. The city will pay the board bill."

Cal held Feathers by the collar as Rachel left, to keep the dog from bounding after her. As soon as the pickup had disappeared down the driveway, Cal got off the bench and walked into the barn. She was already a few hours behind in her daily schedule. She'd get the police horses settled into paddocks, and then she needed to get to work.

CHAPTER SIXTEEN

Rachel drove through a Starbucks on her way back to the apartment. While she was waiting for her triple venti latte, she got her cell phone out of the glove compartment where she had tossed it after calling Cal last night. She juggled her coffee in one hand and the phone in the other, steering with her knee, as she listened to her six messages. One from each mounted officer, asking about the horses, and three from her lieutenant. Hargrove's messages all said the same thing, to get her butt down to the station ASAP.

Rachel decided to take some liberties with her interpretation of *as soon as possible*. She wasn't about to arrive in Abby Hargrove's office wearing Cal's sweatpants and tank top—with no underwear or bra—and smelling like a night of sex. She drove home and sped through a shower before getting dressed. She debated whether to wear civilian clothes or her old patrol uniform since she wasn't going riding, but she finally decided to wear her mounted uniform of breeches and fitted shirt. Until she heard otherwise, she was the team's sergeant. She might as well dress the part.

She detoured a short block out of her way to drive past the police yard where she saw her three team members' cars. What the hell. Hargrove was already pissed, so another five minutes wouldn't make a difference. Besides, the riders deserved to know how their horses were doing. Rachel drove through the wide-open gate and parked by Billie's car. She got out of her truck and stared at the shell of the barn, feeling her palms start to sweat. The roof over the horses' stalls had caved in, and scorched planks from the walls leaned at odd angles. Aside from water and smoke damage, the tack room and office seemed intact. There were sawhorses set up near the arena, draped with saddles and bridles, and as Rachel walked toward the barn, Don came out of the tack room with a saddle on his arm.

"Hey, Sarge," he said, setting the saddle over one of the makeshift racks before he came over and awkwardly patted her on the shoulder. "You look like hell."

The words might have sounded like an insult, but Rachel could hear the emotions behind his words and gesture. Relief, respect, gratitude. She only wished he had chosen her uninjured shoulder to maul.

"Thanks a lot, Don. I'm trying to look real pretty for my ass-chewing with Hargrove. I'm sure she'll find some way to make this fire my fault. How's the tack?"

She was inspecting the saddles when Billie and Clark joined them. Clark shook her hand rather formally, and Billie gave her a one-armed hug every bit as awkward as Don's rough pat had been. Rachel understood. They were all big bad cops, and not about to get mushy over their horses, but every one of them was feeling raw after last night's close call. They were acting as gruff and fake-cheerful as they'd be if visiting a wounded partner in the hospital. All four of them were uncomfortable with the intense emotions they were feeling, but those feelings were definitely there. At least now her officers were looking *at* her, and not through her like before. She was sorry it had taken a near tragedy to bring them together as a team.

"At least the saddles weren't badly damaged," Rachel said, rubbing her hand over the soft leather of Clark's saddle. There were only some surface stains from the firefighters' hoses. "But let's move them to a shadier spot while they dry. It's supposed to be warm today, and the direct sun might dry them too fast and the leather will crack."

She picked up one end of a sawhorse and Clark took the other. "I guess you had a good reason for making us clean and oil them after every damned ride," he said.

Rachel was about to launch into a lecture about the reasons behind proper tack care when her phone buzzed. She answered quickly, surprised to catch herself hoping it was Cal.

"Where the fuck are you, Bryce?" Crap. Hargrove.

"I stopped by the police barn on my way. Be there in ten."

"No. You stay put, and I'll come there. Wouldn't want you getting lost on the way."

Rachel sighed and walked over to help move another sawhorse. She could make up some reason to get the other officers out of there before Hargrove came, but she didn't feel like hiding anymore. Let her yell as much as she wanted. If the team were going to be disbanded, Rachel had no reason to stay with the department any longer. And no reason to care how many people witnessed any further humiliation she might face.

Rachel put the team to work with saddle soap and neat's-foot oil. She showed them how to completely dismantle the bridles so every strap could be thoroughly cleaned. When Hargrove arrived with a spray of gravel, the four were sitting in the bed of Rachel's truck, surrounded by a jumble of leather reins and nosebands. Rachel dropped her soapy sponge in a bucket of water, wiped her hands on her uniform breeches, and hopped out of the truck.

"Care to explain about last night, Rachel?" Hargrove asked without preamble.

Rachel knew Clark had already told her side of the story, but she kept her voice even as she gave an abbreviated account of her jog, her arrival at the barn, and the condition of the horses.

"Yes, great. So you're a hero. But care to tell me how the person who started the fire got into this secured lot in the first place?"

"I don't know. The gate was propped open a few inches when I got here—"

"And who was the last to leave yesterday?"

Rachel stared at her lieutenant. Abby Hargrove's usually composed features and perfect appearance were showing signs of wear. She had dark circles under her eyes and a few tendrils of auburn hair curled along her too-pale cheeks. She looked like she'd been up all night, but Rachel didn't have room for compassion. Was Hargrove insinuating *she* had left the gate open? Or, even worse, that she'd started the fire?

"I fed the horses last night, but I'm sure I—"

"So you admit you were the last one here, and the gate box shows yours was the last key card used. But you have *no* idea how the gate got opened?"

Rachel felt her face flush, hotter than she'd been last night as she battled to get the horses out. She opened her mouth to defend herself, to scream at the injustice of Hargrove's accusations, but Billie's calm voice stopped her.

"No way was it Rachel. I don't believe it."

"Me neither," Don said. "I've seen her out here—she never shuts a gate without double- or triple-checking the lock. Never."

Rachel glanced over her shoulder. The officers were out of the pickup and standing behind her, looking ready to leap to her defense. Their gradual acceptance of her within the fence of this stable yard had been nice, but this was different. They were willing to acknowledge her in front of their lieutenant, and Rachel understood they'd support her within the department from now on. After months of feeling so alone, Rachel suddenly felt an arc of connection with other people—from last night with Cal to this moment with her team. She felt like crying, but for damned sure she wasn't going to break down in front of Abby Hargrove.

Hargrove looked surprised at the show of force behind Rachel, but after a visible struggle, she seemed to accept their insistence on Rachel's innocence. "So how do you explain the open gate with no sign of forced entry?"

Rachel noticed the wary glances exchanged by the people around her. They were the five most likely suspects. The ones with access to the stable yard. But they were also the only ones who had a stake in the mounted unit, who needed to see it succeed.

"We're assuming someone came in and left the gate open," Rachel said. "But maybe they came in another way and used it to get *out*. You don't need an access card to get out."

"Over the fence?" Billie asked.

As if on a silent cue, the five spread out and started walking the fence line. Rachel started behind the maintenance shed, scanning the chain-link fence and the barbed wire tip-in for any signs of tampering. She had only covered three panels before Clark's shout brought the team running to where he stood behind the barn.

"Fibers," he said, pointing at the top of the fence. Small tufts of gray wool were caught on the metal pole connecting strands of barbed wire. "Probably a blanket. And whoever did this climbed over the pole and not the wires, so they aren't sagging much. We probably wouldn't have noticed if we weren't looking for it."

"I'll get the detectives out here to sweep this lot," Hargrove said, walking back toward her car.

Rachel looked through the fence. This was where she and Cal had talked after their fight about Sheehan, and where they'd met Clare. And now someone had used this as an entry point so they could set the barn on fire. Pretty busy for a vacant lot.

"Now what?" Billie asked when they rejoined Hargrove in the parking lot. "Do we keep training? Or is the unit finished?"

Abby sighed and ran a hand over her forehead, tucking her loose strands of hair behind her ears. "Until we're certain the mounted unit isn't being targeted, we should put all training on hold. I'll get us taken off the roster for the Fourth—"

"No," Rachel said. She had finally found her place on this team, had finally gotten enough respect to be able to do her job properly. She wanted a chance to prove herself, but more important, she wanted the team to be a success. They deserved it, and the community needed them. "We'll continue working at Cal's like we planned. And we'll ride on the Fourth."

"Right," Don said. "We can't let some cowardly firebug scare us off. Fancy and I are in."

"Sitka deserves a chance to show off his handsome self to the public," Clark said.

"Oh, please," Billie said, laughing. "You just want a chance to parade around in those tight breeches in front of the poor unsuspecting women of Tacoma."

"Don't pretend you don't want to do the same thing," Clark said.

"Well, Lieutenant?" Rachel asked as the officers' laughter died down.

"Okay. But stay safe, and if anything unusual happens you report it directly to me." Hargrove gave Rachel one of her laser glares. "I said you weren't right for this job, Bryce. That you'd be a detriment to the team. Prove me wrong."

"So what now, Sarge?" Clark asked as Hargrove drove away.

"Now we finish cleaning those bridles," Rachel said, turning toward her truck to hide the grateful tears that threatened to overflow after her team's display of support and protection. "We don't want you out there trying to flirt while your horse is wearing dirty tack."

Cal stowed her saddle, protected by a maroon-edged blue cover, in the tack compartment of her trailer and shut the door securely, turning just in time to see her father come out of the clubhouse and head toward her. Henry Lanford had the long stride of a man who had spent his life walking next to fast, high-strung horses, and the confident air of someone who not only played the sport of kings, but had actually shared the field with princes.

"Ready to go?"

His tone held less question and more assumption, but Cal nodded anyway. She climbed behind the wheel of her truck and started the engine while he got in the passenger seat and fastened his seat belt. She hadn't left the barn's parking lot before he started talking about the merits of her string of ponies, enumerating their strengths and weaknesses and evaluating their ability to hold their own in Virginia.

Cal easily joined in the conversation, adding the information she had picked up while riding in the team's tryouts to the astute observations he had made from watching videos of them. He had offered to postpone their planned horse-buying trip after the events of the night before, but she had wanted to go. Anything to keep her distracted and not thinking about Rachel.

It didn't work, though. Half of her mind was focused on the debate about Raven and whether she'd be speedy enough for high-goal play, but the other half—well, maybe more than half—refused to pay attention to anything but the memory of naked Rachel. Cal was confused. She and Rachel had been steadily growing closer, forming a friendship. But somehow sex had had the opposite effect. She felt the sudden distance between them like a gnawing, aching loss.

Cal maneuvered the large trailer through the pristine white gate of the nearby dressage training farm. She slowed down as the inevitable barn dogs came flying out to greet her, barking and swarming around her truck with tails wagging. A tall woman came out to rescue Cal from the pack as they climbed out of the truck. She was wearing gray jodhpurs and a quilted black vest, with her steel-gray hair in a neat bun at the nape of her neck.

"Sorry about the chaos," she said as she tried in vain to grab collars. "I'm Deborah. You must be the Lanfords."

Cal bent down to play with the dogs while Deborah and her father discussed the horses she had for sale. Cal was happy with her string of horses, but Henry was correct—she needed six solid mounts if she wanted to fit on her new team. He was also right about Raven. As much as Cal loved riding the game little mare—and as linked as she'd always be with Rachel in Cal's mind—the horse wasn't as finished as she needed to be. Not even up for discussion was Cal's young gray gelding, Casper. She bit the inside of her lip, forcing her attention onto the pain and off the sting of tears. She had picked out the colt as a two-year-old and had done all his training herself, but he was far too young and too inexperienced to go to Virginia. She wouldn't have the time or space in her new life for training a green horse, at least until the season was over.

Cal gave the dogs a final pat and followed her father and Deborah into the barn. She was just weepy because of the late night and the stress of nearly losing Rachel and the team's horses. After a good night's sleep, she'd be back to her normal self and able to objectively evaluate not only her horses, but Rachel as well. Anyone would have reacted to the near tragedy with an overflow of sentiment, and she was no exception.

Cal played her role to perfection. She discussed the three horses with her father, checking joints and tendons and evaluating conformation. She got on each one and trotted and cantered around the arena, swinging her polo mallet in wide arcs as the remembered sound of Rachel's moans threatened to eclipse the thud of hoofbeats. Yes, it had been a remarkable night. Yes, Rachel's body had been every bit as delightful as Cal had imagined.

But no, the night hadn't meant more than sex, a release of Cal's long-repressed desire for Rachel and the normal reaction to a stressful event. Cal dismissed the first horse as too stiff and uncomfortable to ride, but the second was perfect, well trained and ready for the rigorous schedule they would face. After a short trial, she dismounted from the third horse, a young chestnut gelding, and handed the reins to Deborah. She had felt a nice connection with him, but he needed more miles before he'd be up to her new team's standards. He'd only hold her back.

Chapter Seventeen

Rachel arrived at Cal's farm before the other officers. She wanted a chance to talk to Cal about their night together, although she still wasn't sure what she needed to say. They had come together in a time of stress, for mutual comfort. Rachel was sure neither of them had any illusions about the relationship beyond that. She would be going back to Cheney—or maybe staying with TPD if the trend of acceptance started by her team caught on—and Cal would be chasing high-goal championships across the country. Rachel couldn't see any gray areas beyond those facts.

So why was she so reluctant to see Cal? Why hadn't she come back to the farm to spend another night with her since the sex had been so much more satisfying than she had expected? The first night had no real meaning beyond the physical. And Rachel couldn't think about Cal's touch without getting so wet she needed to change her underwear. So why hadn't she given in to her near-constant desire and come to the bungalow for more of Cal, more of her tongue and taste and magic?

Rachel turned onto the now familiar drive and slowed to a crawl as she approached the barn. In case one of Cal's dogs ran in front of her truck, she convinced herself, although they could have walked faster than she was driving. Maybe she hadn't come back last night because she would have been admitting sex with Cal had meant more to her than it should have. She had tried to remain distant, just let herself be connected skin to skin after so many months of solitary confinement in her department. But Cal had gone deeper, beyond Rachel's desire for simple social contact and straight to her core. She should have known better, should have seen how her longing for family and permanence and home had somehow—so wrongly—gotten tangled up in Cal.

Rachel parked in the shadow of a huge old maple tree. The police trailer was hitched to Cal's truck and parked in front of the barn. Rachel sat in her beat-up Dodge and forced herself to really look around. To see the money and history in this place. Cal's pickup was a glossy maroon with thin blue and gold stripes along its side. Probably custom detailed, in her team's colors. Cal's clothes, her farm, her truck, they were all surface details, so different from Rachel's faded and worn versions. But they only managed to highlight the true differences between them. Rachel needed to work for her reputation, her apartment, her insurance payments. No one would take care of them for her. Cal worked equally hard, but with a different driving need. She was struggling to stay at the top of her game, to stay in the limelight where her family had predetermined she live. Rachel struggled every day to stay out of the downward trajectory her life had been on before she met Nelson and Leah.

Rachel could understand how the expectations of Cal's family were stifling and difficult to bear. But Rachel couldn't give up on the idea of a family based on love and acceptance and loyalty. She had pictured herself coming to Tacoma, finding a community in the department and a partner in her home. When everything had fallen apart, she had turned to Cal. And Cal had been there for her. A friend when Rachel had been so lonely. A coconspirator in Rachel's search for the still-missing Skunk. An invaluable resource as Rachel tried to stay afloat in a job she wasn't qualified to perform. She was in danger of falling for Cal, of seeing more in their relationship than friendship and sex and a way for Cal to blow off steam between polo matches.

Rachel climbed out of her truck when she saw Cal in the barn's doorway. She had come a long way in two weeks. She had gained Lieutenant Hargrove's grudging respect and her unit's acceptance. She was learning how to lead, how to trust her knowledge of horses, how to temper her ideas of right and wrong in a world devoid of absolutes. She was grateful Cal had temporarily stepped into her life, but now she was ready to move on.

Cal watched Rachel walk across the parking lot, so sexy and confident in her police uniform. She could picture Rachel riding along the waterfront or through the park, with the handsome Bandit to emphasize her strength and beauty. Damn. She'd have women falling all over themselves to get to her. Cal was glad she'd be far from Tacoma, out of the state, by the time Rachel started doing regular patrols. The combination of uniform and horse and power would be attractive on its own, but add Rachel's tall, dark, and gorgeous looks to the mix and no woman would stand a chance of resisting her.

And why would they want to? Cal had learned firsthand—Rachel's sexiness wasn't an empty promise. She was as lethal in bed as the weapon strapped to her hip. Luckily Cal was the kind who could appreciate Rachel's attributes, enjoy her skills, and then walk away the next day. The only reason she had lain in bed awake last night, hoping Rachel would show up at her door, was because she appreciated a good lay when she had one. She wouldn't have minded a second round.

Who was she kidding? She'd take a third and fourth round, too. Maybe more. She needed distance, and she needed it fast.

"Are we going on a field trip?" Rachel asked when she got to the barn.

Rachel's tentative smile and the way she nervously ran her hand through her short hair made her look too adorable. Forget about distance. Right now Cal wanted less between them, not more. She checked her watch to see whether she had time to drag Rachel back to her bungalow, into an empty stall, into the hayloft before the other officers arrived. Ten minutes? She could make it work.

"You have the trailer hitched," Rachel said when Cal didn't answer her first question. "Are we going somewhere?"

"My father has a friend in the Pierce County Sheriff's Department," Cal said, trying to get her mind back onto the lesson she'd planned for the day. "He's going to let us bring the horses to the shooting range. It's the closest we can get to simulating the sound of high-powered fireworks."

"Brilliant," Rachel said. "I should have thought of something like that. Is it okay to bring Fancy?"

Cal shrugged off Rachel's praise, but she was surprised by how pleased she felt. She always enjoyed the feeling of accomplishment when she created an exercise for one of her horses and succeeded in solving a problem. She had felt the same satisfaction as she worked with the mounted riders, but hearing the admiration in Rachel's voice made the feeling even stronger.

"The abscess wasn't very deep, so Tim was able to drain it today and relieve the pressure when he shod the horses. She's doing much better, and we'll only be walking around the range, so I think we should bring her. We…you don't have much time before the Fourth."

"Sorry I couldn't be here to meet the farrier. I had to talk to the detectives about the fire. It took longer than I expected."

"Any more info about it?" Cal asked as she walked into the barn with Rachel following. Talk of the fire only made her nervous, but she couldn't show it. She had come too close to losing Rachel, and the lingering concerns let her know she cared too much. She needed to move to her new team with a clear head and no long-distance ties. She'd never be able to concentrate on her game if she didn't. And she had worked too hard to let one night with Rachel make her lose sight of her goals.

Bandit had his head over his stall door, and he nickered when they came into sight. Rachel walked over to greet him. "Whoever it was climbed over the fence from the vacant lot behind the barn, but we don't have much more. They're trying to connect this with other arsons, maybe find some more clues that way."

Rachel straightened Bandit's forelock, fidgeting with his hair like she had with her own. "Should we talk about what happened after the fire? About us?"

"Us?" Cal repeated, buying herself some time before she answered. For a moment, she wondered if Rachel felt they had something more than a one-night stand. And she was even more curious to find out what her own reaction would be if Rachel *did* want more.

"Well, not *us*," Rachel said, looking at Bandit's mane as she untangled it with her fingers. "But what happened between us. I mean…I understand how people react after traumatic situations. I see it all the time on my job. But I wanted to make sure you—"

"Oh, of course. Don't worry about me, cowgirl. You know I've been looking for an excuse to get you out of those uniform pants, but now they're back on, so we're back to normal." Forget the past and move toward the future. The next conquest, whether in polo or the bedroom. "Hey, come see my new horse. A couple of mine are still too young to compete on my new team, so I needed a more seasoned horse to bring with me. He's a stunner."

Rachel agreed. The blaze-faced bay was absolutely stunning. He stood still as a statue while Rachel and Cal walked around him and discussed his conformation. Rachel's thoughts were distracted even as she talked about the gelding's low-set hocks and powerful hindquarters. She could hear the excitement in Cal's voice when she talked about her move, but it sounded too bright and harsh to Rachel's ears, matching the inflection Rachel heard in her own voice when she responded to Cal's enthusiasm. And she heard the low, gentle tones Cal used when she spoke to her young gray gelding and stroked his neck as they passed his stall—the horse Rachel had seen her schooling in the field, and one she'd be leaving behind when she moved. The conflict between Cal's voices was striking, but Rachel didn't want to dig deeper into Cal's true feelings about her move. Instead, she focused on the crunch of gravel in the parking lot, relieved to hear her team's carpool arriving.

The flurry of preparations for their road trip was a welcome distraction for Rachel. Cal outfitted each horse with boots to protect their legs during the trailer ride and while they were at the range. The team's saddles were still being treated for water damage, so she spent a few minutes finding the right saddles to fit both horse and rider in each pair. Rachel enjoyed that part the most. She was perfectly capable of determining saddle fit, but she let Cal take care of her, like she did with the other riders. Cal definitely took a more hands-on approach with Rachel, and the brush of her hand against Rachel's crotch and ass was very arousing. By the time Rachel dismounted and stowed her saddle in the trailer's tack compartment, she was so wet she wanted to drag Cal behind the barn and fuck her before she lost her mind. Virginia, future, and differences be damned.

Fortunately, Cal moved away from her and lowered the trailer's ramp before Rachel could act on her foolish impulse. She went into the barn and stood in Bandit's stall for a few minutes, taking deep breaths and fighting off the vision of Cal with those tan breeches around her ankles. Finally, she led him to the trailer. Ranger and Fancy had already been loaded, and Rachel waited while Sitka climbed willingly into his place. She led Bandit up the ramp and secured him to the trailer's tie rope.

Everyone piled into Cal's king cab, the three officers leaving the front passenger seat for Rachel as if it was her natural place. She'd rather have squeezed into the backseat and not sat next to Cal since she was already feeling hypersensitive to Cal's nearness, but the nervous riders' questions about the lesson and how to handle the horses near guns made the drive to the range seem even shorter than it was.

Cal drove through the open gate at the range and parked next to a line of Pierce County patrol cars. She went to find her father's friend, leaving Rachel to organize the riders and horses. The pop of pistol shots was a steady background noise as Rachel unloaded the horses one by one. They had been so relaxed and easy to load at Cal's farm, but now—around the sharp and unaccustomed noises—they were agitated as they danced down the ramp. Even Fancy snorted and circled at the end of her rope, her tail waving like a flag in the air as she tried to figure out the source of the noise, the source of danger. She spun in a circle, bumping heavily into Don, but he kept his cool and moved out of the way of her hooves.

Rachel flashed forward to the Fourth. The officers wouldn't be any use on patrol if all they could do was lead the horses through the crowds, plunging and spinning and endangering everyone around them. She tried to focus on Bandit, on getting through this first small step without worrying over the thousand steps to follow.

She pressed her hand against Bandit's quivering side, asking him to move away from the pressure. Then she led him in a series of circles and figure eights. Back up, move forward, move sideways. Quietly taking control of his movement and pulling his focus off the loud noises and onto her. Eventually he gave her his full attention, trotting across the parking lot, circling, coming to a halt, reassured by her unconcern and by the familiar patterns of movement.

Cal paused at the edge of the gravel lot and watched Rachel work with Bandit. And she wasn't the only one. Clark, Billie, and Don were paying attention to Rachel's quiet movements and mimicking them with their own horses. Within ten minutes, without Cal or Rachel saying a word, all four horses were following their handlers through random movements, as unconcerned about the gunshots as if they were the now-familiar horn of the ferry.

Cal stepped forward and the four horse-and-rider pairs circled around her. She explained what they'd be doing the rest of the day, as they moved from the parking lot to the actual range—first leading the horses behind the officers as they did their target practice, and eventually riding close behind them as they fired their weapons. The close-range work with firearms would be helpful not only to prepare the horses for the fireworks they'd encounter, but also as training in case one of the officers needed to fire a gun while riding. Cal heard the catch in her voice as she suggested they should go to Tacoma's range sometime and practice shooting from horseback. The thought of Rachel in any situation dangerous enough to require gun power was more upsetting than she cared to admit.

Cal walked next to Rachel as they went down a gravel path toward the range. She looked over her shoulder at the horses behind them. "For once, Ranger isn't the star pupil," she said. Billie was managing the tall Thoroughbred, but barely. He was as nervous as the rest of the horses.

Rachel took a quick glance behind before she returned her attention to Bandit. "Alex couldn't have exposed him to gunfire without taking him out of the police yard. The others never noticed how much more training Ranger had, so I think Alex was doing it at night, in secret, although I have no idea why. It'd have been too risky to take Ranger off property in the trailer."

"Was he so determined to look better than the rest of the team? Seems like a lot of trouble to go through for an ego trip."

Rachel shrugged, but her attention seemed too focused on Bandit as they neared the range for her to really listen to Cal's questions. Cal moved back as the quarter horse tried to pivot and run back to the relative safety of the parking lot.

Over the next few hours, while two shifts of officers had training on the range, Cal's mind was too busy with her students to give much more thought to Alex's ego. The only reason he occasionally came to her mind was because his leadership methods seemed to be such a telling contrast to Rachel's. She led by example, without shouting or ordering, and seemed more pleased with her unit's progress than with her own. Her natural touch with a horse was more obvious in this extreme environment than it had been in the ring, and the team obviously noticed. They listened to everything Cal said and did what she asked, but just as often they mirrored Rachel's actions.

Rachel had needed Cal's help with the team from the start. She had had no respect, no authority, no confidence in her ability to train the mounted unit. But she had changed so completely, right in front of Cal's eyes. Everything about Rachel was different, from her voice to her posture to her easy laugh as she joked with one of the county deputies. She had seemed self-assured before, but there had been a distance, a barrier between her and the world. Now she was slowly becoming part of it again, part of her team and part of the police community. Cal felt very proud of Rachel because she understood the struggle behind her success. She gradually inched back and let Rachel take over the lesson. She'd still help until it was time for her to leave, but the team really didn't need her anymore. Rachel didn't need her anymore. It was for the best, since this had only been a fun diversion for Cal, but she felt an aching sense of loss as she and Rachel changed places and she became the one on the outside, looking in.

Chapter Eighteen

Rachel ran through the park with a sense of lightness she hadn't felt in a long time. The past week with her mounted team had been a huge success, starting with their marathon session at the gun range and ending with a picnic as they watched Cal's polo match on Sunday. The horses had been given a well-deserved day off Monday, and they'd be fresh and ready for something new in today's lesson.

The first training sessions had been difficult—not only because of her own personal issues, but because the horses were so unaccustomed to anything new and surprising. Not anymore. They seemed to expect the unexpected and often reacted to whatever Cal had brought to the lesson with curiosity rather than fear. At the same time, the riders were growing comfortable with the nuances of desensitization, and the time required to introduce any new object was lessening exponentially.

Rachel jogged around the park's rose garden and startled a raccoon as it scurried along the path. It ran a few steps before turning back, probably hoping for a handout, but Rachel only waved as she ran by. She smiled at the thought of some of the kooky things Cal had devised for the team. Her groom, Craig, had set off a box of fireworks in the farm's gravel parking lot. Rachel had fought to stay out of cop mode and not ask where he had gotten them. By the end of the evening, she no longer cared since the training had been invaluable for the celebration on the Fourth. And on Friday, they had played a raucous game of fake polo, joined by Cal and the rangy bay she'd ridden in her stick-and-ball match with Rachel. The ball had been a huge, multicolored beach ball that was as tall as Rachel's hip when she was astride Bandit. They had used their hands, not mallets, and the horses had eventually become used to having the squishy ball bump against their sides and hindquarters. Fancy had enjoyed her moment to shine when she pushed the ball into the goal with her nose, scoring a point. For the wrong team, of course, but Don had seemed proud anyway.

The best part of the game had been the rivalry between Cal and Rachel. She skirted a tree stump and jogged deeper into the forest, still feeling the rush of pleasure from Cal's aggressive play. After a week of being close to her but not touching, Rachel had been growing tense and irritable. Horny and aroused was more like it, but she hated to admit it. But the shoving match between her and Cal had rapidly accelerated into an all-out war, and the rough physical contact had been a much-needed stress relief. Rachel had done her best to avoid being alone with Cal after the game. She wouldn't have been able to say no if Cal had offered sex. And she wouldn't have been able to stop herself from initiating it if no offer had been forthcoming.

Luckily, she'd always had at least one of her teammates around whenever she was near Cal, during their training or when they had cheered Cal on in her polo match. Except when Rachel had gone into the polo clubhouse to get a beer out of the fridge between chukkers. And Cal had come in moments later, hair plastered on her forehead and maroon polo shirt damp with sweat. Rachel had put her beer on the counter and fairly pounced on Cal, pushing her against the clubhouse's wood-paneled wall and kissing her. Cal's strong arms had pulled her closer, until a loud group of players had come in, nearly catching them writhing against the wall. Now, even in the cold night air, Rachel's face and neck burned with the memory. Her insides twisted and ached. Really, she'd only needed five more minutes alone with Cal. But the players had claimed Cal's attention, and Rachel had grabbed her beer off the counter and left the too-crowded room.

Rachel sprinted up the hill from the ferry landing. She had been in the park longer than usual, and the cars were already lining up for the first ferry run from Point Defiance to Tahlequah, on Vashon Island. Rachel stopped, panting, by the fenced police stables, the darkened hulk of the stable barely visible as dawn approached. She wrapped her fingers around the chain-link fence and stared at the shell of the barn. She was too restless to go back to her apartment, having even less tolerance of the small space since the fire, when she had worried she and the horses might be trapped in one of those stalls. Enclosed by flames, slowly burning to death.

Rachel exhaled with a sigh. She walked behind the stables, into the vacant lot, and climbed onto the pile of concrete slabs near where she'd first noticed Clare. She sat with her back to the barn and concentrated on her breathing and the comforting knowledge that the horses were alive and well, enjoying their stay at Cal's. Airy stalls, room service, afternoons spent napping or grazing in their paddocks. They'd never want to come back, once the new barn was built. *If* a new barn was built.

Rachel hugged her knees to her chest as the heat she'd generated while running gradually dissipated. She felt a sense of peace descend over her as she sat with the dark bulk of the park on one side and the expanse of water in front of her. Lights from the ferry and its attendant line of cars and a sprinkling of lit-up homes on Brown's Point across the bay were comforting, pushing away the deepest shadows.

She sat there, shivering on the rough stone, as the sun started to rise. Mount Rainier was a silhouette at first, but it slowly gained dimension as the glaciers and crags became visible. Vashon Island transformed from a black outline to a lush, green island, and gulls dove and circled as the ferry began its slow journey across the bay. Rachel was chilled in her T-shirt and running shorts, but she didn't want to move, didn't want to leave the scene as it transformed in front of her eyes. She watched a fishing boat chug past her and she wished she could move her apartment to this very spot. Get the full view instead of the glimpse she had from her apartment's little window. Too bad it wasn't legal to live in the park.

Rachel inhaled as a chill, having nothing to do with the weather, ran through her body. This *wasn't* parkland. Not any longer. It had been rezoned so the city could install the mounted unit on the vacant lot. She scrambled off the concrete slab and stood in the middle of the lot, turning slowly around as she tried to piece the puzzle together in her mind. Rezone the land, build a barn, burn it down. The idea seemed too elaborate, too insane. But the more she looked at the property, the less crazy it sounded. Clear the rubble and build a high-rise. With easy access to the beach, the ferry, the park. A short drive to downtown and the amenities provided by the growing community of condos on Ruston Way. This single lot could support hundreds of condos, selling for over a million apiece.

The lot—except for the police yard—was ugly and cluttered, but it didn't block the park's view. A massive building would spoil the pristine sweep of the park and the ferry landing, it would infuriate citizens who wanted to protect parkland. But Rachel didn't doubt there'd be people who wouldn't care, as long as they got a cut of the money. They'd be willing to sacrifice the view from the park, cheat the community out of its property, and probably even burn down a barn and a handful of horses if they stood in the way.

Maybe even kill Alex Mayer. Standing here, so close to where he was shot, Rachel could believe it. She spun around and ran up the hill to her apartment. She needed to talk to someone, figure out if this idea of hers could possibly be true.

Cal showed Clark how to wrap the mallet's strap around his right wrist before she stepped out of his way and tossed a ball next to the wooden horse. Rachel was uncharacteristically late for their lesson, and she had been fielding questions about polo since the team had watched her match on Sunday. Instead of explaining the game, she had brought the group over to the practice cage. Clark was first to try, with Billie and Don providing less-than-helpful commentary from outside the wire fencing.

"That's it," Cal said. "Lead with your elbow, straighten, and swing."

The head of Clark's mallet missed the ball by at least a foot.

"It's not air polo," Billie said.

"Hey, wait until you get in here and try," Clark said, puffing as he swung even harder. "It's not as easy as it looks."

"Maybe he needs the beach ball we used last week," Don said to Cal. "He can't find that little one without his glasses on."

Cal waited until Clark tried one more swing before she stepped over to the wooden horse. "You have to lean farther, so your shoulders are over the ball."

"Are you kidding? I'll fall off."

"No, you won't." She took hold of his knee and rotated it toward the saddle. "Remember how we worked on counterbalancing in our first lesson? Brace yourself against the saddle here, and—"

"Guys, I have to talk to you," Rachel said.

Cal looked over at the door of the practice cage. Rachel was standing there, her hands gripping the frame. Cal frowned at the distracted, agitated expression on her face. She let go of Clark's leg and closed the distance between her and Rachel in two long strides.

"What's wrong? What happened?"

"Nothing happened. Just…come on." Rachel jumped off the small staircase leading to the cage and walked to the clubhouse.

Cal trotted after, followed closely by Don and Billie. She heard the thump as Clark dropped off the wooden horse behind them. Rachel was pacing in front of the fireplace. She gestured for them to sit, and Cal perched on the arm of the sofa while the other three found seats.

"What would you say if I offered you a chance to get in on a sweet deal?" Rachel asked. "I've got a piece of land in Tacoma. Great view of the mountain and Puget Sound, close to parks and schools. Big enough lot for high-rise condos."

Cal glanced at the other officers. They looked as confused as she was. Had Rachel taken on a second job selling real estate?

"Is this some sort of pyramid scheme?" Don asked.

Rachel rolled her eyes. "No. But think about it. Wouldn't it be worth a fortune? And wouldn't you want a piece of it?"

Cal shrugged. Rachel seemed very intent about something. Cal wasn't sure what the game was, but she'd play along. "I'd be interested. Hypothetically. A friend of mine bought one of those waterfront condos and she spent a fortune even though her view wasn't as good as…Oh. You really think…?"

"I do," Rachel said. "It'd be crazy if it were small scale, but—"

"You're talking millions. Even a small kickback would—"

Rachel nodded.

"Would someone mind telling us what the hell is going on?" Billie asked. "Are you two talking in code? And sorry, Rachel, but I don't have the money to invest in whatever you're selling."

"Not me," Rachel said. She pulled a chair in front of them and straddled the seat, facing the straight back of the chair and curling her arms around it. "I don't know who, or even if. But I'm talking about the property where the police stables are. What if someone stands to profit from getting rid of the barn and selling the property?"

"That part makes sense," Cal said. "But why build the stables in the first place? Why not just sell off the property."

"Zoning. Shit," Clark said. "I remember Hargrove talking about the fuss over zoning when she was trying to get approval for the unit."

"Right," Billie chimed in. "It was park property, but they had to rezone it and sell it to the city. You don't think this is the reason Hargrove pushed so hard for the team, do you?"

Rachel shrugged. "Maybe. Or maybe she really wanted this mounted division, and one of the other supporters wanted it for a different reason."

"So they wanted us to fail," Don said quietly. "First they stick us with…Sorry, Sarge."

Rachel clasped the back of the chair tighter, and Cal could see the tension in her arms. She wanted to go over to her, hold her, but she let Rachel talk without interrupting.

"Go ahead and say it, Don. They stuck you with me. The person least likely to succeed. It's the only reason that makes sense—I couldn't figure out why, especially since Hargrove said she didn't want me here but someone higher up did."

"Did she say who it was?" Billie asked.

Rachel shook her head. "No. And after the screw-up with Skunk, she said the same thing. You heard her. She wanted me out, but someone was fighting for me."

"She might have been lying," Cal said. She hadn't been very fond of the lieutenant after watching her publicly berate Rachel. "Saying that to cover up her own part in this."

"We're not sure this is even what's going on," Clark said. "We don't have any proof. And until we do, how do we know who can be trusted?"

Rachel watched as her team looked at one another warily. She had her doubts as well, but she had to bring the unit together, not let it be pulled apart by suspicion. "Stop, guys. We have to trust each other. But I think Cal and Clark are right. We shouldn't bring this to Hargrove until first, we know whether this is true, and second, we're sure Hargrove isn't involved."

"What about Alex?" Billie asked, voicing the same question Rachel had been mulling over since the morning. "Do you think he found out and someone shot him?"

Cal gave a snort of humorless laughter. "If anything, he was in on it from the start."

Rachel could see the three original team members bristle at Cal's words. Cal apparently did, too.

"You're all so ready to defend him, but he did everything he could to make the unit fail. What do you think would have happened on the Fourth if Rachel hadn't taken over? I almost killed you with an umbrella. What better way to get the unit disbanded than by proving you're a danger to the public?"

"Ranger," Billie said. "The flares, the tarps, the raincoats. He was training Ranger to keep himself safe while the rest of us fell to pieces."

"Billie—" Clark started.

"She's right," Don said. "Rachel saw it from the start. The way we'd been trained, the horses we'd been assigned. Corona was a nut job. I like Fancy, but Rachel was right. She's the hardest horse to ride and I'm the least experienced rider."

Billie nodded. "Hargrove even told Rachel that she was supposed to follow Alex's lesson plans and keep doing things the way he had."

Rachel watched Clark as he tried to process what they were saying. She knew he and Alex had been friends for a long time. He wouldn't want to believe the worst about Alex, but the evidence was too damning.

"Shit," Clark said again. "So when Rachel goes against orders and trains us so we might actually be a success, someone tries to burn down the fucking barn with all the horses in it?"

They were silent for a few moments. Rachel rubbed her bruised shoulder. Her nose twitched as the smell of smoke seemed to linger, and the walls threatened to close in and suffocate her. She looked up and saw Cal watching her with an expression of concern, support, understanding. They might not have had much time together, but Rachel was grateful for Cal's presence. She had gone from being ostracized to feeling like part of a team. A leader of a team. She didn't believe she could have made it this far without Cal's help.

"One thing in Hargrove's favor," Rachel said. "She told me to hire Cal to train us. She didn't do that for Alex, and if she really wanted us to fail she would have left me alone."

"So, now what?" Billie asked, after a pause.

"We keep training," Rachel said. "We're riding on the Fourth, no matter what else happens. But I think we need to find another place to board the horses. I don't want to put Cal and her family in danger."

"No," Cal said. "I'm part of this, too. The horses have been fine out here. Maybe someone only wanted the property, and now they can have it."

Rachel sighed. She had learned not to argue when Cal got that stubborn look in her eyes. "Okay, but we should take turns sleeping in a stall near the horses until we know what's really going on."

"I'll stay tonight," Don volunteered.

Billie and then Clark added their names to the rotation. Rachel would stay every fourth night. She had been torn between wanting to stay on the farm, to be close to Cal, and wanting to avoid it for the same reason. At least she'd have a few nights to prepare for being in such close proximity to Cal, and her bedroom.

"What else can we do?" Clark asked. "How do we find out if there really is something going on with the property?"

"I was down at the County-City Building this morning, looking into the property and the zoning laws," Rachel said. She could have done most of the research on her computer, but the laws were tangled at times. She had spent over an hour with a clerk, asking questions and taking notes. "All I really discovered is that the idea is plausible, but there's no proof it's happening. Why don't we each do some investigating on our own. Check out the other condos in the area—who's winning bids, who's selling properties, whatever we can dig up. Maybe a name will jump out. We can compare notes when we meet for lessons."

She stood up. The team looked stressed and preoccupied. She wanted to get them back to work, but they didn't seem ready to be a steadying influence on the horses right now. "Why don't we go back to the cage and let Cal finish the polo lesson she was giving you when I got here," she said. She winked at Cal. "I'm anxious to see if Clark can actually hit the ball this time."

CHAPTER NINETEEN

Rachel jogged into the moonless night. The darkness breathed over her like a sigh as she released the tensions of the day and concentrated on the sound of her light running shoes. The squish of damp grass, the crunch of pine needles and dirt, the slap of pavement as she crossed the Five Mile Drive. The shock of impact reverberated up her legs and her spine and disappeared into the cool black park.

The lesson at Cal's had gone surprisingly well, given the tense discussion beforehand. She felt as if the whole team had something to prove now, not just her. They had spent a hilarious hour in the practice cage and then had ridden out to the large polo field and tried the various mallet swings while on horseback. The training was good for the horses, as they grew accustomed to having the mallets slice through the air near their bodies and heads and having the balls drifting underfoot. The riders benefitted, as well. They relaxed and had fun because the work was disguised as play, but in reality they were learning to lean and move in the saddle, to balance and counterbalance. Rachel and Cal had raced each other as they fielded balls from the wayward swings of the inexperienced players.

The rest of Rachel's day had been less physical and much less satisfying. Hours in front of the computer screen, staring at lists of people involved in the waterfront expansion and searching for any relevant information in a vast sea of unfamiliar names. She had been so excited by her epiphany and hopeful the person behind the attacks on the unit would be easily spotted. But she had only researched two of the new buildings, and she had several more to go. She hoped one of the other team members had been more successful.

Rachel hopped over an exposed tree root and jogged across the pavement without slowing down. The sudden rev of an engine startled her and she stumbled to a halt, staring into the dark. Like a deer in the headlights, only there were no lights. Just the screech of motor and tires as an unseen vehicle accelerated toward her.

She snapped out of her frozen state and ran toward the shoulder, feeling a rush of air and heat as the car missed her by inches. She dodged off the trail and into the trees so the car couldn't come after her. She heard the slam of doors and muffled voices before the noise of her passage through the branches and shrubs drowned out everything but her own flight. They'd come after her, of course. There was nothing random about the attack—someone had been lying in wait. Anticipating the jog she took every night, all alone in the park.

They wouldn't need night-vision goggles to find her, since the sound of her crashing through the brush would keep them right on her heels. Her only hope was to outrun them, get to safety before they reached her. She tried to formulate a plan, figure out which direction to go, while part of her mind had to concentrate on each step. She stumbled over a large boulder and managed to catch herself against the trunk of a tree before she fell. Her eyes had adjusted to the dark night, but she was unable to make out more than shapes and shadows. A twisted ankle was not an option.

The park covered over seven hundred acres of peninsula, and Rachel was deep inside, close to its point. She could head to her right, her normal route. Try to get down to Owen Beach or across the grassy bowl to her apartment. To roads and people and civilization. But an easier and more open route for her would also be easier for her pursuers. Maybe she could continue to run through the woods, trying to shake them in the dark. A shot echoed through the night, and she heard the thud of a bullet in a tree close by. The woods were definitely out. She couldn't get far enough ahead to be safe, or to hide.

A large pine branch smacked her in the face, a stinging blow against her cheek and left eye. She swore silently and kept one arm in front of her as she ran, shielding herself as much as she could. Her breath was growing shallower, burning in her throat and lungs as she gasped for air and grasped for some avenue of escape. She was near the Bridges Viewpoint, above Salmon Beach. She tried to reconstruct the geography of the area in her panicky mind. Unlike the Owen Beach side of the peninsula, with its steep but manageable bluffs, this side had cliffs over two hundred feet high. She had been on several calls over the past few years, watching as search-and-rescue teams plucked stranded people off the side of the cliff. Idiots who tried to scale the steep precipice.

She heard the whine of another bullet and made up her mind. She'd have to go with idiocy. She had only a vague idea of her location, but she thought she could veer left, follow the cliff for another hundred yards or so before she plunged over the side. If she was correct, she'd be on a section of the bluff with more vegetation, hopefully enough to break her fall. If she was wrong? She'd rather die falling off a cliff than let these bastards shoot her.

The trees were thinning in front of her. Open sky, the end of her run through the forest. She wanted to slow to a walk, control at least her first steps over the side, but she couldn't take the chance. She heard her followers but couldn't accurately gauge their closeness because of the racket she made as she struggled through the undergrowth, fought to breathe.

She couldn't stop her startled shriek as one moment she was on solid ground, and the next her foot sank through the air. She managed to twist her body as she slid, grabbing the edge of the cliff long enough to break her fall. And then she let herself go.

She had picked the right spot, heavy enough with trees and brush to slow her downward progress. She tried to be grateful as she skidded from trunk to branch to shrub, dropping down the bluff as if she were in a pinball machine. She had a brief moment of worry as she descended, wondering if the tide would be low enough for her to safely land on the beach. But as she scraped through a thick berry bush, its thorny tendrils wrapping around her legs and lacerating her skin, she decided drowning would be okay as long as it meant her bruising fall was at an end.

She couldn't see more than a few feet in front of her—when she wasn't shielding her eyes from another sticker bush—so her sudden thump onto the damp beach came as a shock. She sat still, frozen in place as the concussion of her landing traveled through her tailbone and into her back, knocking the air out of her aching lungs. She battled for breath as she listened for any sign her attackers had followed her down the cliff.

The world was silent, except for the soft lapping water a few yards away from her. There was no way anyone could sneak down the cliff—her own tumbling progress had been accentuated with gasps and yelps. She had been helpless to stop her involuntary cries, but the crash of brush had rendered any attempt to be quiet completely useless.

Rachel collapsed onto her back, waiting for her diaphragm to relax enough for her to breathe normally again, but a sweep of light, probably from a high-powered flashlight, arced over the beach. She scrambled backward, pressing against the cliff face. She still wasn't safe. She needed to move.

Rachel hurried through the deep sand, her instinct to run still vibrating through her body even though she was certain she was no longer being followed. She hurt everywhere, and her already injured shoulder was so painful she wanted to cut the whole arm off, but nothing seemed to be broken. Thank God, because she still needed to climb off the beach.

After what seemed to be hours, she finally saw the lights and shapes of the community on Salmon Beach. She had been there before, responding to calls. Especially when she had been a rookie, because no cop willingly went to Salmon Beach if there was a newbie to send instead. Originally built by hippies in the sixties, the secluded community was only accessible by boat or by the narrow staircase leading to the top of the cliff. A two-hundred-foot-plus bitch of a staircase.

Rachel walked along the tunnel-like footpath, the neighborhood's main street. Houses built on stilts loomed next to her—old shacks sitting next to fancy homes costing hundreds of thousands of dollars. She could stop at one of them, ask the occupant to call the police and give her a boat ride back to the park's marina. But for the first time in her adult life, she didn't trust the police. Had someone in the department called this hit on her? Had Hargrove sent the car into the park, telling its occupants where to wait for her? Or had Hargrove herself been one of the people following Rachel through the woods and shooting at her?

Rachel didn't know. But until she found out, she wasn't calling the cops. She'd get out of here, get back to her home. She felt like a kid again, hiding from the authorities, trusting no one. But it was different this time. She had her team. And she had Cal. The thought of their support gave her the strength to keep forcing her cramping and sore legs to move until she got to the base of the staircase, winding upward in the dark. She reconsidered asking for help, for a nice easy boat ride, but she put her hand on the railing and sighed. And started to climb.

CHAPTER TWENTY

Cal cross-tied her bay, Roman, in the aisle near the stalls where the mounted unit was getting ready for their lesson. She was looking forward to the afternoon. For the first time, she'd be a student and Rachel would be the instructor. They'd managed to convince Jack to play the role of a fleeing suspect, and Rachel was going to teach them how to chase and apprehend him from horseback. She could hear the excitement in the voices of the officers as they groomed and tacked their horses. For her, this would be yet another chance to play cop—a real Mountie this time—but for Rachel's team, it was finally a chance to learn something associated with their day-to-day job.

"Don't get me wrong," Don said. He leaned his elbows on the top of Fancy's stall door. "It's been interesting taking lessons from you. And I know the desensitizing and riding parts are important. But it's parade stuff. We're not going to be exhibition riders. About time we learned to do some good old-fashioned police work."

Clark laughed as he stood near Sitka's door and untangled his bridle. "Come on, Don. We've learned to arrest enormous beach balls and umbrellas and raincoats…"

"And don't forget the pretty little dolly and stroller you brought to the barn," Billie said. "If we have any infant felons, we'll send you after them."

"Ha!" Clark said. "Fancy'd probably step on…oh my God. What happened to you?"

Cal had been quietly enjoying the banter, but she followed Clark's gaze and saw Rachel striding with a slight limp down the barn aisle. The left side of her face was scraped and raw, and her arms were covered with bruises. She looked furious. Cal felt her chest tighten and grow chill, as if she'd been stabbed with an ice pick.

The officers gathered around Rachel, all asking questions at once. Cal stepped past them, taking Rachel's arm and leading her into the lounge next to the tack room.

"Sit," she said, pulling Rachel over to the leather couch. She ran her fingers over Rachel's cheek, feeling nauseated at the sight of dried blood. Cal had never been squeamish about bodily fluids but this was different. This was Rachel. "I'll get some ice for your eye."

Rachel grabbed her hand. "No, I'm okay," she said. But she kept her fingers wrapped around Cal's and tugged until Cal sat down close to her. The gesture worried Cal more than Rachel's visible injuries did. Rachel was always very careful to keep a professional distance between them while they were around the team—although Cal enjoyed challenging her boundaries at times—but today, Rachel seemed to need her close.

The others had brought chairs over so they were sitting in a tight cluster around their sergeant.

"Talk," said Don.

Cal tightened her grip on Rachel's hand as she described the attack in the park, her flight, her crashing tumble down to the beach. Cal had been to the Bridges Viewpoint many times. The vistas were spectacular, and she had often seen eagles hovering in updrafts where wind blew across the Sound and hit the cliff. She had even spotted a seal once, its tiny head bobbing in the waves, but that was rare because the cliff was so high. So fucking high.

Rachel finished her story with the climb up the staircase and her cautious jog through the residential streets and back to her apartment. "I figured they might guess where I'd have to go to get off Salmon Beach, but I didn't see any suspicious cars. Maybe they didn't know about the beach-access road. Or they assumed I was lying on the beach either dead or too injured to move."

Cal had already conjured up the image of Rachel crumpled on the rocky beach, her body floating out to sea at the next high tide. "Did the police find any clues in the park? Any sign of the car?"

"I didn't report it," Rachel said. She disengaged her hand and ran it through her hair. "Don't look so mad, Cal. I don't know who to trust anymore."

"Did you see the car?" Clark asked. "Or the passengers?"

"No. It was so dark. I know there were at least two of them, because I heard two doors shut and they were talking to each other. But by then I was running, and I can't say if they were men or women."

"Why now?" Cal asked. "It's been so quiet since the fire. If you're right about the rezoning, isn't it enough that the horses have moved off the property?"

"No," Rachel said. "The city might rebuild the barn and give us another chance. I guess it depends on how we do in public, whether we can regroup and pull together in time for the Fourth. The land is still designated for the mounted division, even if the horses aren't actually there."

"I think you're right about the fire," Don said. "It was set to destroy the barn and the horses. But this is personal. Killing you wouldn't necessarily mean the unit is disbanded. Someone wanted you dead."

"Maybe someone found out you were snooping around the land-use records yesterday," Clark said.

Rachel nodded. "If so, it means we're on the right track. Getting close enough to make people nervous. Did you find anything suspicious when you researched the condos?"

Cal listened vaguely to the talk about dead ends and clueless searches through the waterfront high-rise's records. She hated the matter-of-fact way they were discussing Rachel's attack as if it were happening to a stranger. The distance between them and the events happening to them—mainly to Rachel—bothered her. She wanted Rachel to feel as close to the crimes as she did. To feel afraid, to back out of this insane mounted division and follow through with her plan to transfer to a nice, quiet spot with the Cheney police department. Better yet, take a nice, quiet desk job.

Jack poked his head around the door. "Are you about ready for me to rob a bank and…Rachel, are you okay? What's going on?"

"I tripped and fell when I was jogging through the park," Rachel said. "But, yeah. Let's get on with our lesson. I'll get Bandit ready."

"I'll take care of him for you," Jack said. He disappeared, and the rest of the officers followed him.

Rachel stood up. "You coming, Cal?" she asked.

"Are you crazy?" Cal asked, hearing a very unaccustomed note of hysteria in her voice. She fought for her usual control and equanimity. Or at least the appearance of them. "Someone's tried to barbecue you, to run you over, to shoot you. Don't you think a normal person would be getting scared about now? Giving up? The mounted unit would be nice for the city, but it sure the hell isn't worth risking your life for it."

"Hey," Rachel said quietly. She sat down and took Cal's hand again, lacing their fingers together. "Of course I'm scared. And I've considered giving up. But I can't let fear run my life, or I'll never make it as a cop. Besides, I've seen you taking plenty of chances when you play polo. You could be seriously injured out there, but it doesn't stop you from playing."

Rachel smoothed her thumb over Cal's cheekbone and cupped her chin. Cal leaned into the caress even though part of her wanted to clobber Rachel for being so foolhardy.

"It's not the same thing," she said.

"Maybe not, but you don't let fear dictate what you do. And I won't, either. Someone is behind all this. The attacks on the horses, me, probably Alex. If he or she is trying to cheat the city out of its land, and is willing to kill to do so, I have to do whatever I can to stop them."

"I'd have to tie you up to keep you from training these people and riding on the Fourth, wouldn't I?"

Rachel leaned over and kissed Cal, the pressure of her lips and breasts pushing Cal against the soft cushions of the couch. Rachel pulled away and rested her forehead against Cal's.

"I'm going to train my team. And tomorrow, we're taking the horses to the park to prove we're not running scared. And we're riding on the Fourth. After that, if you're still in town, you'll be free to tie me up any way you want."

Chapter Twenty-one

Cal had a feeling Rachel might try to keep her from joining the mounted team when they went to the park, so she was up at dawn to make herself indispensable to the team. The police trailer only had room for four horses, so she hitched her six-horse gooseneck to her truck and backed it into place by the barn door. She hung the unit's saddles over the racks in her roomy tack compartment and got the police horses and Roman groomed and ready to travel. He had been an ideal mount for the lesson yesterday, and his polo training had proved to be a useful base for police work. He was accustomed to crowding and close quarters, and he had quickly learned to hold Jack against the arena wall at Cal's command. Only Bandit had been more adept at perp-catching, but Rachel had an unfair advantage since she'd been preparing and practicing the lesson for a week. The other three had had varying degrees of success, and Cal knew Jack would be limping for a few days after his encounter with the heavy-hooved Fancy.

Roman was already in the trailer, munching on a net full of hay, when Cal went into the barn and woke Clark. He was sleeping on the cot they'd put in a vacant stall next to the police horses, although Cal didn't see the use in having him there. She'd been banging around the aisle for over an hour, and he hadn't heard her, probably because he had been snoring loud enough to drown out her noise. She left him yawning and stretching while she went back to the trailer and loaded Sitka in the stall next to Roman.

She was leading Ranger out of his stall when Rachel's pickup arrived. Cal could see the shapes of Don and Billie as they emerged from the cab and into the mist-covered parking lot.

"Whatcha doing?" Rachel asked when she reached the trailer.

Her voice sounded sweet, but Cal knew she was about to put up a fight. She walked past Rachel and stepped into the trailer, followed by Ranger. She tied him next to a hay net and hopped out of the trailer before answering.

"I knew you wanted to get to the park early, before it got crowded. I thought I'd get a head start on loading."

Rachel held out a to-go cup of coffee. Cal recognized the name on its side. The coffee shop was halfway between Tacoma and her farm, and four police officers had been fatally shot while having an early morning meeting there a few years ago. Cal accepted the cup, brushing her fingers against Rachel's as she took it.

"How nice of you to load the horses," Rachel said, taking a drink from her own cup. "But what's that big brown horse doing in the front of the trailer? He's not one of mine."

Cal was prepared with her list of reasons why she should go. The main one—she needed to be close enough to keep an eye on Rachel, to help keep her safe—was the only one she didn't mention. "You and I have both ridden in the park, so it will be better to have two people who are familiar with the grounds and with riding outside of an arena. It's always best to have experienced riders in front and behind on trail rides. And when Fancy dumps Don on the ground and steps on his head, one of us can chase her and the other can call for an ambulance."

Rachel laughed. "I doubt she'll run far. Is there anything I can do to get you to unload that horse of yours and stay here?"

Cal shrugged. "You can try tying me up."

Rachel patted a little pouch on her duty belt. "Tempting. And I even carry my own handcuffs."

"If you two are going to make out, will you at least get out of the way so I can load Fancy?" Don asked.

Cal stepped back at the same time as Rachel. Don walked between them and into the trailer with his mare.

"That's everyone," Cal said, hurrying to shut the door before Rachel could start unloading the horses to get to Roman. She dangled the keys in her fingers. "I'm driving."

❖

By the time the unit left the park, well into the afternoon, Rachel was freely willing to admit she was grateful Cal and her stowaway horse had come along. Even early in the morning, a mild June day drew a crowd to the Point, and the officers and horses had been overwhelmed by the attention at first. Adults and children had clustered around them, asking to pet the horses and take photos of them. Rachel would have been hard-pressed to answer questions and keep the citizens around her safe while still helping Don, Clark, and Billie control their mounts. Cal had quietly stepped in, giving instructions and a helping hand where needed, freeing Rachel to concentrate on Bandit, and on the PR dimension of her job.

Rachel hadn't really expected anyone to attack her or the team in the busy park, surrounded by witnesses, and her attempts to dissuade Cal from going with them had been halfhearted at best. She did have second thoughts when they rode to their first stop for the day—the place where Rachel had nearly been run down. Not because she believed Cal might be in danger, but because her tanned face had turned pale as they retraced Rachel's steps. It had been easy to push through the trees, off the regular path, and follow her clear track to the cliff. Rachel stood at the edge and looked down at the gouge she had made in the dirt, until it disappeared into a clump of sharp-leaved bushes. She was grateful it had been dark when she'd flung herself over the edge because she doubted she'd have been so willing in the daylight. She might have taken her chances with the gun.

They hadn't found any clues about who had tried to run her down, but they'd certainly established their presence in the park today. And they'd managed to do it without incident. At times, there had been rings of people surrounding each horse, and Rachel felt a hesitant and hopeful sense of confidence about their ability to ride on the Fourth. She had first come up with this idea as a way to prove she wasn't about to back down, but it had turned out to be an excellent training day.

Rachel glanced over at Cal, sitting in the passenger seat with her head propped against the window and her gaze focused on the passing scenery. She had seemed tired and thoughtful most of the day—probably because she had been up since early morning plotting her way onto this field trip—and she'd accepted without hesitation when Rachel offered to drive the truck and trailer back to the farm. Cal had been amazing today. She had subtly assisted the team, never undermining their authority or doing anything to make them look inexperienced or inept. And once the riders had grown more comfortable, she had backed off and let them work through small problems on their own.

Rachel had noticed how great Cal was with the older kids. The teens and preteens had been drawn to her, and she had talked about horses and polo without any hint of condescension or conceit. Rachel had seen the almost hungry look in some of the kids' eyes as they got close to the kind of animals that were so often out of reach to them. Cal had seemed happy to share Roman with them, as generous with the kids as she had been with Rachel's riders.

Rachel slowly maneuvered the huge rig up the winding Lanford Farm driveway. The drive home had been quiet as everyone relaxed after a busy and stressful day. Once they were unloading the horses, however, the reality of their success seemed to finally sink in. They really might make it through the Fourth. Rachel hadn't fully believed it until today, and she doubted the others had, either.

It was dark once the horses were settled in their stalls, and Billie and Don got in Clark's car for the ride back to Tacoma. Rachel got her bag out of her truck and brought it into the spare stall. Guard duty. She hoped it would be a quiet night because she felt like she could sleep for ten hours straight.

"I'm heading to the main house for dinner," Cal said, leaning on the stall door as Rachel unrolled her sleeping bag. "Want to come?"

Rachel smiled at Cal's choice of words. Coming would be great. Coming to dinner with Cal's family was an entirely different matter. Besides, her body was sore and bruised from her fall and the long day in the saddle. She wasn't sure she'd be able to stay awake long enough for either sex or dinner. Well, she might be willing to try for the first one, at least.

She summoned some common sense. "No, but thanks. Do you mind if I use the shower in the clubhouse?"

"Go ahead. There's usually some snack food and beer in the fridge, so help yourself."

Cal turned to go but Rachel stepped toward the door. "I'm glad you were there today," she said. "I would have had my hands full on my own."

"I had a really good time," Cal said. The overhead light cast deep shadows on her face, and Rachel couldn't tell if Cal was tired or if she had something on her mind. "I'll see you later, cowgirl. Sleep well."

"You, too," Rachel said quietly, even though Cal was already out of earshot.

Rachel wandered through the barn long after Cal left. The smell of horses and clean shavings, hay and saddle oil filled her lungs. Healthy smells. The world outside seemed so dark, but inside the barn was a peaceful world filled with the sound of equine teeth crunching on stalks of hay, an occasional snort, the barely audible rustle of hooves through shavings. Rachel went into Bandit's stall and leaned against his shoulder while he ate, sharing his warmth and vitality. She finally pulled herself away and followed the dimly lit path to the clubhouse.

The water stung her scrapes, hurt her bruises. But her muscles needed the hot shower, so she stayed in it, swaying gently under the pounding spray, until the skin of her fingers was wrinkled. She toweled off quickly and pulled on some comfortable sweats.

She rummaged through the cupboards and fridge, collecting a bag of chips, one of cookies, and a few beers. She draped the duty belt and riding uniform she'd been wearing over her arm, tucked her haul under the other, and headed back to the barn. She was looking forward to spending the night in her cozy stall, with the sounds of horses surrounding her.

Rachel frowned as she came around a clump of maples and neared the barn. She felt a distinct sense of unease, something wrong. She stopped near one of the trees and dropped her clothes and food on the ground, pulling her gun out of its holster. She crept forward, scanning the barn and parking lot in front of her, searching for whatever it was that had triggered her subconscious alarms.

There. Near the back fence of the shadowed parking lot. A car? Rachel could barely make out an outline, a shape. She backtracked a few yards up the path to the clubhouse and turned to her left, edging around a row of horse trailers. She stood on the tongue of the police trailer, pressed close to its concealing bulk, and leaned out for a better look. Yes, a car. Were there passengers inside, or were they in the barn? Or somewhere else on the vast property, looking for her or her horses?

Rachel searched for a way to get closer to the car. Walking across the parking lot was out. She might as well paint a target on her head. She could sneak up behind the vehicle, but she'd have to go the long way, behind the barn, to do it. She retraced her steps to the maple trees and was about to cross the path and make her way around the outside of the barn when she saw a movement in the aisle. A silhouetted figure walking toward the door. Cal.

The occupants of the car must have noticed her at the same moment Rachel did. The engine revved to life and the car spun in an arc that would bring it right in front of the barn. Rachel sprinted toward Cal, desperate to beat the much faster car.

Cal's world erupted into the chaos of Rachel's shoulder shoving her, their impact against the barn wall, the screech of tires spinning on gravel, a single and earsplitting gunshot. As quickly as Rachel had slammed into her, she was away again, running toward the parking lot. Cal stumbled after her, unable to take a deep breath, when a flash of white streaked by her. Feathers. She tried to scream, but her words were choked as she called to her dog.

"No!" she yelled as the dog ran into the car's path, ignoring Cal's order as she chased the intruders.

"Feathers, stop!" Rachel's voice, her cop voice, carried across the noise of engines and barking. Feathers immediately skidded to a halt and reversed as the car sped past her. She ran to Rachel's side and obediently sat down.

"Stupid dog," Cal said, kneeling next to Feathers and burying her face in the dog's furry coat. Stupid, stupid dog who had just risked her life trying to protect Cal and the farm. She kept her face hidden, wanting to hide her tears of relief. She felt a cold nose against her neck, and she reached one arm around Tar, who had sidled close to her.

Cal felt Rachel's hand in her hair, caressing her, and then Rachel was gone. Cal wanted to go after her. Hug her and thank her for saving her life, for saving Feathers's life. But she didn't. She had spent too many years avoiding connection. Trying not to care. Now, in the space of a few weeks, she had felt more than she had in a lifetime. And in the space of a few seconds, she had experienced a range of feelings too intense to process. No wonder she'd been avoiding them for so long.

Cal sat back on her heels. Had someone been shooting at her, or had the bullet been intended for Rachel? From the dark parking lot, and backlit by the bright lights in the barn, Cal and Rachel would have been nearly indistinguishable. Similar height and build. Cal had come here looking for Rachel, too. Hoping to turn out the lights, crawl into Rachel's sleeping bag, and create a space free from danger, where they were the only two people in the world. But Rachel hadn't been there.

The two dogs licked Cal's face, pushing even closer as if they sensed her inner turmoil. Everything in her life had been the same. Training, dating, competing. Her family, her farm, her dogs. Nothing was different, but since Rachel had walked into her life *everything* was different. Cal hadn't realized how much she'd changed—how much she'd been changed—until today at the park. She'd worked with the officers until they seemed to settle into their job, handling their horses and the crowds with a quiet confidence she hadn't seen in them before this day. Then Cal had been able to turn her attention to the people around her. The city kids had shyly approached her and Roman, eager to pet him and to ask questions and stand close to such a powerful, beautiful animal.

One of them, a dark-haired girl wearing scruffy clothes and a guarded, distant expression, had tugged especially hard on Cal. Was this what Rachel had been like as a teen? Cal had been given small glimpses into Rachel's childhood, and she knew how her foster family and their horses had turned Rachel's life around. Who would be the one to make a difference in the life of this girl, whose eyes turned from hard and defiant to full of wonder as Roman nuzzled her hands? Cal had been given every privilege in life. Fancy clothes, money, a dream lifestyle. But she was most grateful for the horses. For their quiet and devoted acceptance even when she failed to measure up to her family's standards. For their companionship when she learned money couldn't buy an end to her loneliness.

Cal stood up and headed to the barn, with her dogs following close on her heels. She had spent months attempting to train some sense into Feathers, and Rachel had apparently accomplished the task in a matter of seconds. Cal couldn't handle the strain of caring about Rachel, the stress of knowing she was facing danger every day in her job and in her determination to be true to her ideals. She should walk away from her now. Be glad she'd had this chance to know her, to be changed by her, before they went their separate ways. But Cal couldn't. She'd been changed too much to go back to her old life. As much as it scared her to feel so much, to be so involved in life instead of looking at it from the edge, she didn't want to stop. She loved Rachel for being so strong, for fighting for her beliefs and values. And she loved her for seeing more in Cal than she'd ever really believed was there. Cal grew more confident with every step. She loved Rachel.

Rachel picked up the uniform and snacks she'd dropped in the dirt. She saw Cal heading back to the barn at the same time, relieved to see Cal's posture and cocky walk back to normal.

"The police will be here any minute," Rachel said when they met in the doorway, halfway between the brightly lit interior and the blackness beyond. "You'll need to give a statement, but I can handle most of it. As soon as you can, you should get to bed."

"Rachel, I don't know how I can thank you for—"

Rachel held up her hand. "Don't," she said sharply. She fought to soften her voice, keep her guilt and fear out of it. "Please don't thank me. I'm the one who put you in danger by coming here. By ignoring the warnings and continuing to train the team."

"You're doing the right thing. You can't quit."

"I can, and I will. Someone already tried to hurt the horses, and me. And now you." Rachel paused, struggling for control. Her mind kept replaying the scene, except each time she was a fraction of a second too late and Cal was dead. Cal's concern over Feathers's safety had somehow managed to divert her attention from her near miss with the bullet. Rachel was relieved about that, for Cal's sake, but her own mind wasn't so easily distracted. What if she'd lost Cal? "I'll get the horses out of here first thing in the morning, get them to a safe place. And I'll have my letter of resignation on Hargrove's desk soon after."

"So, fine. Leave the team," Cal said. She moved closer and took Rachel's hands in hers. "But what about us, what we have together?"

Cal's voice sounded steady, seductive, but Rachel could feel the tremors in her hands. She had caused them, had been the one to put Cal's life in danger. Her bad decisions had almost gotten Cal killed. Rachel didn't deserve the tempting possibility Cal was offering.

"There is no us. There was a team. I was the sergeant, and you were helping with training. But it's over now, and so is everything that happened between us."

Cal pulled her hands away and stepped back. Rachel had been lonely in her life, but the feeling was nothing compared to the emptiness at the loss of Cal's touch. But this wasn't about her anymore. Or the team. Now it was about Cal.

"Do me two favors," Rachel said. She waited until Cal gave her a seemingly reluctant nod. "Until you move back East, I want you to stay in the main house with your family. Not alone in the bungalow. And make sure someone is always with you when you're training in the fields."

Headlights traced across them as two Pierce County cars drove over to the barn. Rachel turned away from Cal, from the hurt expression on her face, and went to meet them.

CHAPTER TWENTY-TWO

Rachel parked her truck in front of her apartment building, yawning widely as she reached behind the seat for her overnight bag. She had spent most of the night talking to the county deputies. Yes, there had been a prior attack on the horses. No, she didn't know who was behind it. Yes, she thought the shooter had been looking for her and had mistakenly aimed at Cal instead.

She honestly believed it was a mistake, but it had been by far the best card the shooter could have played. Any bullet aimed at Rachel, unless it had been a clear hit and killed her, would only have made her furious. Made her even more determined to continue with her mission. But a bullet aimed at Cal scared the shit out of her. She was done—off the mounted unit, out of the department, out of town as soon as she could get her things packed.

The flashing images of Cal being shot, of Rachel not getting to her in time, were as relentless as a cold dream. They were occasionally swapped for scenes of a determined furry dog, the thud of impact, a white coat stained with blood. Rachel had managed—somehow—to keep both horrors from occurring, but it was her own damned fault they'd even been possibilities. Maybe if she ran fast enough, far enough, she could eventually make her imagination stop.

Rachel climbed the steps to her apartment, constantly scanning the streets and parking lot for any sign of her attackers. She kept her gun in her hand, but shielded by her coat, until she was inside. Then, after she made sure the apartment was clear, she bolted the door and sank onto her recliner. Finally inside, safe, locked away in her own private world. She never should have left in the first place.

After the deputies had left and Cal had been forcibly led back to the main house by her frantic parents, Rachel had spent the rest of the night curled on the cot in the spare stall, her gun cradled in her lap as she used Cal's laptop to search for local pastures for rent. She had found one that sounded decent and isolated, and she had called about it even before it seemed polite to do so. She had already hitched the police trailer to her truck once the first light of dawn made it bright enough to see, and she and Jack managed to get the horses loaded and on the road before Cal got back to the barn. A quick stop at an ATM for cash, and she had her horses safely stashed on a huge field two hours away from Cal's farm. The long rural roads made it easy for her to be certain she wasn't being followed. The fake name and cash payment reassured her no one would be able to trace the horses before she was able to return them to their owners. Bandit would, of course, go back to Cheney with her.

Rachel raised the footrest of her recliner and leaned her head back. She'd close her eyes for a few minutes. Cal and the horses were safe, so the letter to Hargrove could wait a few minutes. She was slowly drifting to sleep when a loud knock startled her. She kicked the footrest down while scrambling for her gun. So far, her attackers hadn't seemed the kind to knock, but she was cautious anyway. She kept her back pressed against the wall and looked through the peephole.

Her team. And her lieutenant. Yay.

Rachel tucked the gun in the waistband of her sweats and answered the door.

"Lieutenant Hargrove, come on in. You saved me a trip to the station. I quit."

"No, you don't," Abby said as she pushed past Rachel and walked into the apartment as if it were her personal office.

"What a shithole," Clark said as he followed Billie and Don into the room.

"Hey, I have a view and I'm close to the park," Rachel said, closing the door behind them. They wandered into her living room and sat down. Why the hell was she defending her home to these intruders? "What are you doing here?"

"Cal called. Said you absconded with our horses," Don said. He plopped into her recliner and leaned back. "Comfy chair. But I want my Fancy back."

Rachel stayed by the door, hoping everyone would be leaving soon and she could lock it behind them. "The horses are safe. I have them on a pasture until we can return them to their owners. Someone nearly killed Cal last night. Did she happen to mention that?"

"Yes," Hargrove said. "And she said you saved her life."

"No. I put her life and every member of this unit's life in danger. I should have listened to you when you said to sit back and not try to play sergeant for this team. Or when you told me to stop investigating Alex's murder. Or when those thugs tried to run me over in the park."

"Yes," Abby said, glaring at the other officers. "I heard about your little jog through the park and over the cliff. Did you honestly think I was chasing you?"

"The thought crossed my mind," Rachel said, crossing her arms over her chest. "But none of it matters anymore. I quit. And I strongly recommend you disband the mounted unit."

"And I refuse to accept your resignation." Abby leaned forward on the couch, her elbows on her knees. "Listen to me, Bryce, because I'm only saying this once. I was wrong. If you had obeyed me and followed Alex's lesson plans, the team wouldn't have been the success it was yesterday in the park. And if you hadn't looked into Alex's murder, Randy Brown would be paying for a crime we're quite certain he didn't commit."

"And if you hadn't figured out how valuable the police property could be, we wouldn't have found out who's behind all this," Clark added, sounding impatient. "Tell her, Don."

Don made a show of fishing a sheet of paper out of his pocket and unfolding it. Rachel was intrigued enough to leave her post by the door and walk closer.

"So, I was looking into one of the condos, like you said to do," Don said. He smoothed the paper against his knee. "Seems one of the prime-view properties was owned by a man who planned to build a hotel. The vacant lot was fenced and covered with no-trespassing signs, but it had an old pier on it, held up by some rotting pylons. Anyway, one night, an idiot named Jenkins climbs over the fence onto this man's property, walks out on the pier, and a pylon gives way. He crashes into the water, busts up his leg pretty good, and sues the property owner for millions. I looked into the case. Fishy, but Jenkins won and the guy had to sell the property to pay him. A company called J and L buys it and puts up one of the cornerstone condos in the new waterfront community."

"Yeah, so?" Rachel asked. "Attractive nuisance laws are a pain in the ass."

"This one stood out for me. Kept trying to place the name Jenkins." Don closed the footrest and leaned forward, his voice getting quieter as he got further into the story, as if he was worried someone might overhear. "A few years back, I did an off-duty gig at Eugene Varano's mansion. He had a big celebration after he was elected city manager. His in-laws were on the guest list, including his wife's cousin, Drew Jenkins."

Rachel plopped down on the edge of her coffee table. Varano. Wealthy enough to hire people who'd kill for him. And, rumor had it, corrupt enough to take a kickback or two. "So this cousin was the guy who fell on the pier?" she asked.

"No. The trespasser was Mike Jenkins. I haven't untangled the roots of Varano's family tree yet, but I'm sure he's a distant relative. But guess who's the *J* in J and L."

"And guess who was not only instrumental in helping me get approval for the mounted unit but also suggested the vacant lot as the stable yard," Hargrove added.

"Fuck," Rachel said, fitting all the pieces together in her mind. "Varano helps you get the unit started, but he pays Alex to make sure it fails. Then the city sells the property and J and L surprisingly wins the bid to build the new high-rise. Varano keeps it in the family and gets his cut from Jenkins. But why kill Alex? He seemed to be doing his job."

"We don't know," Hargrove said. "But you could ask him."

"Me? No way." Rachel laughed at the ridiculous suggestion. "If this has been Varano's handiwork, I want to stay as far away from him as possible. Besides, I quit."

"Yeah, we've been spreading that rumor around the department all morning," Billie said. "You bailed on us, and we're pissed."

She didn't look pissed. She looked excited and secretive, and so did Don and Clark. Rachel didn't have a good feeling about whatever plan the group had concocted.

"Varano must have been behind your posting to the unit, Rachel," Hargrove said. The use of Rachel's first name, combined with the atypically friendly tone in Hargrove's voice, only increased Rachel's unease. If she were in a doctor's office, she'd be expecting some very bad news. Some bad, untreatable, low-chance-of-survival type news.

"He'd have known about your reputation in the department, and I was very clear about my, well, distaste for you," Abby continued. "And he had you posted where you could do the most damage to the unit. He must have been as shocked as I was when you actually started showing signs of progress."

Rachel snorted. "Thanks for the vote of confidence. Now get out. I quit."

"He's getting nervous, and getting sloppy," Hargrove said. "The hit on Alex was well planned and would have succeeded if you hadn't overstepped your position and chased after Skunk."

Even Hargrove's compliments sounded like insults. Rachel got off the coffee table and stood by her front door, her fingers tapping on the doorknob.

"The detectives found him, by the way, but they're keeping it quiet until we can go after Varano. You were right, Rachel. Someone paid him to set up Randy, but he doesn't know who."

"Varano wouldn't have done it himself, anyway," Clark said. "He'd have someone else do his dirty work."

"Right," Abby said. "But chasing you down in the park, the shooting at Cal's. Those are reactions, not strikes. He's on the defensive, and we have a chance to get to him."

The mention of Cal made Rachel feel physically sick. If Varano was really behind the bullet that almost hit Cal, Rachel wanted to make him pay.

"What do you have in mind?" she asked. The four people in her living room exchanged smiles, looking confident they'd lured her in.

"It's simple, Rachel," Billie said. "We want you to live up to your bad reputation."

CHAPTER TWENTY-THREE

Cal got a bag of dog treats from the cupboard and gave a few to each of her dogs. They had been frantically circling her legs ever since she packed their dog bowls and food into a box to take to her parents' house. They seemed to take it as a sign that they were never going to be fed again, and she hoped a handful of treats would appease them. At least they let her walk without tripping as she finished gathering what she'd need for a few nights away.

Cal didn't want to leave her home. She liked her privacy, and she wasn't afraid of a repeat of last night's shooting. But she had told Rachel she would go, and somehow fulfilling this small promise made her feel closer to Rachel. It was all she had left.

She had spent the day training, riding each of her horses in succession until her mallet arm was weak and her thighs ached, trying to drive Rachel out of her head. Trying to convince herself what she thought was love was only a reaction to the stress of the moment. Someone had shot at her, had nearly run her dog down, had invaded her home. Of course she'd be upset and shocked, grasping at the first person she happened to see. Mistaking gratitude for something much deeper.

But as Cal had galloped up and down the field, she had eventually realized she hadn't fabricated her love after the shooting. It had been there, growing inside her, since Rachel had first walked onto this farm. Proud, but willing to ask for help. Lonely but loyal as she patiently trained her team's horses even though the officers ignored her. So determined to find value and meaning in life, no matter how much personal adversity she faced. Cal loved her, in her faded jeans and worn chaps, or her tight and sexy uniform, or her black street clothes. Or naked. Well, especially naked. Maybe the bullet had made Cal acknowledge her love, but the bullet hadn't created it. It had been there all along, growing sure and strong.

"I thought you promised to move into the main house," Rachel said.

Cal nearly dropped the box she had been carrying. She set it on a table and casually wiped at the tears that had been welling in her eyes at the thought of never seeing Rachel again. Now, here she was, leaning against the jamb of her open door, wearing jeans and a navy T-shirt under her leather jacket. Cal liked this outfit, too, although Rachel could have shown up in a feed sack for all she cared.

"I'm packing," she said. She turned her back on Rachel and fussed with the box, rearranging the clothes so she had something to do with her hands. Rachel didn't want her, she had been very clear about her lack of feelings, and Cal wasn't about to embarrass herself again.

"Good," Rachel said. "Because I worry about you."

Cal stiffened. Rachel's voice came from so close behind her she imagined she could feel Rachel's breath against her hair.

"Funny, you didn't seem to care this morning," Cal said. She wanted to sound casual and unaffected. The sniff she gave at the end of the sentence didn't help.

"You mean I didn't care when I saw you in the barn aisle and realized I only had seconds to save you? Or when I threw you against the wall and hoped I'd feel the bullet ripping through me because then I'd know for sure you hadn't been hit? Or when I had to walk away because knowing I had put you in danger made me hate myself so much I couldn't stay?"

Cal turned around when she heard the catch in Rachel's voice. She was close, close enough for Cal to lift her hands and cup Rachel's cheeks in them, to use her thumbs to gently wipe away Rachel's tears.

"I love you, Rachel," she said. She started to kiss her but pulled back when she sensed Rachel's hesitation. Rachel didn't feel the same way.

Rachel grabbed Cal's hands before she could move them. "I love you, too. Everything about you. I want to be with you all the time, to spend my nights and days with you. No matter what happens in my life—good or bad—you're the first person I want to call, and I want to be the one you turn to as well. But you're moving out of the state, and I'm…"

Cal's heart jumped at Rachel's words. "I know. You're going back to Cheney. But I'm not leaving, so we won't be too far apart. A few hours. We can make it work."

"You're not…? But I thought…"

Cal took Rachel's hand and led her out the front door, over to the porch swing. "When I came to the barn last night, I wanted to talk to you about this. I'm not moving to Virginia. I'm not accepting the place on the team. I'm going to stay here."

"Because of me?"

"Yes and no," Cal said. She leaned back, still holding Rachel's hand, and moved the swing with her foot. "I made the decision before I realized I love you. But if it hadn't been for you, I wouldn't have been able to figure out what I really want."

Cal watched her dogs race across the lawn. "I was going to join an established team. They're already champions, they've been playing at the top of the game for years. I'd be expected to fit into their program, do things their way. But I want what you have with your unit. A chance to build something from scratch, write your own rules, really build a team." Cal shrugged, feeling awkward about her next admission. "I thought I wanted to take the easy way out and get to the top by riding on the coattails of a group of people who've been there already. But I want to go through the process of getting there, and I want to train the people I'm bringing with me. Hell, if I'm willing to move across the country to join them, I'm sure I'll find plenty of top players who'd want a chance to come ride on *my* team."

Rachel had been listening in silence, but when Cal paused she squeezed her hand. "You were a strong leader on your USC team. You're a great player, but you encouraged everyone on your team to be great, too. I've watched you training my riders, and I've seen the effort you make to find creative ways to teach. Don't ever sell yourself short and think you need someone else to make you a star."

Cal rested her head on Rachel's shoulder, smiling when she felt the brush of Rachel's lips over her hair. "If it wasn't for you, I'd never have figured out how much I love teaching. I thought it'd be more convenient to have somebody else do the work, but I want to do it myself. There are a few riders with a lot of potential in our club here, and I know I can help them grow. I've always been so caught up in my own riding, I never focused on anyone else's."

Rachel wrapped her arm around Cal, rubbing her shoulder and nuzzling in her hair. She wanted this to be the happy ending she'd always dreamed of. Cal was staying here, following her dream in a way Rachel believed she'd find satisfying and rewarding. Cal loved her, and she loved Cal. The end.

But not yet. "Cal, we think we've figured out who's behind all this. Alex, the fire, the shootings. Eugene Varano."

Rachel felt Cal grow still in her arms. "The city manager?"

"Yes. But we can't prove anything…yet."

Cal pushed away and sat up abruptly, making the swing jerk underneath them. "What do you mean, *yet*? What are you going to do?"

Rachel held out her hands to steady Cal. "I'm meeting him tonight. Wearing a wire. I'm going to pretend I want to screw the department and work for him, like Alex did."

"Rachel, if he's done these things he's dangerous. Ruthless. If you can't convince him you're—"

"But I will, sweetheart," Rachel said. "Because when I do, I'll be able to keep my team safe. I'll be able to stay here with them. With you."

Rachel tangled her fingers through Cal's hair, pulling her close again. She could feel Cal trembling against her. "Shh, I'll be okay. It's something I have to do. Like I said before, this is bigger than I am. But I'll convince him, and I'll come back to you. Because this isn't bigger than us."

Rachel held Cal against her side as she stared across the green fields. She hoped she was right. And she hoped the future she saw for them when she looked out at the horizon was a true prophecy and not a foolish mirage.

Chapter Twenty-four

Rachel sat on top of a concrete slab, her arms wrapped protectively across her chest. A half hour ago, Lieutenant Hargrove had lifted her T-shirt and strapped the wire under Rachel's sports bra, tucking the receiver down the front of her jeans. And only a couple hours before, Cal had lifted her shirt and blazed an erotic trail of kisses over her breasts, down to her abdomen…

Cal. She had insisted on coming back with Rachel and was now stuffed into the tiny apartment with Hargrove, Rachel's team, and Chief Darnell. Waiting for her to convince Varano she wanted to turn and join the side of the devil. And if she couldn't convince him? She couldn't outrun his bullets. She hadn't wanted Cal to be here for this. Just in case.

A sleek black sedan, its windows tinted black, slid into the lot, and Varano got out of the backseat. Probably unarmed, but Rachel figured there were plenty of guns in the car. Without his fingerprints anywhere near them. Was this the car that had nearly run her down in the park? Were the people who'd chased her over the edge of the cliff sitting comfortably inside? The person who'd shot at Cal? Rachel had to fight for control. She wanted to run over to the car, drag the occupants out, and somehow avenge the attack on Cal. She knew she'd be dead before she got within fifty feet of the sedan, but she wanted to try.

She concentrated on Varano as he walked toward her, looking as ill suited for this back-alley, seedy-underbelly type of meeting as she looked made for it. She hopped off the pile of concrete and walked toward him, her hands tucked in the pockets of her black leather jacket. He was darkly handsome, with a little too much gel in his black hair. Finely featured and elegant, in a dangerous vampire kind of way. So different from Rachel's golden and beautiful Cal.

"Sergeant Rachel Bryce," he said formally, as if they were innocuously meeting at the mall or in a grocery store. "How pleasant to finally meet you."

"Cut the crap, Varano," she said, apologizing silently for making Cal listen to the harsh conversation she was about to have. Cal's ears were meant for much more delicate situations. Like Rachel's tongue, tracing the soft edges of her earlobe as it had just a few hours ago. "I want you to call off your goons."

"I assure you, I have no idea what you're talking—"

"I'm talking about the morons you hired to run me over and shoot me." And Cal. Rachel let her surge of anger rise up and give her strength. "Pretty inept group of assassins you've got."

"Is that a challenge, my dear?"

Rachel took her hands out of her pockets and spread them wide. "Go ahead and shoot me," she said. "I hope you have another scumbag like Randy Brown ready to take the fall."

One of his delicate eyebrows rose slightly. The message she had left this morning with his answering service had been vague. He wasn't sure how much she knew. Keep him guessing. Keep herself alive until she got enough information to nail his ass, and then get the hell out. Back to Cal for a repeat of this afternoon's activities. Although, if she was about to be killed, she couldn't imagine a better last meal than the one she had today. Cal, sitting in the porch swing, pressed against the side of the house as Rachel knelt in front of her…

"I have no idea—"

"What I'm talking about. Yeah, I got that. No need to keep trying to convince me you aren't all that bright. If you'd been smart, you'd have offered to pay me like you did Alex. Then I wouldn't have been fighting against you so hard."

"And you have been fighting hard, haven't you, Sergeant?" He walked closer to her. "I had no idea you'd be such a good trainer. Perhaps I underestimated your abilities."

Rachel shrugged. Nonchalant on the surface, but seething inside. She calmed herself by replaying the vision of Cal moving over her, the porch swing rocking lazily and then rapidly beneath them. The maples giving them privacy, and the fields offering an expanse of air and space and freedom. "I know how to make horses perform well. And how to keep them from performing well."

Varano threw his head back and laughed. "Gutsy," he said. "Foolish, but gutsy. You want what I offered Alex, but do you want to end up where he did?"

"I'm not foolish," she said, her voice sounding harsh and dangerous even to her own ears. Would Cal even recognize her as she listened? "But I'm assuming Alex was. Did he threaten to rat you out? Or did he want more money?"

Varano tapped his finger against his nose. "Very good, Sergeant. You go to the head of the class. Alex learned the hard way, it doesn't pay to be greedy. But his death was an honorable one, even though it could have looked otherwise. His widow gets his pension, roughly the original offer, and so justice is served."

He was talking too much. Either he planned to kill her and was just playing a game of cat and mouse, or he really believed she'd sway over to his side. Rachel felt a moment of panic as a trail of sweat trickled between her breasts and down to her navel. Think of Cal's tongue, dipping into her belly button and making her arch her back with pleasure. Think of the future, of her lover, of her partner. Anything but the fear this man generated with a simple smile.

"I'm not greedy," she said. "If I make a deal, I stick with it."

"Oh, really? My sources tell me you recently backed out of a deal you made. You've quit the mounted unit, so what use are you to me?"

Rachel desperately needed to be of some use to him if only for the next few moments. Otherwise, she was dead. She paused for a couple of breaths, hearing the sounds of the sleepy park around them. She pulled her strength from the quiet chitters and creaks of the forest at night, the slap of waves against the beach and pier, the distant drone of an occasional car on the late-night city streets.

"They're trained and ready to go. You'd need to kill all of them to stop them now. But if I ask for my post back? I can guarantee the unit will fail, and you'll be free to sell this land. You and J and L Enterprises can build your condos and make your millions."

A slight hitch in breath, a momentary widening of the eyes, a tense pause before the masks fell back into place. Small signs, nearly invisible, but Rachel saw them and she knew he hadn't expected her to have so much information.

"So now what?" he asked. "Do you tell me you have this information in a secret envelope in a secret bank vault, only to be mailed to the authorities on the occurrence of your death?"

"Something like that," Rachel said. "But I don't care about bringing you to justice, and I sure as hell don't want to die before it happens. Do whatever the fuck you want with this scrap of land. You either pay me to help, or I'm out of town by morning. You can waste the next few days killing off the mounted unit one by one."

Varano reached out and traced her jawline with his index finger, forcing her to raise her chin as he applied gentle pressure. Bastard. Cal's lips had traced the same path. Her body was Cal's property now, and he had no right to trespass on it. She didn't try to hide her disgust or fury at his touch. He laughed.

"Ah, little one. You and I are so much alike." He smiled when she inhaled sharply. "Yes, I've read about your past, your youthful indiscretions. I, too, was abused, was shunted from home to home—none of them any better than the one I originally had. State sponsored abuse. And I, too, spent some time in the juvenile detention halls. But I rose above my upbringing, and I've made something of myself. You, it seems, are no better off than you were. Whether being arrested, or wearing the uniform and doing the arresting, there is no difference."

"I tried to change," Rachel said, her jaw clenched so tight she could barely grind out the words. "But the whole fucking department turned against me. My lieutenant seems to get off on public displays of embarrassment. I have no friends here, no ties to this city or this park or this shit piece of property. So you either pay me to make sure the mounted unit doesn't survive past the Fourth, or let me disappear."

"Yes, gutsy," Varano said with another oily laugh. He let go of her chin and handed her a slip of paper. "Fine. I'll make you the same deal I made Alex. To be paid either to you or to your next of kin, providing the unit fails miserably on the Fourth."

She glanced at the paper, not needing to be an actress to look impressed by the number on it. She could buy a new car, one of those waterfront condos, a string of polo ponies. "They'll fail. Don't worry."

He brushed her cheek with his palm, and she flinched. "I should have picked you over Alex from the start. He was useful but too concerned with trying to come out looking good. You seem to have no such desire. I assumed you'd screw up on your own, but you managed to clean up the mess Alex had created. I only wish I could see the faces of your team if they were to find out the one person they really trusted is the one who's selling their fates like a lowlife in a vacant lot."

Rachel stepped back, out of his reach. "Be my guest," she said as the night erupted with sirens and flashing lights. In seconds, a ring of officers had Varano at gunpoint, and she walked away from them, heading back toward the burned-down police barn. Toward Cal, who was running down the hill to meet her.

CHAPTER TWENTY-FIVE

Rachel carefully maneuvered Bandit through the crowds and over to where Don and Fancy stood. The main street along Tacoma's waterfront, Ruston Way, was closed to cars but jammed with people celebrating the Fourth of July. The Blue Angels roared past, but Bandit merely flicked his ears in their direction. Rachel gave a brief—and surprising—sigh of gratitude for the barn fire. Cal's farm was in the flight path of Joint Base Lewis-McChord, so the horses had quickly become accustomed to low-flying aircraft. The city's airshow was no big deal to them.

She halted a few yards from Don. He had ridden Fancy over to an ice cream truck for a snack and had immediately been surrounded by the children who had been in line. He was standing next to Fancy and feeding her a crunch bar while he answered questions and let the kids pet her. Rachel decided to save her lecture about inappropriate horse treats. The mare was as still as if she were carved out of stone, and Don had a relaxed and happy smile on his face as he showed her off. Rachel waved when he looked her way, and he extricated himself from the crowd and mounted his horse.

"She's doing great," Rachel said once he had reached her side.

"I knew it from the start," he said, giving her shoulder a pat. "She's made for this job."

Rachel wouldn't have agreed with him a few weeks ago, but she had to admit the mare was performing well, remaining steady and calm even as a group of skateboarders flew by. She'd rather be on Bandit, of course, especially if she had to move faster than a walk, but she was proud of the little pinto mare. She was proud of all the horses.

"Where'd Clark and Billie go?" she asked. "I thought we could stop by the staging area and get some lunch."

"I think they're competing to see who can get the most phone numbers," Don said. "Last I heard, Billie was beating his ass. No surprise there. But I'm hungry."

Rachel steered Bandit off the main road and away from the crowds. Billie and Clark could find them later on if they wanted to leave the city streets. From what Rachel had observed, the unsuspecting women of Tacoma were more than willing to welcome the mounted officers to town. Rachel wasn't interested in that particular benefit of her job. She urged Bandit into a trot along the grassy shoulder, anxious to get to the fenced area where the department had set up some tables and a few barbecues so on-duty cops had a private place to take their breaks. She wasn't hungry for food, but she knew Cal would be there, waiting for her.

Don and Fancy headed straight to the picnic tables, but Rachel scanned the area for Cal's dark gold hair before she dismounted and led Bandit toward her. Cal had been talking to Lieutenant Hargrove, but she broke away and came toward Rachel as soon as she spotted her.

"Hey you," Rachel said when they got close. She was in uniform and on-duty, so she wouldn't give Cal the kiss she had in mind. She had to be satisfied with a quick bump of her shoulder.

"Hey you, back," Cal said. She rubbed Bandit's shoulder. "How's he doing?"

"Awesome," Rachel said with a smile, scratching Bandit's neck in his favorite spot. "And so are the others, although I think Don has Fancy all hopped up on sugary treats."

Cal looked over at the mare. She was standing with her head low and one hind hoof cocked while Don ploughed through a plate of brats. "Yeah, I can tell."

"You did this," Rachel said, giving in to her urge to touch Cal's cheek. Hell, the whole department knew they were together.

A little touch wouldn't do any harm. "I never would have realized how much they'd be exposed to on a day like this, but you really prepared them well."

"*We* did this," Cal said. "Are you still planning to leave before the fireworks?"

"We'll watch them from back here this year," Rachel said. "By then the horses will be tired and we'll have been riding all day, so I don't want to overdo it. But they'll get to see and hear them, so we'll be more than ready for New Year's. And we start regular patrols day after tomorrow."

Rachel rubbed Bandit's forehead. He sighed and leaned against her hand. "What were you and Hargrove talking about?" she asked. "I didn't think you liked her."

"I don't," Cal said. "I still haven't forgiven her for yelling at you like she did, even though she apologized. And sending you out alone to meet with Varano? Not cool. But she's agreed to help me with my new program, so I'm starting to come around."

"What new program?" Rachel asked, her attention focused on Cal's fingers as she adjusted one of the straps on Bandit's bridle.

"I want to bring city kids out to the farm. Kids who wouldn't normally have a chance to be around horses. They can learn to ride and take care of them. Learn responsibility and maybe find a support group."

"Oh," Rachel said. Her chest felt tight as she tried to control the love she felt for Cal, keep it from spilling out in public. "I think it's a wonderful idea. You'll really make a difference in their lives."

"We'll really make a difference," Cal corrected her once again. "I expect your help with this."

"Anything you need," Rachel said, meaning it with all her heart.

Cal moved an inch closer. "What I need is a kiss," she said, smiling at Rachel. "But I know you're too disciplined to make out while on-duty. So I'll just have to remember how you kissed me last night, when you came to my house after work and found me on the porch. When you pushed me up against the banister, and your hands reached under my shirt and—"

"I remember," Rachel said. She felt Cal's hard nipples against her palms, Cal's tongue sliding over her own. She took a deep breath and felt the grassy, cooling air from the polo fields flow into her lungs. "I remember the kiss very well, and I also remember what happened next. A variation on what I plan to do to you tonight."

Cal grinned. She shifted her hips, and Rachel knew Cal's mind had followed her into the bedroom. "I love you, Mountie Bryce."

Rachel laughed, pulling Cal close for a quick kiss, not caring who could see. "I love you, too."

About the Author

Karis Walsh is a horseback riding instructor who lives on a small farm in the Pacific Northwest. When she isn't teaching or writing, she enjoys spending time outside with her animals, reading, playing the viola, and riding with friends.

Books Available from Bold Strokes Books

First Love by CJ Harte. Finding true love is hard enough, but for Jordan Thompson, daughter of a conservative president, it's challenging, especially when that love is a female rodeo cowgirl. (978-1-60282-949-7)

Pale Wings Protecting by Lesley Davis. Posing as a couple to investigate the abduction of infants, Special Agent Blythe Kent and Detective Daryl Chandler find themselves drawn into a battle over the innocents, with demons on one side and the unlikeliest of protectors on the other. (978-1-60282-964-0)

Mounting Danger by Karis Walsh. Sergeant Rachel Bryce, an outcast on the police force, is put in charge of the department's newly formed mounted division. Can she and polo champion Callan Lanford resist their growing attraction as they struggle to safeguard the disaster-prone unit? (978-1-60282-951-0)

Meeting Chance by Jennifer Lavoie. When man's best friend turns on Aaron Cassidy, the teen keeps his distance until fate puts Chance in his hands. (978-1-60282-952-7)

At Her Feet by Rebekah Weatherspoon. Digital marketing producer Suzanne Kim knows she has found the perfect love in her new mistress Pilar, but before they can make the ultimate commitment, Suzanne's professional life threatens to disrupt their perfectly balanced bliss. (978-1-60282-948-0)

Show of Force by AJ Quinn. A chance meeting between navy pilot Evan Kane and correspondent Tate McKenna takes them on a roller-coaster ride where the stakes are high, but the reward is higher: a chance at love. (978-1-60282-942-8)

Clean Slate by Andrea Bramhall. Can Erin and Morgan work through their individual demons to rediscover their love for each other, or are the unexplainable wounds too deep to heal? (978-1-60282-943-5)

Hold Me Forever by D. Jackson Leigh. An investigation into illegal cloning in the quarter horse racing industry threatens to destroy the growing attraction between Georgia debutante Mae St. John and Louisiana horse trainer Whit Casey. (978-1-60282-944-2)

Trusting Tomorrow by PJ Trebelhorn. Funeral director Logan Swift thinks she's perfectly happy with her solitary life devoted to helping others cope with loss until Brooke Collier moves in next door to care for her elderly grandparents. (978-1-60282-891-9)

Forsaking All Others by Kathleen Knowles. What if what you think you want is the opposite of what makes you happy? (978-1-60282-892-6)

Exit Wounds by VK Powell. When Officer Loane Landry falls in love with ATF informant Abigail Mancuso, she realizes that nothing is as it seems—not the case, not her lover, not even the dead. (978-1-60282-893-3)

Dirty Power by Ashley Bartlett. Cooper's been through hell and back, and she's still broke and on the run. But at least she found the twins. They'll keep her alive. Right? (978-1-60282-896-4)

The Rarest Rose by I. Beacham. After a decade of living in her beloved house, Ele disturbs its past and finds her life being haunted by the presence of a ghost who will show her that true love never dies. (978-1-60282-884-1)

Code of Honor by Radclyffe. The face of terror is hard to recognize—especially when it's homegrown. The next book in the Honor series. (978-1-60282-885-8)

Does She Love You? by Rachel Spangler. When Annabelle and Davis find out they are both in a relationship with the same woman, it leaves them facing life-altering questions about trust, redemption, and the possibility of finding love in the wake of betrayal. (978-1-60282-886-5)

The Road to Her by KE Payne. Sparks fly when actress Holly Croft, star of UK soap Portobello Road, meets her new on-screen love interest, the enigmatic and sexy Elise Manford. (978-1-60282-887-2)

Shadows of Something Real by Sophia Kell Hagin. Trying to escape flashbacks and nightmares, ex-POW Jamie Gwynmorgan stumbles into the heart of former Red Cross worker Adele Sabellius and uncovers a deadly conspiracy against everything and everyone she loves. (978-1-60282-889-6)

Date with Destiny by Mason Dixon. When sophisticated bank executive Rashida Ivey meets unemployed blue collar worker Destiny Jackson, will her life ever be the same? (978-1-60282-878-0)

The Devil's Orchard by Ali Vali. Cain and Emma plan a wedding before the birth of their third child while Juan Luis is still lurking, and as Cain plans for his death, an unexpected visitor arrives and challenges her belief in her father, Dalton Casey. (978-1-60282-879-7)

Secrets and Shadows by L.T. Marie. A bodyguard and the woman she protects run from a madman and into each other's arms. (978-1-60282-880-3)

Change Horizons: Three Novellas by Gun Brooke. Three stories of courageous women who dare to love as they fight to claim a future in a hostile universe. (978-1-60282-881-0)

Scarlet Thirst by Crin Claxton. When hot, feisty Rani meets cool, vampire Rob, one lifetime isn't enough, and the road from human to vampire is shorter than you think… (978-1-60282-856-8)

Battle Axe by Carsen Taite. How close is too close? Bounty hunter Luca Bennett will soon find out. (978-1-60282-871-1)

Improvisation by Karis Walsh. High school geometry teacher Jan Carroll thinks she's figured out the shape of her life and her future, until graphic artist and fiddle player Tina Nelson comes along and teaches her to improvise. (978-1-60282-872-8)

For Want of a Fiend by Barbara Ann Wright. Without her Fiendish power, can Princess Katya and her consort Starbride stop a magic-wielding madman from sparking an uprising in the kingdom of Farraday? (978-1-60282-873-5)

Broken in Soft Places by Fiona Zedde. The instant Sara Chambers meets the seductive and sinful Merille Thompson, she falls hard, but knowing the difference between love and a dangerous, all-consuming desire is just one of the lessons Sara must learn before it's too late. (978-1-60282-876-6)

Healing Hearts by Donna K. Ford. Running from tragedy, the women of Willow Springs find that with friendship, there is hope, and with love, there is everything. (978-1-60282-877-3)

Desolation Point by Cari Hunter. When a storm strands Sarah Kent in the North Cascades, Alex Pascal is determined to find her. Neither imagines the dangers they will face when a ruthless criminal begins to hunt them down. (978-1-60282-865-0)

I Remember by Julie Cannon. What happens when you can never forget the first kiss, the first touch, the first taste of lips on skin? What happens when you know you will remember every single detail of a mysterious woman? (978-1-60282-866-7)

The Gemini Deception by Kim Baldwin and Xenia Alexiou. The truth, the whole truth, and nothing but lies. Book six in the Elite Operatives series. (978-1-60282-867-4)

Scarlet Revenge by Sheri Lewis Wohl. When faith alone isn't enough, will the love of one woman be strong enough to save a vampire from damnation? (978-1-60282-868-1)

Ghost Trio by Lillian Q. Irwin. When Lee Howe hears the voice of her dead lover singing to her, is it a hallucination, a ghost, or something more sinister? (978-1-60282-869-8)

The Princess Affair by Nell Stark. Rhodes Scholar Kerry Donovan arrives at Oxford ready to focus on her studies, but her life and her priorities are thrown into chaos when she catches the eye of Her Royal Highness Princess Sasha. (978-1-60282-858-2)

The Chase by Jesse J. Thoma. When Isabelle Rochat's life is threatened, she receives the unwelcome protection and attention of bounty hunter Holt Lasher who vows to keep Isabelle safe at all costs. (978-1-60282-859-9)

The Lone Hunt by L.L. Raand. In a world where humans and praeterns conspire for the ultimate power, violence is a way of life… and death. A Midnight Hunters novel. (978-1-60282-860-5)